COLLECTION

COLLECTION

By

LARRY SIGNY

"There is something delicious about writing the first words of a story. You never quite know where they'll take you."
— BEATRIX POTTER

"You never have to change anything you got up in the middle of the night to write."
— SAUL BELLOW

"Write a short story every week. It's not possible to write fifty-two bad short stories in a row."
— RAY BRADBURY

CONTENTS

COLLECTION

I was clearing out a long neglected drawer in a desk recently when I discovered a stash of old thin and flexible magnetic storage floppy discs, those antiquated gadgets used by old codgers like me to store various writings in the earlier days of computers—contraptions which were the must-have latest thing in "modern" electronic technology from 1982 for about forty years.

There were seven discs and it took about a month before I was able to find someone with the right equipment to open them up and it was only then that I was re-introduced to some two hundred and fifty old friends I had written about all those years ago.

I remembered a few (particularly the glorious research trying to find a Native American phrase for a romantic saying—I managed to speak to several people from the Lakota Sioux tribe via transatlantic phone to America, and one told me, with exquisite, intricate detail, that he'd deliberately wiped out all memories of the language because of a messy divorce before I eventually got the phrase I needed), but the majority came as a delightful surprise and I read through their forgotten tales in a glorious state of reunion. *Collection* contains some of those characters—all (well, the vast majority) are fictional imaginations of my mind—and I'm glad I've found them again.

Humans have always told stories. Storytelling, in fact, was a way of community life long before writing… There were no films (movies as they have become) or televisions, remember. There were no newspapers or radios to get the news. And believe it or not, no electronic media! Most people learnt about their world by actually talking to each other.

But it didn't take too long before professional storytellers took over, passing on their tales, legends, fables and myths—and entertainment.

In those ancient early to middle medieval days, storytellers were the "celebrities" of their time. They were known by many names. In England they were apparently scops or bards (although bards were really poets speaking out loud) while in Scandinavian countries they were known as skalds and in France musical storytellers were called troubadours or *jongleur*, who were musicians, poets, jugglers and acrobats as well as storytellers.

They performed in marketplaces, and in England, in particular, they went from village to village telling stories to groups of people gathered in a semi-circle round them in the central square in return for an evening meal. If they were especially good at it, they were often called in to live in the castles of noblemen, who sponsored them for their own personal pleasures.

I like to romantically think I'm following that traditional line. I'm a storyteller, but instead of travelling from village to village I simply sit at home in my centrally heated easy chair and relate my anecdotes on a three-year-old laptop. That's when I'm not telling a story off the top of my head face to face with an individual when we strike up a conversation. And I microwave my own ready-made meals!

I'm lucky, really, that I have always found it easy to write, and discovered the ability to use writing at secondary school. I was about eleven (around then anyway) and was a very bad pupil who just didn't want to do as he was told. One day I turned up early-ish for the daily assembly to be asked by my mates if I had written the essay set by the headmaster a week earlier. I hadn't, of course, and didn't even know the subject he'd set, but in front of everyone I sat down and scribbled the words out and handed it in (within the deadline I might add).

The next morning the head singled my piece out for praise and told the whole school how it proved that hard work, concentration and a willingness to spend time making sure it was as good as it could be to ensure an excellent result paid off.

I was the school hero for a week, because everyone—apart from the teachers—knew the essay had taken just five to ten minutes to write and had not required any hard work. I had bluffed the headmaster.

I shouldn't be proud of that (but I still am!), particularly as it showed me that I could have a relatively easy life without too much effort. I don't think I've ever done a hard day's work since.

I have never thought of myself as a "Writer" (with a capital letter), although from those early schooldays I have always written in some form or another.

I can remember that when I was quite young—a very shy younger brother who always looked up at the very forceful character of Big Den, my older brother—I heard my father tell someone that, "Larry seems to have a certain number of words he has to say every day, and he has to say them." Well, I did, but I was so shy I did it by writing rather than saying them. Throughout my life it has earned me a living and above all given me huge pleasure.

I told stories, too, when my daughter was a little girl. It was a sacred weekly duty that we would go out together every Sunday morning, I would ask which of the two railway stations she wanted to go to ("the upstairs station or the downstairs station") and after she had seriously deliberated the question, off we would go. Sitting on the platform we would wait for an old steam express to roar through and I would then weave some sort of fantasy literally off the cuff about the train or one of the passengers.

I must have done something right because Helen has now developed into a very good storytelling author herself.

Right now though, I don't get paid for writing (book sales only earn me peanuts!) but I'm living what's called the "Rest of My Life" and I hope to carry on doing what I've always done: listening to the birds, looking at trees, watching the people and telling stories.

Although it is no longer my job, I still try to write something every day—often just an over-long text or e-mail replying to a message—simply because I love the act of writing. I couldn't say where the ideas come from, but the characters in my stories have become quite real to me—quite often coming to me in the middle of the night, waking me up so I can write them. I have often pushed back the duvet at three or four in the morning to tap them out one fingered on my mobile phone ready to transfer them to the laptop later in the day.

There is no underlying theme, no message, in their writing and I don't know exactly when these stories were written, only a few had dates on them and the earliest of those was 2002. A small point, but perhaps I should point out that in those earlier days when these stories were written, people smoked cigarettes far more than they do today. Please excuse any references to the noxious habit.

With a couple of recently written extras they are my musings over the last twenty to twenty-five years or so… a really random and very loose look at stories, characters and happenings that have entered (and left) my mind over the last quarter of a century.

But the people in all of them are my friends. As you browse through them I hope you, too, find some who give you brief pleasure in their company.

They are my people. Let me introduce them.

THE ANGEL WITH
THE CINNABAR LIPS

The painting was called *The Angel with the Cinnabar Lips*. Cinnabar is simply a vermilion pigmentation known as "dragon's blood", and the girl on the canvas had lips of that colour. She was a blonde, with hair that fell freely round her heart-shaped face. Her cheekbones were high, and her pink ears were flat to her head, and she had wide-apart, honest eyes.

But it was her blush red lips that were the main feature of her face; her simple, unadorned, beautiful face. They were lips that wore a permanent, slightly apart, just-licked sheen of moisture, and they were rich and full and desirable. They were lips that demanded and deserved an embrace. They were dragon's lips. Her lovely canvas lips.

The Angel with the Cinnabar Lips hung in the studio where the girl had been painted. The artist, a middle-aged balding man called Henry Truman, was now busy with yet another canvas, a new project, yet occasionally he spared a glance for his old work, still in her unframed splendour, before returning to his new subject with bold, firm, decisive strokes from his brush.

Henry was the sort of painter who had to "feel" a subject before he could paint him or her. The sort of artist who searched for the inner self or meaning, and tried to project that onto the canvas in place of the usual photocopy likeness of the person as he or she would like to be.

Henry often claimed that he was only one part painter and four parts psychiatrist. Emotions were as essential to his art as features; feelings and moods matched limbs and colouring. The results were good, controversially good, and they made Henry Truman into a success both commercially and critically.

Success, however, is measured by the artist against satisfaction, and Henry never let the panacea of wealth dull his over-riding desire to paint people as he felt they were, and as he saw them with his subjective mind's eye. It meant that every now and then he would paint a subject that he could not sell, a portrait that was either too different or too real to please, a canvas that held out a latter-day Dorian Gray quality to the eye of the beholder.

The Angel was such a canvas. It had been in his studio for many years, but Henry had only recently restored it to a place on view. It was one of his least successful commercial works, yet he now looked at it with a pride in his own consummate craftsmanship, reliving once more the warmth and friendliness, the beauty, charm and basic innocence of the model whose name he could not now remember.

Names, however, did not matter, because *The Angel* worked a magic and gave Henry a feeling of creative power that sizzled through to his stubby fingertips and expressed itself in the new canvas at which he now stood.

One day in the summer, as Henry worked and looked now and then at his canvased "angel", an old friend called on him. A bell rang in the distance as Henry painted, and a cleaning lady opened the door. There were muffled footsteps, then the friend walked into the room and stood quietly waiting recognition. As Henry turned from looking at *The Angel*, he spoke.

"She's rather beautiful, isn't she?"

A beaming smile rushed to Henry's face and he held out his hand and walked to the studio door. "Roger! It's good to see you again. Come in and tell me how things have been. It's been an age."

The words spilt out in a genuine burst of pleasure. Henry paused and wiped his hands on an old rag, then he put an arm round his friend's shoulders as he led him firmly into the bowel of the studio room.

The friend's name was Roger Ruark, and he was a big man with a rugby player's body and a mop of fair, curly hair above a boyish face. He was smartly dressed, almost soberly in style, but with a quiet air of sartorial quality. He wore clothes well, and he looked at home in them. His smile, too, was worn easily, and showed true and genuine feelings.

"When did you get home again? I didn't even know you were coming."

Henry ushered Roger to a comfortable chair, one of a set of two in the studio, as he asked the questions, which still rushed out in a torrent of good feeling and surprise.

Roger grinned and waved the painter to quiet. "Give me a chance, old boy," he said. "One question at a time."

Henry Truman sat down on the twin chair. "Well then," he said, "Tell me all about it. Where did you get to in the end?"

Roger grinned again, and it was still a sign of friendship. He offered cigarettes from a slim, gold case that he took from the right-hand pocket of his elegantly cut jacket, and reached for a box of matches from a hexagonal-shaped ornamental table between the two seats.

When they had lit the cigarettes, the two friends spoke. It had been almost three years since they had last met, three years in which Roger Ruark had travelled almost completely around the world, had seen sights and experiences beyond the dreams of the most wild-minded adventurer. He had met strange people and had eaten strange foods. He had smelt strange smells, had handled strange objects, and had done things that shattered the eye and marvelled the mind and the brain.

And in his easy, soft-spoken manner he brought the next three-quarters of an hour to life as he told his artist friend of his enjoyments, sketching scenery and verbally painting in the detail with a short flurry of words and sentences.

During the time he spoke, Roger's eyes were alight with a passion of vividly remembered thoughts, a fire that slowly burnt down until he ended his story. Then, and not before, he lit another cigarette and stood up. Henry was enthusing over his friend's itinerant ramblings, but by now Roger had forgotten the past and was back in the present. He walked to *The Angel* and, standing in front of her, his eyes grew wide, and then the internal glow of excitement returned to them.

"I didn't remember her," he said, interrupting the painter. "She is beautiful. By God, she is."

The Angel looked down at Roger Ruark, and for a moment there seemed to be a spark across the space between adventurer and canvas painting. Roger smiled his boyish smile, and *The Angel*'s cinnabar lips glistened and smiled back at him.

* * *

In the next few months, Roger Ruark paid many visits to Henry Truman's studio, calling in both by invitation and by inclination. Henry was involved in a hectic spell of painting that kept him hard at work from first light until early dusk, and he could rarely spare the time to pause when his friend dropped in. They spoke one-sidedly as the artist worked, leaving Roger to drift restlessly around the studio.

As time progressed and the seasons passed from one into another, Roger found that he was spending more and more time in the studio and that, once there, he was deviating to a place in front of *The Angel with the Cinnabar Lips.*

As the cycle of summer and autumn, winter and spring aged into another year, Roger Ruark grew to love the beautiful "Angel". He bathed in her smile, luxuriated in her rich warm colouring, her blushing vermilion lips—they all came to life and communicated across silence in a way that only lovers can know.

When he was apart from the studio, Roger knew the deep frowns of grief and wished that he was with his coarse-clothed "Angel". When they were together, it was a fulfilment of being, a concord, a unity. It was a full affection that reached the natural climax of love in a silently verbal intercourse, in a mental disgorging of tender, exciting enchantment.

Henry Truman was far too busy to notice the growing silences in the increasing visits that Roger paid to the studio. He failed to realise that around him as he worked, an atmosphere of love and drama was building up to a catastrophic collision in the mind of his friend.

Then one day, when the spring sunshine was fading into a pale turquoise-blue sky and there was a hangover chill of winter in the air, Roger asked Henry to sell him the painting of *The Angel*.

"But you couldn't afford my price," answered the artist with a grin, barely looking up from his easel.

Roger did not answer the smile. "Money doesn't worry me particularly, Henry. The painting does," he said sombrely.

The artist waved a hand holding a brush as if to push the idea away. "I've grown used to her myself, you know," he said. "I've got used to the idea of having her here with me. She helps me in my work."

Roger had a feeling of heartburning. He felt a sudden pang of jealousy, and he wanted to do something to prove himself above the sudden interference of this unexpected adversary for the love of *The Angel, his* "Angel".

"You wanted to sell her before," he said, with a harsh edge creeping into his voice. "Why do you suddenly want to keep her away from me?"

"Come now," replied Henry, "Don't get worked up, just because I don't want to sell you one of my paintings. I'm not selling, and that's all there is to it."

Roger continued the argument for over half an hour, but the more he wheedled, persuaded, ranted and raved, the more determined became Henry to keep his painting of *The Angel with the Cinnabar Lips*.

Finally, even Roger had to admit that further argument was futile, and he stormed out of the house in a bad grace that was to last for a week. It was the most hideous week of his life. A lonely week away from his beloved "Angel". Seven days of tortuous thought and counter-thought. A generation of fear and aching. A millennium of apprehension, misgiving and despair.

But after a week he returned to Henry Truman's studio, where the painter greeted him as he always had as though there had been no argument, and let him stand before the beautiful canvas of the lovely "Angel". Time was as before, and Roger felt the tenderness come over him again. The fears and pains of the previous week flowed away into a past that ceased to exist, and the love of Roger Ruark and his painted "Angel" flowed smoothly once more. Roger stood there, and silent communication and love sparked across space.

As evening fell and the light began to fail, Henry Truman ended his day's work and started to clean up. Roger said a mute "au revoir" to his "Angel" as he crossed the studio to join the painter.

"I'm sorry," he said simply. "Forgive me, old boy."

Henry gave his friend an amused glance, then nodded serious faced. "Just one of those things," he answered lightly and tenderly. He offered Roger a cigarette, then accepted a light.

"Would you paint me?" Roger asked the question on the spur of the moment. "It could hang with *The Angel* in that very corner."

Henry raised an eyebrow slightly. "Just like that?" he said softly. "You just want to come in here, sit down and let me paint you?"

"Why not?"

"It's not all that easy," said the artist. "For one thing, I'm not really certain that I understand you anymore. It was different before you went away… but somehow you've slipped away from me. I don't *feel* a painting."

Roger puffed at his cigarette. "I don't see what you're getting at," he replied after a moment. "You can see me. Why can't you paint me?"

Henry Truman looked at Roger, then beyond him to the painting of *The Angel with the Cinnabar Lips*. His eyes narrowed and his brow creased and puckered with concentration. "Both my subject and I have to learn from my painting," he continued slowly. "We both have to learn about a personality. It's a voyage of exploration into the subject's unknown—to find out what makes him tick—to see what sort of personality he really has. My brush simply records it on canvas. It's more of a psychoanalysis than a painting. I can see you; at this very moment I can see your face and your features. But I can't paint you. Not yet."

Roger listened to his friend, and a muffled stillness seemed to take over his body. He nodded twice, then he stood and walked silently to the door. He looked back into the studio, and as he looked at the painting of his "Angel" a calmness settled on him. "Goodbye" was all he said, but it was more to the painting than to the painter. Then he was gone into the fast falling dark of the night.

*　*　*

Henry Truman heard about his friend's suicide a few hours later, and immediately went into his studio. He stood silently in front of *The Angel* for some time, then he made preparations so that he could begin painting at the first light of morning.

The portrait of Roger Ruark from memory was finished in two days, and was sold in a pair with the beautiful "Angel" at a sale a week later. Henry Truman insisted that they stay together, always together. They were Roger and his "Angel", his lovely *Angel with the Cinnabar Lips*.

THE MERMAID OF ZENNOR

There is a legend about the mermaid of Zennor. As with all legends there is a lot of confusion as to exactly what happened, but it is generally believed that the mermaid, whose name is lost in antiquity, met and fell in love with a young chorister in the ancient Cornish mining village of Zennor. His name is also lost in time, but some believe that he was the son of a vicar. This theory is backed up by the fact that there is still a trace of the mermaid in Zennor Church, where she is depicted by a carving on one end of the heavy wooden church seats. And the fact that there is a small pew bench quite near the door of the church on which, it is said, if you feel very carefully and believe, you can still feel the dampness of the mermaid's body where she rested while revisiting the place of her lover.

But that is digression. The point is that this lovely mermaid, half fish and half woman, fell in love with a man. It was, and it had to be, an unfulfilled love, yet it seems to have been a true love. Because of that, the young man, the poor, unhappy, fate-struck young human, the lover, went with his mermaid, lured by his hopeless passion for her, to some place that we who are earthbound can never know. Some subaqueous Valhalla which is, no doubt, populated by the souls of some millions of drowned sea salts.

Be that as it may, he has never been heard of since, and we can only presume and hope that the poor wretch of a lover found his happiness in that eternally submerged Olympus.

That, of course, is where the legend should finish, but unhappily legends never seem to know when they are well off, and they often continue and sprout tentacles of sadness.

This particular legend has one such tale of sorrow which points out that the mermaid also had a merman who paid his court for her hand. And it goes on that, when the mermaid disappeared with her earth man, her human with his legs, the forsaken merman caused there to be such severe storms along that rugged coast that the fishermen and those others of Cornwall who earned their living from the oceans were driven from their homes, there to stay until his rage had died down and the seas were stilled and safe once more.

The merman, it is said, still has angry spells in those cold, cold waters of the Atlantic, and then the rugged coasts are beaten and lashed by tantrums of waves again.

But that is a digression once more; on with the story…

*   *   *

The fog settled in quickly once the first early blanketing wisps had tucked themselves in at the corners of the headland. Visibility cut back until it was almost nothing; the haunting, sneering wail of a ship's siren drifted landwards, and there was a dampness in the air that got into the linings of the body and the clothing so that everything was wet and chilled. It was an unhappy night.

It was the sort of night you find now and then on the coast, and now in Cornwall it was the sort of night that had crept in across the Atlantic bringing with it an eerie something that all sailors have felt and will know.

I was staying at the small fishing village of Zennor on the northern tip of Cornwall, resting at a hotel up the hill with a name that was a Chy-an-something, and on this sad, wet night I had strolled through the streets that were so narrow you could touch the houses on both sides while walking along their rutted cobblestones, and had reached the part of the village that was called Down-Along.

Across the bay, about two hundred yards from me, a muffled flashing showed where the tower over the harbour master's office signalled to the fishermen caught in the bay by the fog. The lighthouse, away across to the far side of the bay, had long disappeared into the enveloping mists.

Behind me there was the occasional flash of light as a car pulled slowly round the corner of the coast road, The Digey they called it, and went straining in second gear into the night, vanishing bit by bit until even the red of the rear lights was gone. As I looked out to sea, the lights of one car flashed over me, and

I saw my shadow thrown sharp against the amorphous wall of fog. Then it was gone, and for a while I did not believe it had happened at all.

A few moments passed before I saw the stranger by the wall. He was looking out across the bay with eyes that seemed to pierce the fog as if it simply did not exist. I was strolling across, meaning to walk quietly behind him to continue into the town, when he turned and saw me.

"It's not very nice, is it?" he asked. His tone was flat, but he seemed friendly. I had the feeling, an unaccountable yet unquestionable feeling, that he was lonely.

"Not very," I answered, stopping by his side. To tell the truth, I welcomed the chance of a talk with someone. "It came down pretty fast though."

"It often does in these parts. Summer or winter, it makes no difference."

"You come from around here?" I asked, offering the stranger a cigarette.

"No thanks, I don't smoke," he said, holding up a hand as a refusal. "I never learnt."

There was a pause as I lit my own cigarette, blowing the smoke upwards so that it became a part of the fog, swirling away across the harbour.

"Yes, I do come from here." The stranger picked up the conversation. "This," he said, waving a hand expressively in a vast gesture that took in the whole of the bay, "This is all a part of my home."

I noticed suddenly that he rested on crutches. I had not seen them before, and I wondered what was wrong. I wanted to ask him, but I did not have the courage.

"Are you on holiday?" he asked.

I nodded, letting more smoke into the mist, and he went on.

"It's a good place. The people are fine, and they're pretty good to strangers, although they are not always so kind to their own. But fine people. Fine people." He looked into the fog with a deep penetration. "And there are some sights in these parts. It's good land around here and all around the bay."

I noticed that he did not have the normal West Country burr, and there was nothing that marked him out as a Cornishman. Yet he seemed to fit, to be in place here among the mists, looking over the fogbound harbour and sea.

"I wonder, could you tell me some of the places I should see?" I asked him, the sentence tapering away as I finished weakly. "If it's not too much trouble."

He laughed, a little laugh and not too deep as I would have expected. "Of course, of course. Would you like to know the historic or the beautiful places?"

"It's up to you," I answered.

"Right. Then let's sit down, and I'll try and think of the best places for you."

He led the way across to a seat against the far side of the low sea wall, and as he went I tried to see if his legs were plastered or bandaged. I was fascinated by his ailment, but he swung along so quickly on his crutches that I did not have a chance to see a thing.

We sat down, him on the left and me on the right. Another ship's siren cut in from the sea.

"There's the pilchard fishing, that's interesting," he began. "They stand up on the cliffs near here and watch out for 'em. And when they see a shoal out in the bay, they raise the cry."

"But don't they use trawlers?" I asked, baffled.

"Trawlers?" He sounded bewildered, almost as bewildered as I. "Seine nets, that's what they use here. A regular menace they are too. I wish they'd change them. Downright dangerous."

I dropped my cigarette to the pavement and trod it out with my heel. The fog got into my throat and made me cough. The stranger, his eyes now narrowed slightly, looked at me sharply.

"But you want to know about the surrounding places. How about St Just? That's where they mine all the tin, you know."

"Tin?" I interrupted again. "Surely the tin mines are all abandoned now?"

The stranger ignored me and went on. "St Helen's Chapel stands there, and the Brison Sisters just offshore. They've caused many a shipwreck, I can tell you. You've got to know where you're at to miss them, if you happen to sail around there."

He seemed to be distant when he spoke as if the rolling fog was a curtain between us, as if we were miles apart instead of merely a few inches. His eyes shone with a sudden brightness, but there was a feeling about his overall expression as if he were asleep or unconscious.

"They take the tin round to the Mount, on the other side of the headland," he said. "They sell it there, to some strange people from across the other side of the seas."

I listened, fascinated now but slightly frightened for some strange and peculiar reason.

"We used to go round there a lot, my friends and me," he went on, still seemingly ignoring me. "All the way round to Lizard Point and Kynance Cove. Then back to Godrevy Point across the bay there." He pointed out in a general direction across the mist enshrouded sea.

"We used to have fun swimming around past Cape Cornwall and Land's End, you know. We made friends with quite a few of the boys on the Longship's Lighthouse. Mind you," he continued as I listened in a silent awe. "Mind you, we had to be careful of those big ships churning up the seas as they swept into Penzance."

He lapsed into a sudden quietness.

"How about those places nearer to home?" I asked after a moment. I subconsciously lowered my voice, and the stranger shook his head as if someone had suddenly slapped his face.

"Nearer?" His voice sounded puzzled, as if he had just woken up and come back out of the fog and the chill of the night. He paused again for a moment, and looking at him I noticed that the brightness had dimmed slightly in his eyes.

"Yes," I said softly. "This place, and along the rocks… to the tin mines…"

"Oh yes," he replied, wrinkling his brow and half closing his eyes with concentration. "You want to know about Gurnard's

Head, and the castle on the headland, and Zennor. Now there's a place, Zennor. You might have heard of the stone there."

"The Giant's Rock?" I queried. I had heard of the famous logan stone, a rocking stone that balanced precariously on one corner, swaying as it had swayed seemingly for centuries.

The stranger showed interest. "That's the one," he said enthusiastically. "The Giant at Zennor Head." He seemed to have woken up again. "Some people say it's associated with witchcraft, that rock," he went on, winking knowingly and nodding in a curious idiotic-sensible gesture.

"There's a legend at Zennor, something to do with the church, isn't it?" I asked, not really knowing why.

He looked at me closely. I needed another cigarette, and lit one with a hand that shook slightly. It might have been the cold night air, but I didn't think so.

"A lot of people talk about that legend," said the stranger. His voice was taking on a harder texture. "They all say the mermaid fell in love with a chorister at the church."

For some reason my brain clicked up the date 1271. That was when the church was built. I remembered it from somewhere.

"They say she lured him away to sea so that she could be with him for all time."

His voice stopped suddenly, and he stood up, levering himself off the bench with his crutches. "I must be going," he said sharply, and started to move away.

"It's not true, is it?" I asked quietly.

The stranger stopped and turned back to look at me for a moment. "No," he said, so quietly that I had to strain to hear him. "No, it's not true. He pleaded to go with her, and she hadn't the heart to refuse him."

He turned away again, and I tried again to see the bandages or the plaster on his feet. They were hidden in the mists as the stranger moved into the night, supported on his two crutches.

The fog had practically covered him when he turned back to me once more.

"We grew up together, that mermaid and me," he said.

Then he turned away again and disappeared into the night. All of a sudden the noise of the scraping and the steady click-clump of the crutches that had followed him into the mists were silent. I stood up and started to walk after him into the fog, but he had vanished and seemed to be no more.

Then his voice came over to me, over from the side of the low wall, over from the sea he so obviously loved. "Tell them," said the voice, "Tell them that she really loved me, not the chorister. Tell them that we really loved each other."

* * *

* I revisited Zennor Church again many years after this story was written. There was then a separate chair carved in oak and standing in front of one wall. It was noted as The Mermaid's Chair, carved, apparently in the fifteenth century from an old pew. The main pews seemed to have been re-arranged or replaced... and there was certainly not a damp pew at the back this second time.

LONG NIGHT
IN THE CITY

He looked at his watch for the forty-fourth time in this seemingly long, but in reality so far short, night. Half past three. He groaned and rolled over onto his right-hand side.

Next to him, the girl grunted. "Me neither," she said, and he understood that she couldn't sleep.

The night had a million sounds, and each one seemed a personal insult to the two of them on the strip of harsh horsehair that padded together for a mattress.

The man rolled onto his back. What a place to stop over for the night. What a place after the quiet they had just known. A holiday. Huh! To the city-bred man, the country is full of anguish and noise. But to come back to the city…!

He reached out and held his watch sideways to the narrow strip of light reflecting from the ceiling.

The girl grunted again. "Don't they ever go to sleep here?" she asked in a low, plaintive voice.

A car revved right outside the window, and an anxious Romeo slurred the gears together in a way that would not please his father when he got the car back the next morning.

"What's the time?"

The man reached for his watch for the forty-sixth time. "Three thirty-three and forty-four… check, forty-six seconds."

"Give me a cigarette."

The man reached out and pulled on the slim chain that hung slightly to one side of the bed and was fixed by a piece of string to a central light high on the ceiling above them. Nothing happened, not even when he pulled the chain again. He swore and swung his legs over the side of the bed and stood up. He walked across the cool lino on the floor and flicked up the switch by the door. The room flooded with light, and he padded back to his own side of the bed yawning deeply.

He looked at the girl as he went, but hardly noticed her. Hours of work to weave the expensive transparent material of her nightgown. Hours of work to stitch it and hem it. Hours of work to earn the money to buy it. The man did not notice. He handed over a cigarette, flicked another casually up for himself, and took it direct from the packet with his lips. Then he noisily scratched a match. Another noise in the night.

He held the flame up, and both lit their cigarettes at the same time. They both blew smoke up at the ceiling, and a tight ring formed from the girl's. They both watched it rise an inch or two, then slowly melt into the air.

"It must be nearly a hundred degrees."

"Well, give or take a degree here or there. What's it matter?" She took a draw from her cigarette. "It's hot."

"Too hot."

They both puffed again, At the side of the room, a faulty tap continued its steady drip-drip into the cracked basin.

"In China, they use dripping water as a torture, don't they?"

"Uh huh."

"And I read somewhere that water can make a hole even in the hardest of stone if it drips long enough. Did you read that?"

"Yes, honey, I read it."

"Christ, but I never knew a night as hot as this before. It must be nearly a hundred degrees."

The man puffed his cigarette. "Nearly," he replied.

Outside, another car hooter rang through the night, echoing from the sides of the tall buildings lining the road. Tyres squealed as another driver hurried home to a wife who wanted to be unfaithful like him but who didn't know what time he would arrive back. A tram clanked. Two students argued in a semi-shout as they walked past the front of the hotel. The night porter made a sign at them, through the window, then turned back to the pictures on the sports page of the American edition he could not understand.

A moth flew in through the open window of the couple's bedroom and beat itself against the lampshade.

"That damned tap."

"It only needs a new washer, honey."

"Those Chinese sure know what they are doing."

The man stubbed out his cigarette in a metal ashtray advertising Dubonnet. He held out the metal to the girl, and she took a last, long drag at her cigarette before she, too, doused it, blowing out smoke at the same time.

The man put the ashtray back on his bedside table and checked that the girl's cigarette was fully out. He stamped the stub viciously on an ember the girl had missed, then he looked at his watch for the forty-seventh time that night and pulled the cord to put out the light. He was too tired to be surprised when the light actually went out.

"Good night, honey," he said.

"That all you're going to say?"

"Sleep well."

"No, not that. Aren't you going to say anything else?"

"What d'you mean?"

"You know. Like you usually say."

"What d'you mean?"

"You always say it before we go to sleep." Her voice was plaintive again.

"You really think we're going to sleep with that noise and all?"

"You could say it, just in case though."

"You really want me to, huh?"

"Uh huh."

"OK then. I'll say it."

"Don't make it sound such a favour. You don't have to say it if you don't want to."

"I want to."

"Well, say it then"

"I love you."

"D'you really?"

"Yeah. I love you, OK?"

The girl leant over and kissed the man. More tyres squealed outside as a driver jumped the traffic lights. The girl pulled back.

"Don't they ever do things quietly in this damned city?"

"Try to get some sleep, honey. Try to get some sleep."

The man lay back and shut his eyes. *She must be damned near right*, he thought. *It must be getting on for a hundred degrees. How hot can the body take it?* he wondered. *I bet the Chinese have a torture like that too.*

A clock chimed the quarter hour somewhere in the distance. And the man opened his eyes as he made an involved mental calculation to find out that there were five hours or so to go before they had to get up, wash, shave, make up and dress.

"That damned tap," he muttered, and lay there with his eyes wide open.

The girl heard the dripping too. She heard the man mutter, and she groaned. The two students returned along the street outside, and she wondered what they were arguing about. Politics, maybe. Students seemed to do that a lot nowadays. She wondered why. In her own student days—long ago, and very brief—the important things were the tennis results, or the boy friends, or the necking in the park with the boys you knew but whose names were a mystery when you were asked who you'd been with. But politics?

She turned over on her side and wished she had the energy to get up and answer the call of nature. *I hardly ever went in the country,* she thought, then drove the idea from her mind, not so much because thinking about it was vulgar but because it would only make her want to go all the more.

She felt, rather than saw or heard, the man reach out for his watch once more, and wondered why he wouldn't wear it in bed. Something to do with breaking the glass, she supposed. Or maybe his first wife wouldn't let him. She wondered for a moment and was positive she had read that watches only used unbreakable glass. So that couldn't be it. She wrinkled her brow as she tried to figure out where, and if, she had read that.

The man put the watch back on the bedside table. He sighed, and immediately wanted to look up the time again. *This could become a habit,* he thought. *Like drugs. Or cigarettes. Or sleeping with girls in transparent nightdresses you don't even have to look through anymore.*

He sniggered mentally as he pictured the scene. The doctor would be wearing one of those large mirror things on his forehead, with a light in the middle. He would be grey haired, kindly, dressed in a white and quite clinical.

"What are you suffering from, son?" he would ask.

"I've got the habit of looking at my watch," he would answer, and the doctor would cluck and make sympathetic noises.

He sniggered again to himself, yet damn it he wanted to look at the watch again.

The man rolled onto his back and stared at the strip of light on the ceiling. He tried to work out by the angles where the streetlight was situated outside, but then gave up because he knew that if he went on he would have to get up and look out of the window to see if he was right.

He rolled over again to face the still dark outline of the girl next to him. She was dozing now, her breath deep and steady. He could only guess that her eyes were closed and her forehead smooth, and he could only vaguely make out the rise and fall of her breasts. But he knew where they were and what they were doing.

A fly came in through the open window and buzzed around the now dark and cold shade round the ceiling light bulb, where the moth that had flown in earlier was sleeping. The man muttered an oath, and the fly went back out into the hot air of the night.

The noises in the street were quieter now. *Perhaps the city is going to sleep at last*, the man thought. *If only the tap would stop dripping.* He closed his eyes and tried to doze. A tram squeaked in the distance. Its driver yawned and was thankful that this was his last trip of the shift, and tomorrow was his night off.

The man rolled onto his other side and reached out his right arm, feeling for the bedside table. He looked at his watch for the forty-ninth time in this long, long night.

WAITING FOR MY WIFE TO DIE

Life is really miserable at the moment. You see, I'm just waiting for my wife to die. I don't know when it will happen, but I know it won't be too long. Days probably, a couple of weeks at the most. But I know it *will* happen.

Let me tell you about it.

My wife's name is Harriet, and we've been married for fifty-seven years. We met when she was just seventeen—I was a somewhat immature twenty-one at the time—when we were introduced at a friend's house. We got on well from the start, and within three years were married. Life was good, and we were happy to be together. Neither of us wanted children, so that didn't happen.

Then about four years ago she started to get ill. Alzheimer's. Her memory faded quickly, she became incontinent, she couldn't talk properly or hold a conversation. It was hard work looking after her, bloody hard work, but I managed for a couple of years, getting more and more frustrated seemingly by the minute.

The disease was not only killing her, looking after her began to take its toll on me as well, and during that third year I even had thoughts of hatred towards her. She became the cross I had to bear and I didn't want to carry it.

Eventually though, Harriet got so bad she couldn't walk or feed herself, and I had to send her to a care home so she could get the professional medical help she so badly needed. I visited her every day, but it was making me even more miserable, and the fact that I know it's the biggest killer of today—even more than cancer—has got me to the stage where I can't take much more.

The staff at the care home have been magnificent, and a carer called Pari has been particularly helpful. Well, much more than helpful actually. You see, she walked out of the home with me one afternoon and on an impulse I invited her for coffee in a cafe down the road. I was delighted when she told me her name meant angel, beautiful, a fairy. She was all of those things.

After that coffee we started seeing more and more of each other. I took Pari for a drink, then a meal, and after a couple of weeks we began seeing each other regularly. One thing led to another, and it wasn't too long before she let me kiss her. Her lips were like nectar, and after a few of them we soon became lovers.

Our feelings for each other grew quickly after that, until we finally committed our love for each other, and I can't think of being without her. We plan to get married.

The trouble, of course, is that I am still married to Harriet, and although the illness is slowly killing her, she is standing in our way. So I have decided, one day soon, I'm going to murder her so I can live with Pari and get my own life back. And that's why I know my wife hasn't very long to live, why I'm just waiting for her to die.

Tomorrow, or the day after. This week or next.

AT THE END OF THE TRAIN RIDE

For fifty years, Old Harry had waited by the bridge at ten past four to watch the London express go through. For fifty years he had not missed a single day; only once had the train been late, and Old Harry had sulked for a week.

Now, he ambled slowly through the narrow back streets of Little Milfield, walking slowly across the main road that led on to Great Milfield and Hazleton and then who knows where. He kicked a stone to one side, and as the clock on the church tower struck four he pushed his old felt trilby to the back of his head.

For some reason, everyone called him Old Harry. It had been so for as long as anyone could remember, even when Old Harry had been a young man. He nodded sagely as he thought of his younger life, walking silently with his hat on the back of his head by the village store and nodding a greeting to two of the wives of the village.

Old Harry walked out into the clean green countryside, leaving the musky smell of the village behind him. He breathed deeply, savouring the freshness of the afternoon, the bite and nip of the autumnal air, the beauty of England as nature began to rest for the winter. There was a purpose in everything around him, and a purpose in his step as he sped slightly, eager now to reach the bridge in plenty of time. Ready to settle and anticipate; aglow inwardly as a lover on his way to an assignation.

A slow-flying bird, a crow, worked its way across the sky to the east. A slight breeze awoke, rippling the long grasses and wildflowers. It cooled Old Harry's face as he walked the last few yards to the bridge.

He looked around him, unhurried still, and this time chose to sit on a long-dead log stump of a tree on the bank by the side of the bridge and overlooking the rail line. There were two or three alternative seats, but today Old Harry chose the tree. As he sat and settled himself into a relaxed comfort, a late-living fly buzzed around his ears for a moment, and then flew away into obscurity.

Old Harry sat on his tree stump and lit up an old and favourite briar pipe. He was a medium-height man, but that was the only thing about him that was medium. He had a fine cut face that now wore a thin fuzz of tufted white bristle; his hair under the trilby was also of the same spiky white, but with a few outcrops of ginger red still at the sides just above the curled rims of his ears. He rubbed a gnarled hand over his thin-lipped mouth and against the flat button of his nose.

Old Harry puffed contentedly at the pipe. He judged the time to be a few moments short of ten past four, and sure enough he heard the distant hoot of the express as it passed haughtily by the open wood platform of Milfield station. The train driver always hooted, but it never stopped and Old Harry knew it took just two minutes and fourteen seconds to race on to the bridge where he waited.

Two and a quarter minutes is no time at all, and then the train rushed round the bend and swooped down to the old stone bridge. Old Harry half stood as he saw it, the pipe forgotten in his hand as he watched, enthralled and happy as he had been as a boy, glad at the sight of an old friend.

The driver saw Old Harry and shouted to the fireman on the footplate with him that he was there as always. As the great steam engine rushed past, they both returned his friendly wave of greeting until his figure disappeared in the cloud of smoke that enveloped him as the engine disappeared under the bridge.

As the driver and his mate turned back to the controls of the magical engine, Old Harry watched and nodded back, the excitement now glimmering inwardly. The express roared by, steam surging from the fore stack, pistons racing and jumping like demon jack-in-the-boxes. Then the carriages, swaying and rocking, with wheels beating out a rhythmical beat that stuttered over the joints of the rails, their sound going deep as they crossed under the bridge and then rising up again as they reappeared on the other side.

Old Harry nodded as he watched and thought of the places up the line. Beyond Hazleton and away up to Edinburgh one way, and to London itself the other; there was life and adventure, a life he had never known in sixty years and more. Adventures such as he could never even dream about.

In his dreams Old Harry always knew he would make the journey one day. Up the line or down, it was of no matter. There was the journey, with all its noise, the arrival, and then the new sights that no one he had met had ever seen.

Old Harry puffed at his briar pipe and knew that soon he must turn the dream into a reality. He must make the journey soon. He had enough money in the savings bank, and he wanted to ride in the train, his beloved four-ten express that whistled through the familiar station and roared down to the bridge and away into the evening.

*   *   *

It took Old Harry a week to complete the details, but then he had the ticket: an inch and a bit of thin pasteboard. A return dream that beckoned and invited him to London, with its lights and its people and its different way of life.

Old Harry was surprisingly philosophical about it, and accepted his new status as the owner of a ticket on the express with a grace that surprised most people in the village. In the rough and ready saloon bar of The Plough he showed the ticket to all who enquired, and even to the three strangers from Hazleton who had heard the news and came to ascertain its truth. He never let it out of his hand, holding it firmly as a grandfather holds a baby learning to walk, and smiling with the corners of his mouth at the surprised burr of awe and appreciation that floated up every time the ticket was taken from its place in the top breast pocket of his Sunday jacket, which he had worn ever since the day he had taken the plunge and paid his fare over the counter at Milfield station.

That had been a day. The whole of Milfield had learnt about it soon enough from Jed the stationmaster, and had gone to see where the ticket had been sold. Old Harry himself had crept away to look at it in the privacy of his own cottage, but that privacy had soon been lost and forgotten as Milfield took the news to its slow-moving bosom and rejoiced.

They turned out in force to see Old Harry off, and George Squires drove him through to Hazleton in his trap, and at Hazleton the three strangers who had visited The Plough led a party of twelve who had come to see Old Harry onto the train that was to take him to the main line station where he would board the express.

Then, at last, Old Harry was on his own and climbing aboard the express that waited, with steam raised but under a tight check, for the whistle to blow. He walked down the narrow corridor and found a carriage that was, glory be, alone and empty, and he slid open the door and sat down. A tight knot of excitement and fear banged against the walls of his stomach, and his freshly starched collar dug into his neck.

All of a sudden he felt lonely, and he wished he was back on his bridge. He would sit on the jutting piece of wall today, and he would wave and the driver and fireman would wave back as they always did. His mouth went dry, and he wondered whether he dare smoke on the train.

There was an ageless three minutes before the whistle blew on the platform, and then the express lurched and picked up into a forward motion. *Too late now for regrets*, thought Old Harry, clutching at the strap of the half open window as he swayed with the movement of the carriage.

It was like a dream come true as the express roared along straight tracks and twisting corners. There was a frightening moment as they shuddered into a coal black tunnel, and then the familiar sights as he neared home.

Hazleton dropped behind, then there was the whistle through Milfield (seemingly higher and prouder than ever, it seemed today) and the two minutes and fourteen seconds to the bend and the bridge.

The whole of Little Milfield waved him past the bridge, and then he was gone and roaring into the evening towards the sprawling, grimy mess that was London.

Eventually, with a pitiful hiss and a last despairing toot of its whistle, the express slowed and stopped and became just another train standing in the station. London. Main line. The end of the ride.

Old Harry climbed down slowly and wandered dazed and pensive along the noisy concreted platform. He gazed, awe-struck, at the hurrying, bustling mass of people, rushing like nondescript ants about businesses that were at one and the same time important and yet futile.

He felt, rather than heard, the great hubbub of sounds. He sensed the great throng that surrounded him, pushing here and there without actually touching him or absorbing him. A clanging bell mingled with the shrill blast of a guard's whistle, combining to make him leap like a frightened deer.

The bodies rushing in every direction around him were not humans but self-centred entities with no thoughts or cares for any of the other beings around them. Old Harry was stunned. They were not people as he knew them in the tree-surrounded and suffused village where he had been born and still lived. It was big and busy, noisy and soulless. He had seen nothing like it before, and he wanted to flee.

But he had to wait, anonymous and unseen, before he could catch a return train home to Little Milfield.

Finally, Old Harry from the country found himself in the buffet with a steaming cup of weak tea on the table in front of him. The time by the great four-faced clock high above the platform was just past half past five.

Three hours, fourteen cups of buffet tea, and a plate of baked beans later, Old Harry crept back along the now cold and half deserted strip of platform to board the express for the return journey. This time he puffed at his friendly briar pipe as the train rushed mightily through the pitch black of the night, finally disgorging him and rushing off to the proud and castled city of Edinburgh at the far end of the line.

There was nobody to welcome Old Harry back to Little Milfield in the late night hours of the dying day. Harry puffed at his pipe and crept home to crawl peacefully between the comforting sheets and friendly worn blankets of his bed. The questions and talk would come later the next day, but for now it was enough just to be at home.

Questions there were by the score the next morning: about the journey, the train and the city. All through the day Little Milfield revelled and swayed to the repeated accounts of the ride that had taken Old Harry so far from home.

Then sharp, at a quarter to four, Old Harry wandered through the streets and out into the fields to the bridge. He waited, briar pipe in his mouth again and raising smoke into the evening air. And then he heard the whistle and felt the tremor as the express roared round the bend.

The driver saw Old Harry and shouted to the fireman that he was there again. They both waved, and then turned back to the controls, wondering, perhaps, where Old Harry had been the day before.

Old Harry watched them pass, and he nodded back as the train roared on along the tracks.

A SORT OF IRISH FABLE

I don't care what anyone says, sir, Shaun O'Flaherty was a good Irishman from the right side of that dividing border line the English have set up, and that was the only reason for his ambition. And as you'll know, sir, like every good son of the Blarney, Shaun's ambition was the burning light of his life.

I suppose it was, to be sure, the highest ambition it's been my good fortune to come across since Patrick Duffy himself got fed up with plunking his double bass in the local jazz band and decided that instead of going "boink boink" he had to learn the trombone and go "tara tara" instead.

But of course, you'll not be knowing what I'm talking about, sir, so I'll let you into the secret—although perhaps I shouldn't be calling it a secret as everyone knew what it was about. Let me tell you then, that Shaun's ambition was to own, and be master of, his own indoor privy.

Oh yes, he shared the use of one at the bottom of the garden like all respectable people, but I'm afraid that Shaun got taken with his fancy new idea.

It all started when Father O'Toole and he met up one fine day at the back of the Shamrock Arms.

"Shaun," says Father O'Toole, "Sure it must be wonderful to have an indoor privy like they have in the modern houses in the cities."

"Aye," replies Shaun in that quiet way of his, and off he goes all excited inside and without a word or a nod to anyone, not even the people he knows.

It was there inside of him though, this new idea. An indoor privy, indeed, yet it burnt up every living thought he had, and even when he was asleep he couldn't say a thing in his dreams without it having something to do with this new idea.

Even in the summertime Shaun had it on his mind. An indoor privy, and the sun shining like it was over the mountains in July that year.

But still, pretty soon he began to do more than just think about things. He went to work up at Hennessey's Farm three days a week, and didn't even spend one solitary penny piece at the Shamrock anymore. And pretty soon, to be sure, he'd saved himself quite a pile—about thirty punts all but a penny or two so I believe. Although, of course, it still wasn't anywhere near enough to build himself an indoor privy, especially as Shaun didn't even have his own house, lodging as he did with the Murphys up at their place down in the village.

At the time, of course, no one took much notice of Shaun, although we did all wonder what it was that had bitten him and started him to work so hard and give up the drink. Him, a one-time captain of the Shamrock shove-ha'penny team and all, and he never once came to see us when we went through to the semi-finals of the championships in Cork.

Still, Shaun O'Flaherty had his wits about him right enough, and we pretty soon found out what it was that was eating at his mind. Not that we had anything against the Widow Dooley. She was not handsome, mind, but she did have some money stacked away, and once when I bumped into Shaun on my way home after a day laying up in the sun, he did let slip that it was possibly as much as a hundred punts.

Mind you, I'll never know how hard Shaun had to work to win her hand. Nor how much of his own thirty punts savings it cost him. But I do know that I was as excited as anyone this side of Belfast or Dublin when they came into the Shamrock one night and announced their engagement as bold as brass. Why, I even bought them a Guinness a piece—at near on two punt a glass—to celebrate the great occasion. Out of my own money too.

They were married soon enough after that, and the Widow Dooley put her savings into a legitimate tallyman's business for Shaun. "O'Flaherty and Dooley Associates" they called it, and pretty soon it had grown into a fair sized proposition. I don't think anyone realised how much hard work was going into that business until Shaun mentioned about his expansion one day after Sunday service. We were all on our way up to the Shamrock for a quick one before lunch when he stopped us and told us about it. Shaun—who was completely teetotal by then, it was the Widow Dooley we thought—said right out that if we was all to drink less and save more we, too, could open a second branch and become a tallyman to the county council.

It was a bit of a shock, I might tell you, sir, because we'd all known Shaun when he was as right as Danny Donovan.

Still, things might have gone back to normal if it hadn't been for that terrible ambition at the back of his mind. Shaun worked night and day, and soon his two branches became four, then eight, then a round handy dozen. And soon after that the Widow Dooley and Shaun O'Flaherty started a lock-up shop and that, too, prospered and soon became a chain of stores.

But the moral of it was only too plain to see. You or I could have told that it would happen if we could have got near enough to borrow a punt or two for a drop of the hard stuff from Mr O'Flaherty, as he had become by then.

Sure enough though, Shaun's ambition would be the death of him, and I can tell you that when he had amassed a tidy pile that would see you or I through a century of evenings in the Shamrock, he and the Widow Dooley just upped and built themselves a house just out there on the church side of town, just a short way up the road.

And by the saints above, it had Shaun's indoor privy, as well as the usual one at the bottom of the garden too.

But it was too much, and Shaun was never the same man again. You see, when the house was built and finished he had no ambition left, and no need to work really. After all, what could money buy him then?

He'd left all us old neighbours behind, because you can't have friends *and* an indoor privy, and the Widow Dooley was no use to him anymore because all her original savings had gone a long time since and he didn't really like her.

But to cut a long story sideways, what happened after that is really old history by now, and Shaun O'Flaherty just passed away as he was climbing the stairs to his indoor privy, God rest his soul.

It just goes to prove something or other, I suppose, sir, and it sure does make a fine excuse for a wake. Before we go off to bury the poor old boy though, I'm sure you'll excuse me while I take a walk down to the bottom of the garden. It's for old time's sake, sir, and I won't be a moment.

LONELY IN A CROWD

I am surrounded by a million images I cannot distinguish. There are dozens of people I meet and I am alone. My world is full, but I am empty.

Logically I know I am surrounded by love, yet my own love has been cut away from me. I am alone in the middle of a teeming existence.

All my life I have used words to express what I saw and what I felt. They were the tools of my being. But now I cannot find the right words to tell me how I feel.

In broad daylight and in the silent dark of night I struggle to remember my wife as she was—as a vibrant, beautiful, funny, practical being who embraced every bit of what I was.

In reality I lost my wife to an evil mental condition many years ago. She suffered from Alzheimer's disease, and I watched bits of her slowly disappear for seventeen and a half years. There was always the vague hope that something might come back, temporarily maybe, that there may be a small, sudden spark of old normality, one last conversation.

But it was always a forlorn hope, and now her physical being has also gone, a final underlining to her life, and a huge part of me is missing.

It was inevitable, but it is unbelievable.

In the long years of my wife's illness I consciously discovered that I had emotions that had been bottled up inside me, and now suddenly they are jumping out and prodding at my conscious self at frequent moments as I carry on existing in my own lonely vacuum.

My memories are all, currently, of her as a frail sick old lady, but I pray my real memories of her may soon come back.

Life goes on, but right now I just feel empty. I am lonely in my crowd of love.

THE MAN OF THE MOUNTAINS

The sun scorched down over the cold, hard rock of the mountains, and Walter, relaxing on the lush grass of the lower reaches, stretched his arms above his head lazily. He yawned twice, then rubbed the right side of his jaw with a rough, gnarled hand. He studied the hand; short stubby fingers, a sort of puffiness around the lower joint of the thumb, and a line of ridged scars across the palm.

Walter looked at that left hand. He studied the scars where the forefingers had been torn away at the second joints when a fall of rock had caught him one day in the winter. He studied the scars, and he shook his head sadly, for the loss of his fingers meant a loss of activity to a man of the mountains, and the loss of activity is a terrible thing for such a man.

Down in the village, the church bell chimed its ritualistic call to prayer. The sound echoed throughout the mountains and was answered by a dozen smaller bells from a dozen smaller hamlets. Walter stood up slowly and looked around him sighing as he always sighed when he saw the mountains. The beauty he saw was like none other anywhere in the world, he thought. Not that he had been anywhere else in the world, but throughout his life he had been sure that his beloved mountains were by far the most lovely sight that man could hope to see.

He had always lived in the mountains, working mainly as a guide to the people who came once and looked at the views. He pitied them—they would go back to their towns and only half remember the peaks and valleys and crags. He would see them every day as he had the day before and the day before that, and as he would see them tomorrow and the day after that.

He was not a particularly religious man, but as his eyes took in the pine-covered slopes, the cold, forbidding, yet still inviting slopes of the mountains, he said aloud, "Show me a man who doesn't believe in God, and I will show him my mountains." His voice echoed gutturally from the rocks, and Walter felt ashamed for feeling a moment of weakness.

He started down the path to the village. Soon, he would pass the church, and everyone would be inside at prayer. But he would go past the church, go past it and on to his favourite *stübli* where he would relax with a beer, waiting for his friends of the mountains to leave their prayers and come to join him. A cool beer. Walter licked his lips with a rubbery tongue at the thought of it.

It had been a long time since he had last walked this particular mountain road, but every step, every blade of fresh green grass, seemed like an old friend. Thinking about it, it seemed to Walter that it had been a long time since he had last walked along any of the mountain paths. He racked his brain, but he could not remember just how long. Perhaps he had been away, but he could not remember. Again he passed a hand over his face, and he tried to remember. But what good is memory if it will not serve you when you need it?

Walter sighed once more. "I am growing old, I suppose," he said aloud, but this time he did not answer himself because there is no answer when you realise that life continues. Slowly he carried on down the path.

On his right-hand side, the ground dropped away down to the village far below him, covered with a vivid mass of red, yellow and blue wildflowers, covered with a profusion of minute wildlife that moved and acted and reacted; that lived and reproduced, that built and fought and tore down, and that eventually died.

On his left, the ground rose swiftly in the lower regions of the mountains that towered so many metres above his own puny and too-small body, rose to the snow-covered points where once he had climbed and been in love with life. And on his left, too, the pine forests clung to their precious grip on the hard topsoil that was the many-million-year-old descendent of the mountain.

Walter looked about him as he walked so slowly back to the village. His thick, studded mountain boots crunched the dust down as he moved his feet forward mechanically but with an inbred care that was the result of many years of experience. He paused to adjust the roll of his thick woollen socks over his boots, rubbing the remaining fingers of his hands over the bulging muscles of his legs showing between the socks and the heavy, hard-wearing *kniehosen.*

Sturdy legs, give me speed and power to get back past the church and to the bar where the beer is iced and cool to the throat and belly, he thought. *Hardy legs, stride forward.*

There was no appreciable increasing of speed, but soon Walter was able to make out the symbols that told educated men the names of the tourist hotels. He could not read. Not the writing of men. He could tell the next day's weather from reading the sky. He could anticipate the falling of snow from the smell of the wind. He could foresee a slide of mountain rock from a rumble too low for the ears of most men. But he could not read the symbols that men painted on the wooden sides of their hotels. Not that he needed to. He knew which place was owned by Hugo, where Otto ruled his guests with a frown and a wise word. He knew where his friends lived, and he did not need to read their names on the door.

Walter stopped on the path and smiled. "I know the symbols for my own name," he said aloud. "The schoolteacher showed me one day when the snow stopped me climbing and her class would not learn. Then she showed me how to make my name."

He chuckled to himself, and using the metal tip of the climbing stick he carried everywhere he scratched out his name in the ageless dust of the path. W-A-L-T-E-R G-Y-G-E-R. He stepped back, admiring the roughly formed letters.

"I can write, but I cannot read anything but my name," he said aloud to the wind.

But the wind, now building up as night began to creep up and over the mountains from the distant places on the other side, did not answer; it just blew gently, raking up the dust and blowing it back into the letters Walter had carved on the path.

Walter sighed again and carried on down to the village, where he could hear the funereal clanging of the bells from the tall, pointed spire of the church.

Now he thought only of the beer that he would drink when he arrived. It seemed a long time since he had tasted a cool beer. If he could only remember why he had not tasted a beer for such a long time. Perhaps he had been away, but he could not remember. If he could only think.

Soon he was in the village. He walked down the main street slowly, passing the chemist that was alternatively called *pharmacie* or *drogerie*, past the souvenir shops, the bank that also served as a hairdresser, past the tourist-smart cafes and bars, past the photographic shops with their revolving card racks, past the post office and the police station, and finally past the church to his own favourite *stübli*, where the men who earned their livings on the mountains gathered when they had a free day or in the evenings.

The *stübli* was in the main street, not too far from the station where the tourists arrived, and Walter had been going there almost all his life; so had his father. And if it had been in existence then, his grandfather would also have gone to the same bar. He would have sat in the same seat that Walter and his father always used, over in the corner looking from the end window along the street and up to the tall peaks that towered over the village. He would have sat in the same seat in the same *stübli* drinking the same lager, as cool as a mountain stream falling through the snow that never melted on the heights. He would have sat there, and he would have enjoyed it as much as Walter and his father enjoyed it.

But now there was no grandfather, and no father either if it came to it. Only Walter to sit in the seat and enjoy the lager beer trickling slowly over his tongue and down, past the throat, to the very depths of his stomach. A satisfying feeling that only men of the open air can know.

Walter climbed the two wooden steps into the friendly warmth of the beerhouse, paused for a moment to catch his breath, then took three slow steps forward to go to his window seat. He looked round, but only he and a stranger sitting at his seat were in the bar at that moment.

He thought for a moment of asking the stranger to move, then he thought otherwise. "What can I say to him?" he asked himself. "Can I say I have always sat in that seat, so he cannot? Can I say that my hospitality and the hospitality of the village says he cannot sit in the best seat in the house? Can I say that a stranger must make do with that which is not the best? No. I cannot say any of those things, so I shall sit in another seat myself. I will not like doing it, but I will do it." And so saying, he felt better about it and went to sit in the opposite corner to the stranger.

The two men did not look at each other, and after a while the stranger began to tip his glass to a higher angle as he neared the end of his drink. But when he finished, instead of leaving (and allowing Walter to shuffle into the window seat) he took a thick briar pipe from his trousers' pocket and lit it with a match he struck against his thumbnail.

Walter watched him in silence, running his right hand through the grey mop of hair that topped his weather-worn, browned face. *Soon,* he thought, *soon the men of the mountains will be in from their churchgoing, and things will be all right again and the* stübli *will ring with their chatter.*

And soon they were in. Soon, the half dozen men of the village who climbed and guided others on the mountains as part of their daily lives came into the wood-built bar for their evening glasses of beer. They came in laughing at some joke or another and sat down around the stranger in the window seat. They did not look at Walter, and Walter was upset.

"Perhaps they have not seen me in my strange and different seat," he said softly to himself, seeking as always to defend his friends when they did something he did not fully understand. He stood and went across to them.

"Hello," he said simply.

They ignored the greeting and carried on laughing at the pipe-smoking stranger's jokes.

"Hello," said Walter again, a little more loudly this time. But they still showed no sign of hearing.

Walter pushed past Hans and Hugo and Otto and the other Walter, and he stood in the middle of the group. "Hello, don't you recognise me anymore?" he asked, his voice louder than it had ever been heard before. "Don't you recognise me, Walter Gyger?"

They took no notice, and Walter suddenly remembered. He remembered where he had been. He remembered why he had not walked his beloved mountain paths and looked at the flowers. He remembered why it had been so long since he last drank a glass of glistening mountain-cool beer. He knew why the stranger had sat in his favourite corner seat in his favourite beerhouse, and he knew why no one had come to serve him although he had been there for fifteen minutes or more. He knew, he remembered, and suddenly he wanted to breathe in the fresh air of the mountains.

None of the mountain men looked up as Walter rushed for the door as fast as his sturdy but now aged legs could carry him. None of them looked up as he ran awkwardly up the street towards the mountains, now glistening in the silver light of a fast-rising moon.

On the edge of the village and less than a quarter of a kilometre from the *stübli* he paused and looked up at his beloved mountain, taking in the silent beauty of the majestic power of the scenery with a slow sweeping look. His heart filled with joy as it always did and he knew he was wedded to the mountains and could never leave them.

He started to walk upwards, out of the village and past the church. Dusk was settling and he was looking at the mountain and not where he was going, and somehow he tripped over the low wall dividing the church from the street, and no one heard the low groan as Walter saw the words on the grave in front of him.

W-A-L-T-E-R G-Y-G-E-R. He made out the symbols in the light of the moon. His own name. And now he knew for sure. He remembered distinctly, but now he was not scared anymore.

"I should have remembered," he told himself, speaking out loud to the wind, "But I suppose I am getting old."

He laughed as the wind repeated his words.

"Getting old," he said again, this time to his precious mountain, looking up at it in the moonlight as the wind stroked his roughened face. "How can I get old like you? I am dead!"

MIA ROMANTICA

I t was one of those balmy evenings you only seem to get in Europe. The night darkness flickered against the edges of the Roman city lights, struggling dismally to clamp down its nocturnal curfew against the unwilling wishes of the people and the tourists in the streets.

Somewhere, a far way off, a hooter blared, lost quickly with its hundred others in the night mood of timelessness. A shrill cry pierced the air, a swift correction for some erring babe or pet. Somewhere among it all, a car door slammed and an engine whirred into life. Then it, too, was lost as the confection of warmth and lazy leisure loomed all around.

There was a certain smell to the city of Rome that night; a feel to it in which you knew just why it was called The Eternal City. Time was at a standstill, motionless among a welter of movements all too individual to be of consequence in the pattern of the future and the present and the past.

From close at hand, a recognisable sound came from a radio or jukebox. A song, played perhaps too often these past few weeks, lulled its melodic way into the atmosphere, dividing the creamy paths of the air in its well-worn course of notes. The song was called something *Romantica,* or *Romantica* something, a two-word name that explained itself to the ears of the tourists and residents alike. It was soft and pleasant, tuneful and easy to hear.

In the restaurant of the cheap Albergo des Americaines, the Hotel of Americans, a severe little waitress had just finished serving the last of the en pension guests. They had eaten their green lasagne, had a breadcrumbed escalope and a side plate of mixed salad, and were even now at work devouring large helpings of gateaux filled with a rich, yellow custardy cream and soaked in brandy.

The waitress heard the song wafting in on the evening air. It was instantly recognisable and popular, and it was the reason she had come to Rome just a few brief weeks before. She listened to it, and let the music and words drift over her, as its warmth enveloped and held the city.

Anna Maria, the severe little waitress, had a face that could easily be pretty if she would only smile. Her features were demure and petite; a small, near snub nose below large blue eyes. Unusual eyes for an Italian, but wide open, honest, trusting eyes. Her hair, black as the night above the city lights, was pulled back and on top in a tight bun, adding severity to her features, which she kept held in a grim-lipped scowl even when she was happy.

Listening to the music now, Anna Maria's face kept itself closed, but a tapping foot gave hint to the feelings behind the features.

The song ended, and the city relaxed back into its limbo of never-ending. Anna Maria pulled herself back into the real world and began collecting the plates and forks without a word. Her leg brushed against that of a middle-aged and lonely American who let it happen, and she pulled herself away sharply, the movement a match to the expression on her face.

Later, in her room, she remembered the incident and grunted scornfully. *How American,* she thought, and mentally dismissed the lonely man, whose wife had actually died just a year and a bit before.

Anna Maria let her thoughts take full possession of her.

She recalled the night, about a month or five weeks back, when she had first heard that record of *Mia Romantica,* far off in her small village home some fifty kilometres outside Florence. It had hit her with a feeling she had never known before, a feeling that seemed to shine a bright electric torch into her spirit and light up long hidden corners of darkness within her tough but slight-built frame. The music had kindled feelings within her that she did not know were lurking there, and the smooth voice of the singer had slid into her mind and hooked itself to some waiting niche that was there and ready to receive it.

Anna Maria, although nearly twenty-nine, had not had much contact with men. The boys of the village were all the same, she knew, and there were plenty of other girls for them to cuddle and squeeze in the hiding darkness of the fields around the village. Anna Maria had heard all about it during one incredulous evening with a schooltime friend of hers who had been persuaded, and she knew she wanted no part of that kind of thing.

Her parents had raised her respectably, and a man was there to be loved and married, to cook and care for, give her children to raise, and to grow old with. *Time enough for all that*, she thought, *when I find the man and marry him.*

Then she heard Ricardo Gozzi singing the new hit record *Mia Romantica.*

The song caught on quickly, sweeping over all Italy in a frenzy of melody. It swayed and it lilted, it had reason as well as rhyme, and it said everything that its listeners would want to say but were too shy.

Anna Maria heard it every day that first week, and having saved her lira carefully, she went to buy the record one Saturday when her friends were out. She had no record player, but she bought the record and kept it in her drawer with the fresh-ironed underwear and the white shawl she had worn when she was confirmed. She told no one about the record, and only looked at it in the dim light of the evening, humming the melody and looking at the name printed in small block capitals on the otherwise dark black sleeve. DA RICARDO GOZZI.

Soon, she knew, the song must fade away and another take its place. She dreaded the inevitable, and she knew in her deepest thoughts, the ones she hardly ever dared to think, that her love was absolutely hopeless. For now though, it was something she could enjoy, held nocturnally in a solid, black circle in her hand.

Then three things happened almost at once. Anna Maria was busy at her work around the house one day when she chanced to hear the radio from the house next door. It was turned up loud, and the sounds of her *Mia Romantica* drifted in with the smell of azaleas from the garden. Anna Maria stopped and listened, and then like a young girl eavesdropping at the door, listened wide-eyed as an unknown announcer introduced and interviewed her Ricardo.

He started off by insisting that he was just an ordinary Italian home-loving boy who enjoyed home-loving things. Yes, she heard, he was pleased at his success, and no, he had not been singing to anyone in particular.

"At least," said the voice of her Ricardo, soft and husky and lush, "It was aimed at a girl somewhere, a girl I don't know yet and haven't even met. She will understand the song, and she is the girl I'm going to marry one day."

There was a laugh in his voice, but Anna Maria knew that it was not a mocking laugh. It was a laugh that told her all she needed to know about the man.

She pictured the face she had seen in a dozen posters, and could see the eyes crease up with the laugh, the mouth open to reveal firm white teeth. She had an uncontrollable feeling that Ricardo's scalp would ride back when he laughed, and perhaps his ears would twitch just once when he began.

Anna Maria went to her room early that day and held the record to her body while she hummed the song and heard the laugh in her imagination.

The next day, while shopping, the second event happened. She saw a picture of Ricardo on the front page of a newspaper in the village store and ran back home as fast as she could to take enough money from her hidden store of savings and then return to the shop to buy it. It was the first time in her life she had ever been so extravagant, but she excused herself liberally and promised to give up something the following week so that she could replenish the savings in her drawer.

That night she locked the door to her room, though no one but her ever went into it, and sat on her bed with her record and her newspaper. She dreamt a little, hummed the song a little, and held the two articles in her two hands for a while.

As she daydreamed she thought of the voice, and the lines of laughter that had surely covered that lovely face when he spoke on that interview.

She looked at the newspaper photograph for a while and was sure she was right about the laughter lines, and then slowly, because she had not read much since leaving school, she worked out the caption that hung for about an inch below the picture.

"Ricardo Gozzi," she read, her lips moving. "The handsome thirty-two-year-old singer whose record of *Mia Romantica* has swept the continent, arrives in Rome today to receive the Golden Eagle award of the International Music Association. He will be singing at the Hotel Grand for four weeks before leaving on a tour that will take him around the world."

Anna Maria's eyes read on, but there was nothing new that she did not already know about her Ricardo. She looked again at the photograph and held the record in her hands. But after a while the practical woman who was always inside her made her tell the picture that she would have to leave him for a while. She didn't want to waste the money she had spent buying the paper so she felt she had to read it all—every word—and it was on page seven (of twenty-four) that the third event happened. Tucked away on that inside page, far from the picture of her Ricardo, Anna Maria saw an advertisement for a waitress at the Albergo des Americaines in Rome. In Rome!

She turned the newspaper back to the front page, folding it neatly so that the picture faced upwards. She smiled at it for a moment, then put newspaper and record on the table as she got pen, ink and writing paper and began composing her letter to the manager of the Albergo des Americaines.

Now she was in her room on the third floor of that hotel, and she was counting out the money she still had left. On her first day in the city she had made enquiries, and she knew she just had enough to make her dreams come true. Tomorrow, her evening off, she would go to the Hotel Grand, and then she would see and hear her Ricardo for herself.

She went to bed in a flurry of rare nerves, snuggling deep down into the clean, crisp white sheets as she endeavoured to force herself to a sleep she knew wanted no part of her that night. In her imagination she heard again the soft laughing voice, and then the melodic chant of her *Mia Romantica* swept Anna Maria to her night-time dream meeting with Ricardo Gozzi. Enough time, tomorrow, for reality.

Then it was morning. Anna Maria awoke with a conscious feeling that this day was to be like no other she had ever known before. Somehow, the feeling she had encountered with her erring school friend so long ago came back to her as she hustled and bustled around the tables during breakfast. The middle-aged American was there again, but today he was immersed in a bout of indigestion and made no move towards touching her again.

The day flew past, and by the evening the balmy warm air held the city in its grasp once more. The eternal repeating sounds of Rome held on the breeze for moments, then were gone and the night was silent for a while. Anna Maria was in her room, the record on her bed and the folded newspaper with its photograph of Ricardo brazenly staring at her while she changed.

Anna Maria looked at her body for a moment, conscious of it as a virgin bride on the night before her wedding. She dressed with care, covering her body with fresh underwear and the simple pink frock she wore for festivals. Her face was well scrubbed, and her short snub nose a bit shiny. Her eyes were wide open, and she flashed excitement. She combed her hair and took just a little bit longer than usual to pull it back into its bun on top of her head.

Then she went out, and for a while as she walked her shoes, with their sensible heels, clicked regularly and added their noise to the myriad sounds of the city.

The head waiter at the Grand kept her for a while, but then she was in and tucked behind a small table at the back of the room. A small band played eating music, and she ordered simply from the set menu, giving details of her meal slowly and carefully, making sure the man in front of her had time to write down each dish before she told him the next.

She had a clear soup with rice, then some chicken with a sauce, cauliflower and pasta. She had a trifle and a glass of water, then the lights went down and the band leader appeared as if by magic to announce, amid great applause, the main attraction of the evening.

Rich wives clapped enthusiastically, their husbands wondering about it all, and then there was a sudden hush as Ricardo Gozzi stepped out. A spotlight hunted for the briefest of seconds before finding him, and time stood still for Anna Maria.

Ricardo took a pencil-thin microphone and began to sing. One song, two, three, four. At the back of the room, Anna Maria was as still as midnight in her village as she watched and loved her Ricardo. Twice as handsome as her newspaper, and here in the very same room as she was.

There was another brief pause, then Ricardo began to sing again. *Mia Romantica*. A breathless hush fell over the room, and the words fell clear and pure into every ear. Ricardo put down the microphone and began to walk in an unelectronic sweep around the room. No one moved. Not a thing, not a sound, just Ricardo Gozzi and *Mia Romantica*.

Then he was in front of Anna Maria, and for just a split second she was her normal stern-faced self. But then she smiled without thinking. Their eyes met, and for a moment before her mind went blank, Anna Maria noticed the laughter lines etched deep around his eyes and in the corners of his mouth.

Ricardo saw her honest blue eyes—un-Italian eyes—and his whole face smiled down at the simple girl before him.

"Mia Romantica," he sang, and the room filled with a huge bursting torrent of cheering.

Rich wives, bored husbands. Hungry waiters. They all joined in the echoing flood of applause as Ricardo smiled, with lines at the corner of his eyes and around his mouth, at the girl for whom, at last, he could sing his song. The only girl who would understand it.

THE EIGHTH DAY OF THE WORLD

It was the greatest morning there ever was. A day blooming with a sense of magic, a perception of magnificence, an emotion of splendour. In the heavens, the sun beamed and glinted into the furthest outposts of space, and particles of matter shone with a delightful aura of loveliness.

The colours of eternity were rich and warm, pastels and primaries glowing wholesomely into space even beyond the bounds of godly imagination. It was, indeed, the greatest morning there ever could be, and God was in his office studying it.

Suddenly God sat upright at his desk. *I know*, he thought, *I'll create a world and make it the centre of everything that this morning is. I will preserve the beauty and the tenderness of this day for all time. I will make… the world.*

And God thought, *Let there be an earth*. And there was an earth, spinning and twisting its minute path through some infinitesimal part of space.

Then God thought, *Let there be life*. And a small amoeba and a patch of algae burst into being, created and creating and growing into mighty bundles of life.

And God went further. *Let these small single cells be two cells*, he thought. And there were two-celled creatures twitching and squiggling around the waters of the world.

But God had not ended. He looked at this new-found world of his, and he realised the goodness of the earth. The soil that begged to be used. The mass that pleaded for cultivation. And so God made the plants, which grew and let the earth become used and good.

Then God thought, *Let there be animals on this flourishing earth*, and he created amphibians, who creaked out of the seas and walked the lands, and left a trail of life behind them.

And then God made the amphibians lose their gills and shed their fins and become an equal to the flowers and grasses and plants that abounded. And they became small animals with fur, which grew to be large animals with hides. These were huge at first, so then God created others. Some were striped, some spotted. Yet others were sleek, and yet others that grew fur so long and shaggy that they left the proliferation that had become the jungles and made the plains and the valleys a living world.

Animals there were in plenty. At the two polar extremes. In the equatorial centre. Around the Capricorns and in between. They crawled and they slithered. They ran and they walked. And eventually, still covered in fur, they stood and they used their front paws as arms. The world was nearly complete.

Then finally God thought, *Let there be man*. And Adam came. And shed a rib. And the family of man was begun and grew and spread to all corners of this new, rich, wonderful world.

And God sat back pleased, and watched his creations. Watched man and the animals, the amphibians and the fishes, the two-celled and the amoeba. He watched the plants, the tall trees, the bushes, and grasses and the flowers. It was a wonderous sight that had taken just seven heavenly days since the greatest morning there ever was. And God rested, content.

On the eighth day, God was in his office looking out at the first mortal day on Earth. He dwelt on the beauty of the flowers, on the strengths of the trees, all the hundreds of animals, and at the fertile goodness and loveliness that was this new world he had created. And he thought with empyrean pride of his greatest creation: mankind.

And while he was watching, those humans started a world war.

THE HEDGE

The hedge was more than five hundred years old; half a millennium of growth that had made it like an elder statesman in the garden.

It had sheltered and pleased fourteen generations of the Benedict family, and now it stood tall with its mass of younger brethren—smaller lines of shrubbery that coursed through the magnificent park land of the old abbey. A huge, tall, stately—albeit now commonplace—*Crataegus monogyna* from the family Rosaceae, the common hawthorn.

It was tall, almost six metres in height, and at times of the year its upright, prickly thicket showed sweet-smelling and delicate small creamy pink flowers. For year after year, clusters of deep red berries bore the oval brown seeds that would ensure that the hedge continued life for another year, another generation.

The idea of the hedge was first suggested by Gyles Benedict during a rather one-sided discussion with his wife Elyzabeth as he mopped up the remnants of a rather greasy, thick gravy from his tin plate with a slice of Bannock bread.

"God's death, wife, I think you deserve a special garden for your own privacy and that of the children. T'will keep the peasants from prying," he told her.

Elyzabeth looked back at him steadily. "I thank thee, sweeting…" she said, adding demurely, "But thee are ta'en, for we have no children."

Gyles had hacked another slice of beef, dropping a slither of fat to a rather gaunt-looking dog by his side, and allowed himself a slight grin. "Not yet," he grunted, "But when we do, we will, i'faith, need to keep them from those peeping eyes of the peasants of the village."

Elyzabeth nodded her unheeded agreement.

"Hey-ho then, 'tis done," he replied, then proceeded to tell her what he planned for the hedge, belched, and that was the end of the matter.

It took Gyles a while to find a countryman worker from another nearby hamlet courageous enough to defy popular feeling in the village to first plant and then tend his immature shrub. But as with everything he did, the problem was eventually resolved and the foundations of the hedge were laid.

It grew quickly. In the first year, the roots took firm hold and the bush grew by about a foot, and then it was fed by a steady mix of rain and sunshine that boosted it to a solid and sturdy thicket.

The idea of the hedge was to give Elyzabeth and Gyles' planned children a certain amount of seclusion from the angry villagers after he had moved into his new home.

Gyles had acquired the old abbey after the Dissolution of the Monasteries decreed by Good King Hal the year before. The king had been battling to overcome the power of the church, and when he decided to cut back the power of Rome, he had formed the new English church with himself as leader. He sold off many of the old church buildings to the wealthy aristocrats of the land for use as country estates, and Gyles—although not a gentle himself—had been lucky enough to be rewarded with the grand old two-floor abbey.

Gyles had begun his working life at the age of seven as a fletcher, and by hard work had at last managed to find a place on the team making arrows and other weapons for King Henry's private family army. He had played a large part in helping the soldiers of that army blight the smaller church buildings during the Dissolution, and while his fellows would spend their angels and crowns on women, pleasure, or (at tuppence a time) on the best beers, Gyles, through careful saving and a certain amount of duplicity, had boosted his rather princely six pounds a year wage so that he ultimately had a cache of almost one hundred sovereigns.

When the offer of the abbey outside the village of Hambledon Moreton was made, he offered small vails, bribes to the agents, so that he got priority and plunged virtually the whole of his savings towards buying it.

"Fie me, it will mean we will be landowners," he had told his startled fifteen-year-old bride Elyzabeth. "Our descendants will be real gentry rather than common rustic or townies."

And so they moved into the abbey, despite objections by the ageing supporters of the erstwhile clerics of the village, who protested long and loud but could do nothing about it.

The abbey itself was rather grand for the son of a common town labourer, and within a year Gyles had managed to convert it to a home of even greater magnificence. The great hall was long and tall, the floor covered in rush matting, and a new full wainscoting tongued and grooved to give it the appearance of a palatial palace.

Gyles was something of a forward thinker—he was one of the first to replace the traditional turnip on his daily menu with the new-fangled potato—and he had great plans for expanding the abbey site even further. But he maintained his trickery and wiles in the city, making three or four trips there each month as he slowly but surely built up his savings once more.

He was able to afford three servants, whom he paid a handsome two pounds a year each to help him develop the house and provide for all his and Elyzabeth's home needs. Now he put them to work on the garden and the hedge. Soon the simple hawthorn had grown to a full six metres and was trimmed and neat and a pleasure to the eye.

Gyles used his natural town double-dealing ways to court the still-angry country villagers of Hambledon Moreton by allowing them to use the trimmings from the shrub they called Mother-die for their annual medieval Maypool rituals. And the villagers eventually grew to forgive him and to accept him as an advantage to their community, at the same time craftily making money for themselves by selling the dried hawthorn flowers, leaves and berries to gullible passing travellers as rare country medicinal herbal cures for a single silver groat.

By now, Gyles and Elyzabeth had three children, two girls and a son they named Wylfride, and they all played together as a family in the garden behind the privacy of the hedge. Gyles told the children fascinating stories of the fairy spirits he professed to live in the hawthorn, and like them he believed every word he spoke.

Wylfride loved the garden as much as his city-bred father, and as he grew he took a delight in helping the peasant servants tend and nurture it. When Gyles eventually died at the ripe old age of thirty-five, Wylfride became the master of the estate and continued to work on developing the garden.

Wylfride had all his father's wiles and maintained the same kind of fruitful chicanery operations his father had used to build his funds, so when the rich families began to flee from London to escape the dirt, crime and illness and replace it with good clean fresh country air, he was able to sell them plots of land in neighbouring villages for grossly exaggerated profits. The family fortunes grew, just like the hedge Wylfride had grown up with and loved.

The money he acquired allowed Wylfride to hire gardeners from the now compliant villagers, who had turned their hatred instead to the "furriners fro' Lun'on" and he began developing the rest of the grounds with a further series of hedges and lawns. Soon, smaller bushes of English box, leylandii, gold diosmas, lavender, myrtle and laurel edged away from the central hawthorn to provide the garden with a whole series of lanes and pathways leading to magic open spaces filled with glorious, white-starred eriostemon, hardy *Grevillea rosmarinifolia*, and small-leafed honeysuckle.

Weeds were meticulously removed, and many small animals and birds made their homes in the excellently tended and cloistered seclusion of the many deciduous and evergreen hedges. At one time there were over fifty different birds, twenty small animals and fifteen kinds of butterfly living in the hawthorn itself; they were an essential part of the wildlife habitat of Hambledon Moreton.

By the time Wylfride's grandson, Erasmus, had followed in the line of Gyles, the great gardens of England were beginning to grow, and although it was meant mainly for agricultural use he used his family's natural cunning to acquire money from the government of the time under the new Enclosure Act to add fancy twirls and whirls to the hedges, cutting complex topiary figures in elaborate, whimsical elephant, swan and giraffe shapes with a kind of manic phobia. As Erasmus, and later his children, walked the pathways and alleys of the garden, lively rabbit shapes danced out at them from unexpected corners to make them jump with joy.

But over all of it, the central hawthorn hedge still reigned supreme.

Erasmus and his successors planted tall trees of elm, linden, hornbeam and beech to add high hedges in the growing French style, along with evergreen cedar, cypress and yew. There were squared off areas of hedge surrounding herb and flower gardens, wind-shielding high-sided plots leading into temperate vistas, and enchanting bowers where couples could stroll or sit under parasols on carved wooden benches.

Some sections were extravagantly ornate in their precisely laid out ways, while others were landscaped in the manner of the new British gardeners such as William Kent and his helper Lancelot Brown—later known as Capability Brown.

The abbey and its elaborate garden developed and grew through the ensuing centuries, and fourteen generations of the same family loved, played and enjoyed its privacy and beauty. No matter what befell the family, the house, its garden, and in particular its original, venerable hawthorn hedge, were the link that held them all together.

For generation after generation, age after age, youngsters of the Benedict family would hide behind that hedge, jumping out laughing at their parents, or would hop, skip and jump in mock fright as they made their way playfully along the radiating, scattering arms of its smaller hedges in games of derring-do.

The older members of the clan, too, would use the hawthorn as a hidden meeting place with the girls of the gentry who came to the dances with their parents, and many a stifled giggle was heard inside the house or down in the village as a result of those illicit midnight trysts.

The ancient old hawthorn was so much a part of Hambledon Moreton's one-time abbey that the Benedict family included it on the impressive coat of arms that now hung carved in granite over the original stone lintel of the front door.

And it became so famous for its sturdy surround and imposing girth that after one member of the family around 1873 had famously thrown open the garden to the public for an open day for charity, people began to travel from around the country—and some even from far abroad—to see the garden and marvel at the Benedict hedge, as it became known.

Today, the modern incumbent of the estate was Earl Benedict of Hambledon Moreton, who had inherited the title from his father, given it as an ostentatious reward in a political Honours List just after the Second World War in 1945, and he was just in the process of handing control of the estate to his son Viscount Giles, whom he had named in honour of the illustrious forebear who had begun the dynasty so many centuries ago.

Earl Benedict, like all those others of his kin before him, cherished the garden, and he had brought up his only son with the same loyal and loving feelings towards their family and its home. Viscount Giles relished the thought that he, too, could play a part in its history.

It was because of this, that shortly after taking possession of the abbey, he called all known relatives to the house for a traditional Sunday family lunch. And it was while the roast beef and potatoes were being prepared by the staff in the kitchens, that he called everyone to order to make an announcement.

He was, he told them, about to have a separate, smaller, house erected in the grounds for his father and his second wife. It was to be built in the same style as the original abbey on the far side of the garden by the lane that led down to the village and would be the latest enhancement to the estate so diligently built up by Gyles, Wylfride, Erasmus and the other Benedicts who had lived in and loved the old house and its sylvan, idyllic, peaceful grounds.

"I am determined, however, that although my father and his wife will live in a separate house, we must still stay together," he announced. "We must all be as a single family. Togetherness must be our byword, as it always has been for the Benedict family over the last five hundred years and more."

There was a moment's silence, broken only by the sound of electric shears coming in through the open windows from the garden. Then there was a slight ruffle of applause, and Giles' father silently raised his mug of vintage Olde English beer to his son in acknowledgement of the sentiment.

"And to make sure that we will be as one, that the familial fraternity will always be there, I am having that darned old mangy hawthorn hedge chopped down at this very moment. It means that at last, we will be able to look at each other across the lawns every day."

THE MISSING KISS

Young Archie Bassett knew he had forgotten something. It had worried him all day.

Mind you, at the age of eighty-six, Archie, always known affectionately as "Young Archie", being forgetful was a daily (almost hourly) part of his life. But today was different. He had missed out the daily kiss for his wife Muriel.

Today he had somehow forgotten it, and it worried him. It was a routine—something Archie enjoyed. The daily kiss.

How could he forget the daily kiss for Muriel?

The kiss had been a daily statement of love between them from the very first day they married. It had developed from the early passionate embrace and full-on-lips heart-pounding kiss of the early days, through to the tender kiss on the cheek to finally settle down to a morning kiss blown casually—but meaningfully—across the room. Today he had missed it for the first time.

Archie looked across the room.

"Sorry," he mumbled, but even as he blew the kiss he knew it was no atonement for the "sin" of missing the event earlier in the day. It preyed on his mind and as he prepared to turn out the lights, check the door locks, and go (slowly) upstairs to bed, he worried about it.

He got into his pyjamas, and as he stood ready to turn the light switch off by the bedroom door he blew another kiss towards Muriel. Not that she took any notice—she had been dead for eighteen years. And her photo standing on a small table on the opposite side of the room looked as impassively lovely as always as the daily kiss was blown across.

THE CHAPEL IN THE SAND

Cornwall is a land of history—and legend.

And in all honesty the legend is usually richer than in actual history, although it's often hard to know where one starts and the other ends, so intertwined are the stories that make up the past of this fascinating part of western England. What we do know is that it is a land dating from time immemorial, with strange, beguiling legends that might or might not be full of truth or half-truths.

Take the story of St. Enodoc chapel. It is close by the sea with the breakers rolling in and dates back to medieval times or beyond. And it has an intriguing history.

St. Enodoc is part of a parish set up by William de Sancta Menefreda, who is thought to have been one of the twenty-four children of St. Brychan and who probably came to Cornwall in the sixth century, a time of great Christian missionary expansion. William, like so many of those wise early religious missionaries, did not attempt a clear break with the old religions, but attempted to assimilate and change the old beliefs gradually.

That is why the churches of St. Menefreda were built on the site of pagan altars, as well as the mother church in his own name, that applied to the chapels of St. Michael's at Porthilly (the north chapel) and St. Guinedoc at Trebetherick (the south chapel). Both of them are today part of the parish of St. Minver (the modern name for St. Menefreda).

It is St. Guinedoc, like many other Cornish evangelists, a Welshman, we must look at here. Today his chapel is known as St. Enodoc and it came to more than just local note as the "Sinkininney Church" because it continually sank into the deep sands of the rugged coastline alongside which it was built. By the early eighteenth century the chapel had sunk so deep that sand covered the warped spire to its eastern gable, and in order to keep its ecclesiastic powers a clergyman had to be lowered through a skylight especially cut for the purpose at least once a year in order to carry out a lonely service inside the buried church.

That is the apparent history. But this, could it be the legend…?

★ ★ ★

He first saw her as the opening hymns of evensong were sung. She was at the very back of the chapel, on a lone seat at the far end from the altar almost hidden behind the ancient rood screen and just in front of the stone mortar once used for grinding the corn of worshippers. Despite the dark shadows he could tell she was young and very pretty, although a cowl hid the colour of her hair and part of her face.

For Bartholomew Atterbury, newly appointed deacon of St. Guinedoc, it was like a sudden chorus of angels. He had never seen anyone with such beauty in all his nineteen years, and despite the solemnity of the occasion he felt love at first sight.

When the service was over, Bartholomew went to try to find the girl but she had vanished. He asked around, and people seemed somehow not to want to talk about her. His heart pined, and he determined to find out more.

It was not until several days later that he discovered that the girl was called Jessica Morrow, and that she lived and worked in a small farmhouse over the hill towards Padstow. She had come to the area just a few days before he had seen her—she was new to the district (as was he), but she was in disgrace. A mother at the age of sixteen; a baby out of wedlock.

Bartholomew felt immediately that Jessica was a girl in need of his help, and despite the cautions of his priest he made an excuse to visit her at the farm as soon as he could.

Jessica was, indeed, as beautiful as she had grown in his mind since that first sighting. She had slightly reddish hair, striking auburn eyes, and as he turned into the farmyard and saw her once more Bartholomew again heard the angels singing. Later, he spoke to her in the kitchen of the farmhouse, watching her feed her five-month-old baby oblivious to the apparent shame. "I was attacked by an uncle. I think he loved me, in his way, but he forced himself upon me," she told the young man.

Bartholomew accepted the explanation. "'Tis not what ye've done that may be termed a sin. It's what ye do towards others that's important," he told her. "We must look towards helping our fellow men, 'tis the start of the fifteenth century after all and we must be modern about these things."

Jessica's voice was soft and gentle. It sounded to Bartholomew full of love as she spoke of her baby. "Will always look to this little fellow," she told him. "He is my love, my reason for being."

Although he worked for St. Guinedoc, Bartholomew's lowly duties also meant he had to go back and forth to the other ancient chapel in the parish, across the lowlands district, one and a half miles to St. Michael's at Porthilly Rock near the outskirts of Padstow Harbour itself. It gave him opportunity to call in often to the farmhouse where Jessica worked long, hard hours and raised her baby.

Over the next weeks they met frequently. Bartholomew's priest tried to intervene, but love had such a stranglehold over the young deacon that nothing could be said that would put him off course as he realised that Jessica was slowly beginning to return that love.

When the baby slept at night they would talk of their feelings, and when Bartholomew managed to get to the farm during daylight hours he would make time to walk with the girl and her baby on the beach. One day he turned to her and kissed her. "I love thee, Jessica. Would we could be together," he said.

"How can that happen?" she replied sadly. "I am an outcast, I have a baby out of wedlock, we cannot be together. It is not possible for what people would think or say."

"Love will conquer, I know it will," said the young cleric earnestly. "I will find a way."

They walked on, and before parting kissed again. "T'will be fine, my own beauty," said Bartholomew. "I will find a way that our love can last for eternity."

Bartholomew brooded over his own words during the days and weeks that followed, but he could find no solution. Then one morning at the farmhouse, he and the girl were talking as Bartholomew rested during his daily rounds. He asked if the baby had ever been christened. "T'would be right to bring the little one into the church," he told the young mother. "If t'were, mayhap that would redeem you and we could wed. Then we could have a child of our own."

They kissed, and Jessica's eyes were aglow. "More children?" she mused, then suddenly laughed. "T'would be nice to have another babe," she added. "I like that, one child apiece for every man who hath loved me. One for one—it sounds good."

Bartholomew was a little taken aback, but Jessica grinned at him. "'Tis lucky that a hundred men and more hath not loved me then!" she said with a slight giggle.

Bartholomew's face softened and he smiled back at her, and they kissed once more before he left. "I will see what can be done," he told her.

That lunchtime, before the service, he stood in front of the small font with its cable mouldings and granite base, idly tapping its splayed foot as he daydreamed of what it would be like to bathe the head of Jessica's baby son in its round bowl. Then, when the priest came into the church to join him for the service, Bartholomew leant on the communion table that rested on a small outcrop of stone at the foot of the east wall and asked if it would be possible.

The priest's face darkened. "Ye talk of admitting that child, born out of wedlock to a girl who has committed the most evil of sins known to man, and ye ask that," he almost exploded, his voice rising as he spoke. "I would rather the devil came to St. Guinedoc to ask forgiveness than allow that."

Bartholomew was shocked by the response, but withdrew without a word to carry out his duties as the junior cleric during the service.

Later, as the sun dropped low into the sea below Ler Brea Hill, he told Jessica what had happened. Her face was sad as she listened, because she knew it could mean the end for the two of them. "1 love thee, Bartholomew," she said softly, "But if the church has decided…"

He put a finger on her lips and knew in that moment what he had to do. "Trust in me and in God," he told her. "The Almighty will not, cannot, let a love like ours perish because of the way others think who know not of the world today."

"But what can we do?" asked Jessica, her voice still barely audible. "There is the babe. I cannot do anything without him, and folk will not let me do anything because of him."

"I will leave the church," said Bartholomew firmly. "We will marry and move to another place. That will make things right, and no one will ever then take the wee child away from you. We will be together, and we will make a good life the three of us. T'will be fine."

"Thou wouldst do that for me and the baby?" replied Jessica, and Bartholomew's heart lifted as he saw the absolute adoration in her eyes as she told him once again that she returned his love.

That evening he was full of joy, and when he sang in the evening service his voice projected the full power of his emotions. It was not until after the service that he felt matters starting to slip away from him. Once more he told the priest of his plans, and the priest immediately and irrevocably forbade him from taking the action he suggested. "It will bring the sin, the shame, of that young woman onto the church," said the senior clergyman.

Bartholomew tried to argue, but the priest would have none of it. "Thou must tell the girl it is over," he ordered. "Thou must banish thoughts of her once and forever. The call of the cloth is your vocation, your calling, and a life outside can never be yours for fear of your own damnation alongside that corrupt, dishonourable, shameful woman and that child she bore out of wedlock."

Bartholomew's head was in a whirl when he went to bed. He knew that despite what he had told Jessica, he had to make a decision between his love for her and his devoutness within the church; it was not a decision he could take lightly, for they were strong passions both ways.

In the morning he woke still not knowing what to do. He performed his daily ecclesiastic duties perfunctorily, and as soon as he could he hurried out to the farmhouse to see Jessica. But when he got there she was gone, and no trace.

Later that day the priest called him into his office. "I went to see her last night," said the older man. "She hath been banished from the parish. I know not where she and that bastard child have gone."

Bartholomew turned and walked out. He was never seen at St. Guinedoc again.

Over the years, the decades and the centuries, the church slowly sank into the sands and fell into disrepair. Gradually the winds blew the sand from the dunes above Daymer Bay in through the many trefoil windows, and slowly but surely it covered the whole church higher than its gabled roof. The damp got into the empty, sunless interior, and the pews were covered with mould. Worms got into the woodwork, while insects and other burrowing creatures lived on its floors.

For many years there was a mystery hanging over the site, where just a small part of a crooked spire poked skywards through the dunes like a finger pointing to the sun that never reached its base. Nearby, only the waves breaking on the beaches of the north Cornwall coast interrupted the eerie silence. Silent winds blew over the fields, hardly intruding on the surprising stillness.

Three hundred or more years had passed before someone decided, in his high authority, that if St. Guinedoc were to retain its status as a church something had to be done. In the manner of people of such influence, it was decided with conviction that a local clergyman had to be lowered down through the roof once a year to read a service within the church so that it could keep its tithes. St. Guinedoc was entirely buried under the drifted sand—it was damp, decayed and in a state of utter ruin—but so it had to be.

And so it was that this year a young parson was selected to drop through the roof of what had by now become St. Enodoc Church, to conduct the lonely service in the subterranean dark. By strange coincidence, his name was also Bartholomew—Jed Bartholomew.

Accompanied by a party of dignitaries, along with many worshippers from Porthilly Rock and St. Issey and villagers from other nearby places, Jed led the way from Padstow, crossing the River Amble at Trewornan Bridge, and following the coast before turning inland and through the surrounding fields, climbing the steep Little Petherick Hill before ploughing down heavy-footed across the dunes to the quaint spire jabbing misshapen and twisted from the sand.

Watched silently by the gathering, he slowly, methodically, stripped himself of his warm top garments, then let others tie ropes around his shirted body as he prepared for the drop inside the ancient, submerged church.

A sudden, chilling gust of wind blasted him and the watching crowd as he was lowered through a hole cut in the roof a few years before and into the stygian darkness. Then it was calm, and he breathed in the dank, musty smells as he dropped down and prepared to do his work.

Soon he was on the floor of the church, and slowly his eyes adjusted to a gloom broken only by the thin beam of his torch. He looked round with wonder, for it was the first time he had been inside the deep-set, depressing St. Enodoc.

There was a peculiar feeling all around him, and although he knew he was alone he had a sensation of another being nearby, watching him. He could not explain it. It was just that awareness you get when you wake in the middle of the night and know there is someone else in the room.

He could not put his finger on it, but he had an inexplicable impression that there was something around him that did not want him there. His torch probed through the dark, and he forced himself to ignore the feeling because he knew he really was alone in the buried church deep under the sands.

Jed knew what he was about. He had read a lot of the past history of St. Enodoc, and he had its history at his fingertips. As he untied the ropes that had lowered him from the roof he took a further look round.

He immediately noticed the font with its granite base, and way to the back the fifteenth-century carved oaken rood screen. His glance took in the now darkened gable windows higher up and all round, and he could see, too, the old communion table, askew now, with two short legs showing it had once been attached to something at the foot of the east wall.

He moved forward, taking care when leaving the altar to step gingerly down the three treads to the floor of the nave, then he moved towards the back of the church to look at a recessed piscina that seemed to him, curiously, much too high. *Probably the floor of the sanctuary had been lowered at some time*, he thought.

Quickly, too, he spotted a circular stone box which he knew was supposed to have been a holy water stoop until fitted with a lid to convert it to receive alms. He lifted the lid and looked inside, but it was empty.

For some reason he still had the uncanny feeling of a mysterious presence observing his every move. He was not normally a man given to supernatural feelings, but he could not explain why he suddenly felt he was not alone.

Although he tried once more to put the feelings to the back of his mind and concentrate on the job in hand, Jed was uneasy as he walked slowly back along the central aisle through the Cornish church columns and arches, and he looked anxiously around him. With his torch picking things out with tiny stabs of light, he soon reached the entrance on the left to the old north transept, the oldest part of the church standing two steps above the floor of the nave, and raising his eyes he looked up into the gaping darkness inside the curved spire.

He thought he heard a noise and jerked his glance back to the inside of the main church. There was still the perception of another being close by, but now it seemed to be changing. The malevolent aura seemed to have altered—now, the ghostly feel was of something warm and welcoming.

Without knowing why, Jed called out. "Who's there? Who are you?"

There was, of course, no reply, just the same suspicion of a presence he could not understand.

"Jed," he said aloud. "Get control. There is no one here."

He moved back to cross the central aisle, looking into the transept on the other side where he could see the remains of a gabled lychgate which he knew had opened onto the churchyard. He knew from his readings that outside was a tomb with the portraits of a father and his daughter, who died within six days of each other a couple of hundred years back, and he paused for just a few moments to wonder about them before he retraced his steps down the main aisle.

Perhaps it was their spirits he had felt. Perhaps.

But Jed somehow knew that the contrasting manifestations he had felt were not the ghosts of the father and daughter. Instead, he now had the impression that there were two separate apparitions, malevolent and loving, fighting for his very being.

He moved back along the central aisle, but before returning to the altar he looked into another recess, spotting a Celtic cross of the type often found on the Cornish wayside.

He carried on, but in his mind there was the feeling… A Celtic cross? There was an association there with the supernatural, wasn't there? He wondered and shivered involuntarily.

The mystical feelings stayed with him, but bravery was now running out quickly so Jed said the few necessary official prayers before pulling the rope around his body again and signalling to the people above to pull him out. Daylight was a welcome relief.

The peculiar feelings he had felt inside the church stayed with Jed for weeks, and eventually he went to the bishop to ask for an explanation. The bishop could give none, and Jed began to withdraw into himself. He became remote, almost as if he were living in a different world to everyone else, but despite his apparent loneliness he never felt alone.

It was a new experience for him. He had a permanent feeling that he was in another place as an outsider in his own body, and he frequently spoke to this new self he felt had taken over his whole being. Then in the middle of one night he woke in the darkness, calling a strange name to the sinister shadows. He could not remember what he said, but in the morning his landlady asked him who "Jessica" might be.

It was a name he did not know, had never heard before, but it stayed in his mind—and with it a feeling of relief from the abnormal, uncharacteristic feelings that had beset him since his foray into the church buried in the sand.

During the days that followed, the name Jessica kept repeating itself in his mind. He knew it was absurd, but he somehow felt that she was real and that he was falling in love with her, although he knew she did not exist.

Then months later, like another priest in another time, Jed Bartholomew, too, disappeared from the parish of St. Enodoc.

It was many years later, in 1864 to be exact, before St. Enodoc Church, which by then had been retrieved from the sands, was reopened after a restoration had restored it to something of its old glories. A sum of six hundred pounds had been raised by voluntary contributions from the local villagers, and with a tax levy of another seventy-five pounds, St. Enodoc was ready for its formal resurrection.

Everything was ready for ceremony, and there was an aura of expectancy in the air. Grand speeches were made, then finally the doors opened and people began to push forward. But they didn't get very far—those at the front suddenly stopped and blocked the entry.

On the floor of the central nave, just in front of the highly gilded rood screen, they had seen three skeletons that had not been there the day before. There was a girl in the middle, and on either side the grisly bones of two men could be seen holding her hands. At their feet lay the bones of three young babies.

'YMNS & ERRS

St. Probyn's, bang in the middle of a small borough of north London, is a funny place—a Victorian building housing a non-sectarian private residence and place of devotion for a small group of monks while at the same time open to the public for general worship.

Although the old place is a bit grimy and run down, even non-believers drop in for moments of peace and quiet, and no matter what their religion many with problems quickly learn that unburdening them in the ornate confessionals at the side of the chapel provide them with sensible and uncharged advice.

Usually, and for some time, Father Tobias had been taking the lunchtime confessions—a wise old man with experience of the human condition, a man able to conjure up guidance on the hoof in an instant. People knew about him, and trusted him. He would talk just as willingly to non-believers of the faith as others—and for non-believers, where a sin had been committed, rather than ask them to recite a catechism would implore them to join in singing a hymn. He believed hymns cured all sin.

One day though, he was rather taken out of his stride. He was taking confession from a man whose voice he did not recognise but whom he presumed was in his early forties from the sound of it. His mind was tending to wander after the succession of infidelities and household problems he had heard when he was instantly focused on what he was being told.

"Father, I have not sinned, but I am about to," said the man. "I need your advice because, you see, I am helping plan a major robbery—a really big one—and it is worrying me a little."

"Tell me about it, son."

"We plan to hijack a bullion van, me and my mates, and hopefully we'll snatch between half and one million pounds. The trouble is the others are starting to talk about using violence if necessary—shooters—and I'm not too sure about that."

Father Tobias was intrigued, and muttered the usual platitudes hoping it might help the man back out of the grand theft—although he doubted it. He was so intrigued at the content of the interview though, that over that evening's spartan communal meal he told some of his particularly friendly fellow monks about it. "I know I shouldn't repeat what I was told in the confessional," he said, "But…"

Father Tobias felt better about revealing the secret nature of his lunchtime talk with the man, and grew more intrigued as the same man returned to the confessional twice a week over the next few weeks, each time repeating his "confession" of the sin to come—each time giving more details of the robbery. Father Tobias duly passed the information on to his fellow monks, until he and all of them agreed that to ignore the information would be a stupid thing to do. If they could somehow take part, it would be too good to be true… and they felt they would be able to use the money for far greater good than the gang.

"It will save the gang from sinning," suggested Father Absolem.

Between them, the fathers felt they could not only complete the restoration of the abbey, but the money would also possibly help them buy the treasured first edition Goodwood Bible that was up for auction at a million pounds for their library.

But then came the snag. The gangster told the monks that an essential part of their plan was to use a woman to play a part in luring the guards away from the bankroll as the gang moved in.

That evening, the monks singing vespers passed on messages to each other in sing-song voices.

"We could ask Sister Theresa," sang Father Tobias.

"Wo-o-uld sh-e do it?" intoned someone else.

"Well, she's been in my confessional, and she admitted that as she couldn't even begin to dream about the immaculate conception she had always hoped to find a man and have babies. I think may-beeeeeee she-e mig-ht," chanted Father Tobias.

The next day they approached Sister Theresa, who promptly agreed to help. "Maybe I'll also be able to get away from the Mother Superior. It's a dreadful sin, but I've always coveted her job," she said.

So, the information continued to come in through the regular confessions by the original man until finally he revealed the "big news", telling Father Tobias the raid was planned for fourteen days' time.

The monks and Sister Theresa now had something definite to work on. While the gang man laid low for a couple of days they practised the raid as it had been outlined in his various confessions, and after various "trials" in the quadrangle of St. Probyn's quickly had it perfected. They eagerly counted down the fourteen days.

Then came the day of the raid itself.

It was due to happen in the forecourt of a giant industrial estate, crammed between tall square blocks of buildings which they hoped would shield them from outside eyes. The monks got there earlier than the original gang had planned and quickly swung into action. Father Tobias parked their hired white mini-van on one side of the square, and walked along to "suss" the situation.

But he quickly found a whole host of armed police were waiting.

"What are you doing here, Father?" asked one surprised copper.

"Oh, I heard from a confession that there was to be a burglary, and I was just trying to stop it happening," he replied, thinking fairly quickly on his feet despite the surprise.

He thought he had got away with it, but just then the rest of the monks—and Sister Theresa—chased onto the scene from one direction… and as the security guards leapt from the van, Sister Theresa tore back the face mask covering the lower part of her face and clutched at one of them and tried to distract him by kissing him frenziedly as he frenetically (and unsuccessfully) fought to resist her.

At the same time, another gang—this time a group of nuns who had picked up on the raid from weekly briefings by Sister Theresa—turned up from the other end of the building. And while all this was going on, yet another group arrived. There was mayhem, and with three gangs raiding the van, the police were baffled.

To clear things up, everyone was arrested. It took three policemen and a guard to drag Sister Theresa away from the guards, because by this time she was hanging on for grim death—deprived by years of religious chastity she had decided she liked smooching and was kissing all four of them in turn in a mad, frenzied passion. Everyone was taken to the local police station, where Sister Theresa had to be physically restrained by five different policemen (including a weedy inspector), a community policewoman and a traffic warden, from kissing the custody sergeant in charge of the police cells.

When the traffic warden started to respond, Father Tobias stepped in. "We are none of us innocent of sin," he proclaimed grandly. "We'd all better sing a hymn."

The policemen listened, and the prisoners sang, loudly. Then they were all put in the cells and retired for the night, although Sister Theresa insisted on one last goodnight kiss from the weedy inspector.

The next morning, after a traumatising night in the police station, all were released on bail—the monks and the nuns skulking back to the monastery.

"What on earth were you trying to do?" Father Tobias asked Sister Theresa, whose lips were still very sore, but who (on the way out of the police station) had insisted on trying to get at the custody sergeant (who now seemed to quite like the idea) yet again.

"Well, when we knew what you were up to, we, ahem, thought we'd try and stop you committing a grievous sin," she replied, convincingly. "And that guard…"

The next day, as usual, the original burglar turned up for his confession.

"I'm surprised you're here. I thought you'd be laying low," said Father Tobias, "That raid you said was going to take place yesterday went wrong, so…"

"Yesterday?"

"Yes, fourteen days after your last confession."

"You must have misheard, Father. I said *forty* days."

"But apart from us and some nuns, you all turned up."

"Oh no. I heard it was a rival gang—a similar raid—quite a coincidence. And there were some of your guys from St. Anselms. Seems another one of my lot had a fit of conscience too, and he went to confession there. They also picked up the tip and decided to take advantage to restore their place and help them buy that first edition Goodwood Bible that's up for auction at a million quid."

Father Tobias pondered the wonderous wry ways of God.

"Fact is, both of you—St. Probyn's and St. Anselms—both decided to muscle in on our caper. Honour among thieves, Father. You tried to steal an honest crime from us. That's a sin, Father. A sin."

"Ah well," said the monk, "Perhaps we'd all better sing a hymn to honesty. After all, to err is human, to forgive, shall we say, may not be divine but will hopefully mean no fine."

He was, shall we say, right and wrong. Father Tobias and the others did not get a fine, but all of them did unfortunately get forty days apiece in the private confessional that is a prison cell.

BLITZ

Dear Son: I haven't heard from you for a long time. You must be busy. It's getting very bad over here in the East End. We're having a rough old time of it, what with the Germans bombing us in our own homes. Why don't they fight the war on the battlefields?

Dear Mum: I'm back home in Blighty after Dunkirk. It was awful, with the Germans bombing us all the time. A lot of my mates was left behind and some was killed on the beaches.

Dear Son: I do hope you are well and eating properly. The East End is still being bombed most days, and it's becoming a right old mess. The raids are on every night, with the siren wailing almost as soon as it gets dark and going on until daybreak. Wherever you go round here there is bomb damage these days. Even Nelson Street has been hit—an incendiary landed on the house opposite and it was damaged by fire. You wouldn't know them. They are refugees from somewhere and had to move out.

Dear Mum: I haven't heard from you for a long time. I can't say where I am now, but it's very hot and there's a lot of sand. We are ready to go into action.

Dear Son: Just think, 1940 and you've been in the war over a year now. The German bombers still come over the East End every night, and it's getting so a lot of people go down the Underground for shelter. Hundreds of them sleeping on the platforms, not to mention the smell. I can't believe East Enders can be like that.

Dear Mum: I still haven't heard from you, so do write and let me know what it's like on the home front. We met Rommel's army yesterday for the first time—five of my mates copped it, and there's another ten badly injured.

Dear Son: Those bombs still fall on us day and night, but there's a real Blitz humour although some days it's been so bad that they've set up soup kitchens just like the newsreels of Europe, even some spivs trying to get extra above the rations. But us East Enders can take it, although it said on the wireless yesterday that 23,000 Londoners were killed in the first five months of the bombing last year, and things haven't got any better. I suppose here in Stepney and Bow we're in the front line because the Nasties are trying to get at the docks.

Dear Mum: It's been really bad here and fifteen more of my mates were killed last week. I'll be glad to get back to the East End and a bit of peace and friendship.

Dear Son: New Year's Eve 1941, and over two years of war. Over here, the Commercial Road has been badly damaged by the bombers, and round the comer in Myrdle Street four houses were knocked down by a single bomb last night. A land mine, I think I heard someone say. It's quite terrible these days, but everyone's talking about the East End spirit so we have to keep our peckers up. It's difficult though, with all the dirt and the rationing and that.

Dear Mum: Still no news. We're supposed to be going into battle again soon— and me and my mates are really in the front line. Is the East End still as much fun as it was?

Dear Son: We had more raids last night, and I think even I'm going to have to go and sleep down the Tube regular. They have a laugh and a giggle there. I know there's a war on, but being in London is horrid these days. It's not very nice seeing those huge jagged bomb holes in the middle of the terraces. I walked down to Spitalfields Market yesterday to see if I could get some extra to help out a family that's moved in with me because they've been bombed out from Settles Street, and you can hardly even get potatoes there now, let alone bacon and eggs and things. Lucky we've got Vera Lynn to keep our spirits up, not to mention the king and queen.

Dear Mum: We've left the desert now and that will give us time to regroup because we've been in the thick of it and another twenty of my battalion killed. I miss Stepney something terrible.

Dear Son: Still no letters from you. I wish I could hear you're safe. London is really up against it these days. Here in Stepney it's worse than ever, even the Great Synagogue has been knocked down, so much for God being on our side. At least he let Uncle Fred buy some salt beef sandwiches in Blooms kosher restaurant. I went upstairs last night—I don't do that much these days in case a bomb drops and catches me there—and I peeped through the blackout curtains and I could see a big fire over near the Tower. The flames were so high they could be seen over all the buildings in between. The papers showed St. Paul's like that too, but not damaged. Perhaps God is with us after all. Your Auntie Nell told me she went down the Prospect of Whitby last week and the beer there is as good as ever. Hope you'll soon be home to enjoy a pint with us.

Dear Mum: We landed "somewhere in Europe" yesterday. Another three of my mates was killed when we hit the beaches.

Dear Son: It'll soon be Christmas and I'm glad you're back in Europe. It's nearer home. Despite all the bombings the East End is still as much fun as it was, with carols and dancing as soon as the all clear goes. It's now been three years since the air raids started, and now we've got the flying bombs coming down too. I heard the engine of one shut out almost overhead yesterday when I was down Petticoat Lane. My heart stood still 'cause I thought it was going to land on top of me. I knelt down and prayed and everyone laughed at me. East Enders do make you feel better. On the way home I noticed how dark and dirty Stepney now looks.

It was always dirty, but the smoke and dust from the bombs everywhere makes it worse.

Dear Mum: We've seen more action and taken more casualties. All my old mates are now dead, a lot of them buried over here—"somewhere in Europe".

Dear Son: Just think, 1944 already and you haven't been home since the start of the war. Lucky, really, because we're still at the heart of the fighting over here. We've not only got the flying bombs, there's those new rocket things that are knocking down whole streets as well. All very nasty, but we're trying to look on the bright side like Mr Churchill says.

Dear Madam: We regret to tell you…

Dear Son: Those V2s, they land when you least expect them. You don't hear anything, then bang they're here. You just never know when one's going to land in top of yo—

THE SEVEN WISHES
OF MAX ALBION

Max Albion was what you could call a self-made man—only his DIY was somewhat pitiable and flawed.

He had struggled throughout his life to try to make something of himself, to get married and raise a family, to be "someone". Yet he had singularly failed dismally in every individual aspect, every single respect.

Max was now forty-nine years old bordering on ninety-four, and today he was sitting in his back garden on a sun seat with a fading blue, yellow and red strap at the back, contemplating the imminent arrival of his half century. Hanging limply from one hand was a bank statement asking that his latest overdraft of several hundred pounds be repaid as soon as convenient.

Max glanced down at the letter and wondered if repayment would ever be available. He looked up and saw that even the sun was now hiding behind grey clouds, although it had been shining brightly just three-quarters of an hour before when he ventured into the garden at the rear of his shabby, diminutive one-storey house in a gloomy downtown suburb.

"Where has it all gone?" he wondered. "Where have I gone wrong?"

Suddenly the sky above him seemed to dim for a macrosecond, then lightened with a blinding blue flash. What you could call a heavenly flash if you were of a mind.

For a moment Max was scared, then as the accompanying smoky haze cleared he composed himself as he saw a strange figure by his side. He had appeared abruptly as if by witchcraft, but there was something in the stranger's appearance, the cut of his shoulders, the look on his face, that calmed Max in an instant.

The stranger bowed low and, before Max could speak, introduced himself. "I am the angel of sorrowful but deserving causes," said the stranger in a deep, deep voice. "I am here because your whole life is in such despair."

Max looked surprised, as well he might. "An angel? But how…?"

The angel smiled. "Don't worry about how. Just be glad the boss drew your name out of the big miracle wish barrel for today."

Max blinked several times, and he shook his head almost in disbelief.

"You Earth people all do that," laughed the angel, rather cheekily, "But believe me, this really is happening to you."

Max leant forward, his right arm lifting and an enquiring forefinger pointing to the angel. "You… I… The boss…? What, what's it all about?" he stammered.

The angel smiled benignly, angelically if you want. "Your life, as you've been thinking for the past forty-eight minutes and twenty-seven seconds, is a mess," he said. "I'm simply here to try and help. If you want help, that is."

Max sat back in the sun seat. "You're right, my life is a mess. But how can you help? How can anyone help?"

The angel drew up another, similarly brightly coloured sun seat and sat down next to Max. "Well, we've decided that you're a Grade Four case—that's out of six, incidentally—and that means you are entitled to six main wishes. I was told that if l liked the look of you I could offer a small extra bonus wish if it's needed. So you've got that as well."

Max struggled to take it all in, but the angel didn't want to waste time. He had a lot of calls on his books for this millennium.

"OK then, so let's get on with it," the angel went on briskly. "Your first wish?"

Max blinked. "A wish? Her-umph. Let's see." He blinked again. "Well, I guess I've got to ask if you can make me rich. I want untold wealth."

As he spoke the mobile phone on the ground by his side rang. The angel indicated he answer it, and Max picked it up.

"Max Albion," he said into the mouthpiece, then flinched as he heard the voice at the other end say it was his bank manager apologising for the error in his last statement of account.

"It should have read ninety-seven billion, of course," said the voice. "We forgot to add in this month's income, and we dropped off about eight noughts, ho, ho. But we'll send you a statement by special delivery, Mr Albion, just to confirm the new total." The voice emphasised the word mister.

The phone went dead.

"Untold wealth? That was easy," said the angel. "So, what about your second wish?"

Max leant forward with his eyebrows raised. "Can you give me unlimited power?" he asked the angel.

Suddenly he found himself walking to a lift in the huge atrium of a gigantic skyscraper block. He stepped in, and as the doors closed the attendant pushed the button for the sixty-fifth floor.

"G'mornin', Mr Albion, sir," said the attendant as the lift whooshed upwards.

As the doors opened again, Max walked out and into an aisle between several rows of desks at which literally thousands of young men and women were banging away at their computers. A few older men in suits bowed to him as he passed, and two beautiful, immaculately dressed secretaries hovered at his shoulder.

At the end of the corridor, Max came to a T-junction. He paused for a moment to look to the left, and saw an even longer room with even more people at computers. Then looking to the right he saw a large oak door, and taking a step towards it he noticed that on it, in large golden lettering, was the inscription:

Max Albion
President, Chairman and Senior Group Executive
Albion International Corp

One of the secretaries, the blonde, bustled past him, a trifle too close perhaps, and opened the door to the office. Inside, Max saw the largest desk he had ever seen in his life sitting in the middle of a thick, blue, deep pile carpet. Another secretary, just slightly older than the other two, was by its side, already pouring from a teapot.

"Formosa Oolong, especially flown in for you from Taiwan—the champagne of teas. Just brewed, exactly as you like it, Mr Albion," she said with a smile. "And your favourite biscuits," she said indicating a solid silver plate.

Max walked to the desk and sat. The secretary passed the teacup across, and he sipped the liquid. "Excellent. Temperature's just right," he said.

The girl hovered, then she pushed the plate of biscuits gently towards him, and Max took one and nibbled at it. "Exquisite."

"It's from the Peruvian bakery group you've just taken over. We gave them the recipe from your mother's cookery book, and they've produced some for your exclusive use," said the secretary.

One of the fifteen phones on the desk rang, and another of the secretaries, who had followed Max into the office, jumped forward to pick it up. "Yeah. Uh huh. OK. Can you wait a moment, please?" she said, then covering the mouthpiece with her spare hand she spoke to Max.

"It's the secretary of state," she whispered rather matter-of-factly. "Says he wants to know if he can cut the exchange rate before the mid-summer break. He says you promised him a decision two weeks ago, but you seem to be stalling…"

Max gulped and took another small bite from the biscuit.

"You still haven't told the prime minister how you want to play things," said the tea-pouring secretary, "But he's back from America after his talks with the president today, and he'll probably ring you soon. Better delay the secretary of state for a little bit longer, don't you think?"

Max nodded, and the girl on the telephone muttered into it. "Sorry. Mr Albion is not available at this moment. OK, yeah, I'll tell him as soon as I can." She replaced the receiver. "He said he'd be grateful for a decision by the end of the week," she went on smoothly, "And he apologises for interrupting you."

An instant later the aides and the secretaries were gone and Max found himself alone at the desk in the middle of the vast office. Sitting deep in the comfortable leather chair, he looked around the room, The chair itself was about twice the size anyone would need it, while the office was some ten times the size of the home where he had earlier been sitting. There were glass cabinets with delicate Venetian plates, jugs and goblets in them, and there were fine works of art in gold and silver frames on their tops. Great masterpieces adorned the walls.

All of a sudden the angel appeared before him. "I could do with a sip of that tea," he said. "If only I drank tea, not nectar. You get so bored with nectar." He sighed, then seemed to pull himself together. "Now then, Max. You have wealth, you have power—what about your third wish?"

Max relaxed back into the chair. "Well, what I've always wanted is a car. Maybe, could I have a car?"

One of the telephones on the desk rang, and in an instant a secretary was in the office and had picked it up. "Yes, yes. Thank you." She turned to Max. "That was Signor Ferrari," she announced. "The new nine-litre model they're releasing next month is on its way to you. It should be in the garage with the other cars by dusk."

Max absorbed the news with a touch of disbelief. The other cars? He decided he had to find out more. "Is there room in the garage?" he asked, trying to sound off-hand.

The secretary smiled. "Oh, you're teasing again, Mr Albion," she said. "The new Ferrari will only make thirty-seven cars in all, and you know the garage you had built under the mansion will take up to fifty-five!"

Max sat back again, amazed, and the secretary turned to leave the office.

The angel reappeared as the girl slid imperceptibly out of the room. "And the next?" he asked.

By now Max was beginning to enjoy the game. "Oh, I think a luxury yacht. And maybe an aeroplane," he replied conspiratorially, and with a studied insouciance.

The office faded, and Max found himself with his three secretaries, two worried-looking executives in ties, and an aviator in uniform being ushered towards a large, impressive-looking jet with the name Max Albion painted along its side.

"I think this new one's the best choice yet," the pilot was saying. On his uniform, Max noticed he had the initials AC above the breast pocket and just below his pilot's wings. "It's a great addition to your personal fleet. Far better than anything the company, the corporation, has had before."

One of the secretaries was at the foot of the private jet's steps, and she wished him a happy, restful, enjoyable weekend as the pilot stood back to let Max climb aboard. As he entered the plane, the pilot sat him down in a huge armchair-like seat—larger, even, than his office chair—and a slim, auburn-haired stewardess helped him strap in and offered a drink.

"Your usual Kir Royale? Or would you just prefer straight champagne today, Mr Albion?" she muttered softly, sexily.

There was a boom as the jet roared down the runway and took off, then seemingly without a pause Max was back on land, walking down a gangplank and onto the most enormous yacht, the largest by far in a marina that seemed to stretch to the horizon. A crewman blew his bosun's whistle as five smartly uniformed officers saluted him aboard, and there was a flurry of activity around them as the deck hands cast off. The liner, for it was more like a mini-liner than any other craft, sailed towards a bright red sun, settling low into a balmy horizon.

The angel was suddenly lounging next to Max in the immense wardroom. "Everything to your satisfaction so far?" he asked.

Max smiled contentedly and nodded.

"Then what about the fifth wish?" asked the angel.

Max wrinkled his nose and pursed his lips. "I suppose with all this, my own paradise island would be an idea…" he began.

In an instant he heard the yacht's whistle sound, and there was activity on deck. Max walked to a large window along the side of the cabin where he now found himself, and saw that the ship was easing into a small wooden pier in front of a bank of swaying palms.

He walked up on deck as the crew made fast, and ahead of him lay the island, a tropical utopia. The sun was now high overhead in a turquoise blue sky, but a slight cooling breeze kept the temperature just right. Native bearers were carrying huge trunks with the initials MA on their side to the shore, and Max breathed deep. He looked round further and could see the island stretching far to each side. Apart from the palms, there was a massive bank of some deep blue coloured plants, and a whole expanse of some vivid red and yellow flowers with huge spiky leaves.

To the right was a long pure white sand beach, while when he looked the other way Max could see an imposing three-storey mansion on stilts. "Welcome to Albion Island again," said a voice.

Max turned to see who was speaking, and it was the angel once more.

Max smiled at him. "Very nice," he said airily. "All I need now is as many beautiful young native girls as I can manage."

The angel started to speak, but Max stopped him with a confident raised forefinger. "And that blonde secretary in a sarong would be nice," he added.

The angel nodded sagely; he was under orders. "Is that your sixth wish? Your final wish?"

Max beamed back again, enjoying himself. "Sure is," he answered. "Especially the secretary. And make that a skimpy sarong."

Time moved on, and Max found himself on the balcony of the house, which was just as impressive inside as out. Below him, draped elegantly around the sumptuous pool, were some fifteen or sixteen deep-tanned beauties in various stages of undress, while another four were playing tennis on one of the five courts to the back. There were, too, about a dozen more soaking up the sun on loungers draped around the razortrimmed, stretched and tiered lawns.

There was a noise behind him. He turned, and there was the blonde secretary from the office. He smiled, leered at her, and she blushed.

"Why, Mr Albion, what an afternoon…" She slid the bedroom picture window shut, and as she did so, in her place on the balcony, was the angel.

"How goes it, Max baby?" he asked.

"Fine," retorted Max with a smug I've-got-it-all look on his face. He felt good. "What was I thinking of before?" he wondered. "No money, no girls, no prospects. Now look at me. Wealthy beyond belief, immense power, possessions. I've got it all."

"Good. Good. But bear in mind, it's not done with yet," said the angel. "Remember that I said you could have one special bonus wish. What do you want to do with that?"

Max sighed. What more could the man who has everything possibly want?

"There's nothing I can think of immediately," he said slowly, his mind working overtime. "Nothing really."

"Nothing? Surely there must be just one little thing."

Max's brow furrowed. He thought hard. "You know, if I was really pushed to it I guess I would have to ask for happiness," he said eventually.

"Happiness? Are you sure that's your final request?"

"Uh huh."

There was a blinding bright blue flash, and Max Albion was sitting in his well-worn dirty jeans in a slightly soiled sun seat in his old back garden. On his lap was the bank statement revealing an overdraft of several hundred pounds.

"I wonder what I should do for my fiftieth. No money for a party, and no friends to invite to it in any case," he said out loud. "Guess I'll just order a takeaway and make a wish that it's better than the last one which gave me such a stomach ache."

THE NIGHT RIDER

It was just beginning to rain when Rudi heard his name called from far across the upright sentinels of pine trees, the water suddenly dropping out of a sky that was already darkening for oncoming night.

"Rudi. Rudi. *Schnell. Komme schnell.*" The voice was that of his father, and it held an insistent note of urgency that made the young boy take heed.

Rudi was a gangling sixteen-year-old, with a fresh-scrubbed look to his face that was broken only by dark eyebrows which seemed at complete variance to his near-white blonde hair.

"Rudi."

The voice took on a sharpness that made the boy look up guiltily at the vast pines that covered the mountain above his village, then he started to run home covering the soft springy below-ground of moss that filled the floor of the woods with equally springy steps. Soon, he was in the main street and could see his father standing wet haired in the doorway of their all-wood chalet.

"What is it, Papa?" he called breathily as he approached, slowing down instinctively as he got near enough to be heard. "What makes you call me so urgently?"

"There has been an accident," replied his father, his deep voice carrying just enough for the boy to hear. "You must go and call the doctor. The stranger, the Englishman, he is hurt badly. I cannot leave him, so hurry now. Run. Quickly."

Rudi lengthened his pace, and without stopping was gone on his way up the street to the doctor's house at the far end of the village where he stood on the step and banged at the door. But there was no answer, and although he called out, looking up at the window, holding his face up to the rain that now fell quite heavily, it was obvious that there was nobody at home.

The boy turned and ran back down the street to where his father waited in the doorway, half listening for a sound from the injured man inside. Rudi paused for only a second before he was off again.

"The doctor is not at home. I will go down to the town, to Bolzen. There is another there." Then he was off again, back up towards the doctor's house and beyond.

"But how will you get there?" His father called the question up the road.

Rudi called back over his shoulder, hearing the words swirl round over him and back into the waiting night. "I will borrow Herr Rocca's motor car. It is in the garage, and he, too, is away for the day."

"But—"

His father's protest was hidden in the wind and the rain, and Rudi was away to open Herr Rocca's large garage doors and jump into the car. In this part of the mountains, the Dolomiti, the people are part-German and part-Italian, and it was with typical Teutonic thoroughness that Rudi examined the car, checking on the brakes, accelerator and clutch, engaging all the gears in turn to make sure of their positions, pulling levers and pushing knobs to find which worked what. And when that was done, it was the Latin half that felt afraid for the journey to come.

Fear did not stop Rudi, however, and he turned the ignition key that had been left in the switch and started the motor first time. Then, with a sinking feeling to his stomach that he could not stop nor really understand, he engaged the gears, let off the handbrake, let in the clutch and moved forward gently, slowly gathering speed as he moved out into the darkness that the rain and the ending day had draped over the mountains and village.

His father was still in the doorway as Rudi drove by, changing gears until he got into fourth. Rudi did not look at him but concentrated on the twin beams of light he had sent out from the car into the road and blackness ahead.

Soon the car left the village behind, and the road began to drop, twisting as it wrapped itself against the side of the mountain. Rudi held the steering wheel easily, crossing his hands over as he turned corners, and uncrossing them as he straightened out. The speedometer needle crept round to the seventy kilometre an hour mark, and Rudi, noticing it, braked violently and pulled the speed back to a steady fifty.

The road outside the village, and for about five miles below it, was wide and smooth, but then the mountain laid itself against the edges and narrowed it down, making it twist even more as if in an attempt to escape rocks that had spent centuries on the point of falling. The road here was a thin streak between the walls of the mountain, with curves and sudden S-bends, and twists and bumps like nowhere else. Men had built fences on the bends, but they were not there for protection but only as a warning that the offended mountain towered above and below this scar to its system.

As Rudi came to this section, the Latin in him fought with the Teuton, and method and control battled with impulse and a rising hysteria. Rudi had never before been on this road alone after dark. This time there was no one to comfort him against the darkness outside, no figure sitting next to him outlined against the black velvet outside the car. This time there were only the twin headlamp beams that danced and bounded in front of him.

Great gleams of rock loomed and laughed out of the world outside the car, and the giant pines by the side of the road now swayed and sighed in the wind dreaming no doubt of breathing in the sunshine again. Rudi twisted the car round and round, turning corners and steadily dropping lower and lower down the side of the mountain. He had settled into a world of his own. A world in which the bonnet of the car was his horizon and the headlamps the sun. A world in which outer space curved round grey rocks into nothingness, then came back again with a menace. A world of hissing tyres on wet road, the swishing of wiper blades, and the pattering, stamping rain on the roof.

A sudden shaft of lightning lit the rocks into a grey-white flash of terror and beauty. There was a brief pause in which Rudi had the time and the calmness to count up to four, then the thunder curled down onto the mountains, rumbling a warning down and down towards the bottom of the valley. Rudi wished he could travel as fast, but he held the speedometer back to fifty kilometres.

The road levelled for a moment, and Rudi felt rather than saw that a stream rushed and flowed by its side, splashing along in its anxiety to become an ocean. He relaxed into the seat of the car, Teutonic and fatalist now, and for the time being in control of the situation. He felt alive and vital for the moment, and of a sudden he felt like shouting and yelling his exhilaration at the mountain.

"I am not afraid of you," he sang out. "Not darkness nor rock. I am not scared."

The road suddenly spun away to the right, and Rudi had to wrestle the car round the bend. There was another distant flash of lightning, and the thunder seemed to laugh back with the mountain at Rudi's defiance. The road straightened out again, and Rudi felt the sweat beaded on his top lip. He wiped it away with a clammy set of fingers and mumbled an apology to the elements.

"Sorry, I am afraid of you," he whispered.

The road continued to drop down into the belly of the mountain, and the car twisted and swayed along it, alone in a small, perhaps, world of anguish. Behind the wheel, Rudi strained his eyes along the beams of light that danced away from the headlamps and bobbed about on the craggy slabs of mountain rock, lights that seemed to dance a faraway tango on the side of the mountain.

A little blob of rock flung back the light to a gully, which redirected it to a clinging plant, fanning it out again onto a projecting spigot of time-old granite, and then back onto the thin strip of road. Rudi focused his tired eyes on the light, then as the car turned yet another twist he caught a glimpse of the town, a flash of electric light pinpoints in the distance. The road bent away again, but this time Rudi did not mind the darkness, nor the mountain towering above him.

For a moment the road lifted slightly, sending a spray of headlight rising up into the sky and reflecting a million raindrops. Then Rudi turned the steering wheel to the right, and the car drove down again into the town street, suddenly leaving the mountain behind. Immediately a car shot by from the right, hooter screaming, and Rudi settled in to follow it to the heart of the city.

Soon he braked the car to a stop and jumped out, running round it to knock at the door of the doctor's house. When the knock was eventually answered he blurted out his request for help, then paced cagily backwards and forwards while he waited for the doctor to dress and pack his case.

Then at last he led the way out into the rain, back to the borrowed car.

"Jump in then," said the doctor, still sleepy.

Rudi stopped in the road and scuffed his feet.

"Go on then," repeated the doctor. "What are you waiting for?"

Rudi looked down at the road. He squeezed his lips together, then looked up at the doctor. "Could you drive?" he asked huskily, pausing before adding a hesitant "please".

The doctor looked back across the car at him, suddenly grumpy.

Rudi wiped the rain smooth across his face and licked his lips. "You see, sir," he said, "I have never been taught to drive. You'll probably be safer if you drive back up the mountain. Sir."

THE BULLET

I was on duty the night they stretchered Toni Manzino into casualty. I wanted peace and quiet and time to ogle the new pretty nurse who was sharing the disinfectant-clean clinic with me; instead, I found Manzino had a bullet in his right shoulder. A three-eight from the looks of the wound.

Toni Manzino had been around for a long time. He had been the big guy when I was a kid, and all the boys (and girls, too, come to think of it) had idolised, lionised and damn near canonised him and had dreamt of a time when they could go to work for him.

Manzino was the latter-day Robin Hood of the back streets and alleyways of New York's Bronx.

But he never gave to the poor, except when he was being watched by us kids or when the pressure was on him in one of the frequent DA's purges that never got anywhere because of the mass of independent, and newly rich, witnesses.

Now, Manzino was still the big guy. He had a hand slyly dipping into just about every one of the town's dirty rackets, and his interests ranged from gambling to strip clubs to vice, from larceny to protection, booze and drugs, to the unions, and even to murder according to rumours from what the papers call "reliable sources".

To look at, Toni was every bit like the popular conception of the big-time racketeer. He was over six feet tall, had extremely wide and powerful shoulders, with muscles bulging under the sleeves of his expensive-cut jackets, and with huge hams of hands. His face was fat but not flabby, and his jet-black hair was brilliantined down flat. When he frowned, which he seemed to do a lot, Toni's hair line almost sambaed with his thick bushy eyebrows, in which a few white bristly hairs now already showed through.

He was unconscious as I examined him, but he recovered within ten minutes or a quarter of an hour. I had another look then at the ugly, red-rimmed inflamed mess on his shoulder, and as I touched the bruised flesh near it Manzino flinched and clenched his teeth. I saw pain in his eyes.

"Be careful, dam' ya," he growled, and I recalled some moments of terror from my childhood again.

"Sorry, Toni," I answered, as I tried to soothe the skin.

Toni settled back on the bed. "S'OK," he said, and tried to smile. He had firm, pure white teeth behind fleshy lips. "So where are the boys in blue?"

"The lieutenant's using the phone in my room," I told him. "Two officers are waiting outside for me to call 'em when you wake up."

"There's-a no hurry." A slight accent from way-back Sicilian forebears. "I don't want to talk to them just yet." He laughed. "Ya know the name of the lieutenant?"

"Simpson."

"That punk!" He winced and eased the hurtful shoulder slightly. "I must be gettin' old. I could-a eaten him in the old days."

"How did it happen, Toni?" I asked casually. Too casually, perhaps, because Manzino closed up. I saw his eyes cloud over for a moment, his teeth clenched again, and he drew in a deep breath through his nose.

"Sorry," I said.

"That's-a OK, son," said Toni. "I guess I got to tell the doctor." He smiled at me and I grinned back. "So I'll tell ya. Y'see, I was in this bar downtown. Just mindin' my own business and havin' me a quiet beer. Then all of a sudden this jerk comes in, y'see. An ordinary guy. I didn't even notice him and didn't look up. Then he shouts and it's a stick-up. Y'know, like y'see on the television sometimes. So it's nothin' to do with me, but all of a sudden there's this gun—this toy sawn-off shotgun—goin' off, and I'm a-hit in the shoulder for Chris' sake."

It was no Oscar performance, but it seemed genuine. I mopped sweat from Toni's forehead, and he eased himself back onto the pillows.

"That's tough, Toni," I said, "But you're the lucky one. There's no real damage to the bone, and when I take the bullet out you'll heal over. I doubt you'll even be able to see the scar in a year's time."

Toni tried to sit up, but the pain forced him back down again. His eyes were wide open, and his nostrils dilated.

"You not a-goin' to take the slug out." The Sicilian was more marked. "I'm not goin' to let-a you do that to Toni Manzino."

"Why not?" I asked. I cocked my head to the right to emphasise my confusion.

"It's against my principles—religious principles—is all."

I raised both eyebrows. "What religion's that, Toni?" I asked innocently, remembering him from when I was a boy.

"Neve' you mind what religion. It's *my* principles, ain't it? I say you leave the slug where it is."

"What the hell, Toni? Since when have you found religion?" His pain encouraged my frank question.

"I'm-a entitled to principles like anyone. I gotta right to religion. Who's-a to say that I can't have principles? You?" He was beginning to get annoyed. Real annoyed. "Listen, punk. I'm Toni Manzino. I'm still a big guy. I can make or break you if I want. You stop me havin' principles—religion—I'm a-likely to finish you off like that." He clicked two fingers together, then winced.

"OK, Toni, so you've got principles and the Good Lord Above says you can't have a half-inch lump of flattened metal taken from your shoulder." I shrugged and turned away. "I'll have another look at the wound in the morning. Goodnight, Toni."

I walked to the door slowly. As I opened it, I glanced back at the bed and saw Toni with his eyes shut and his face contorted in pain. He was muttering to himself. "I got to stick to my principles, don't I? I can have religion…"

I closed the door behind me and went to look for Lieutenant Simpson.

I found him just lighting a cigarette, and he ignored the medical disapproval I frowned at him. "Toni's awake," I told him.

"Can I speak with him?"

"Yeah. But it'll be tough going tonight."

"Oh, ya think so, huh? What's so special about tonight?"

"He's got a bullet in the shoulder and a principle on his mind. He won't let me operate to take it out."

The lieutenant dropped his cigarettes on the scrubbed, antiseptic hospital floor and stubbed it out with the immaculate toe of his highly polished right shoe. He coughed.

"Tell me, lieutenant," I said. "You know more about Toni Manzino than any man alive. How come he's suddenly got religion? Could it be some sort of conscience? Something that makes him want pain because of all the evil he's been party to in the past?"

Simpson laughed. Not loudly, but coldly and, I felt, with a tinge of helplessness about it.

"Conscience? Not Toni Manzino. Not that son-of-a-bitch gunsel," he said.

Nor Robin Hood, I thought.

"He's only got one thought in that mind of his. He won't let you take that slug out 'cause he knows what it'll mean to him. Y'see, he was in a fight-out with a night patrolman he ambushed just before we picked him up. Killed him. Cop killer, first degree murder—"

"But he said he was shot up by a stranger in a bar," I interrupted.

Simpson laughed again. "So that's what the man says, eh?" he replied softly. "I say the patrolman shot back after being hit the first time by our Mister Manzino. He was hit in the shoulder before Toni put another fourteen slugs into him." He sighed and picked up his hat from a desk. "I could prove it too, if I could get that cop's slug as evidence."

THE GUEST ROOM

There was something about the room—a presence he couldn't quite fathom. It was a certain aura that seemed to hang in the air like a manifestation of something he couldn't understand.

But Max Falke was too tired to do anything about it. He was getting on in years, and he'd driven more than two hundred and fifty miles during the day, and now all he wanted to do was rest. But he methodically, almost fastidiously, unpacked his bag, hanging up his shirts, trousers and jackets before stretching out on top of the wide green and yellow duvet that extended over the two single beds that sat side by side as if a double.

He yawned and let his eyes wander around the room, trying to discover what it was that gave it the peculiar atmosphere he could feel. There was nothing to see. The room was tastefully decorated in the Louis Philippe style more usually associated with large chateaux or five-star hotels, with a copy of a restful Monet painting on the wall opposite the window.

Max let his thoughts drift. He was on a journey of rediscovery, touring the areas where he had served as a young officer during the war, and he had stayed in the Auberge des Deux Bières at that time as well, but it was so very different then to the way it was now.

The hotel in those days had been known as the Chateau de la Paix following the First World War, although chateau was far from an accurate description. It was far too small, having been turned into a family hotel following three generations of beer brewers and wine-makers whose successive descendants had built it up with a series of outhouses for their work. Although it was now a guest house, it had developed a formal garden at the back that enjoined today's visitors to enjoy a game of boules or to simply sit with a glass of the traditional beer, now fermented especially for the house by a new brewery nearby.

Max knew that beyond the garden was a serenely relaxing lake that was home to geese, ducks, swans and various other water birds. They were quiet now it was dark, and Max quickly fell asleep in the countryside silence despite the weird, almost supernatural feeling that he could still feel suffusing the room.

The noise of the birds squawking in the nearby fields woke him early. He glanced at his watch, then swung his feet to the floor and stood up, looking out of the window while rubbing his scalp through his still-thick white crop of hair with the fingers of his right hand. He heard a gong in the distance, and quickly took off the previous day's clothes he had been wearing when he fell asleep before showering, shaving and dressing for the traditional communal breakfast buffet that always started the day and consisted of local ham, fresh rolls and butter, homemade jams, melon and that rich black French coffee that could never be replicated anywhere else in the world.

Max was one of six guests in the house, but their meaningless chit-chat in an assortment of accents and languages over breakfast bored him. He spoke to them quietly and replied to their questions civilly, but they in turn thought of him as an ageing, compliant, rather shy upper middle-class man: harmless, insipid and rather ineffectual.

Max quickly finished his early morning snack and, as there were many things he wanted to see in the area, he left as soon as he could. As he drove off, he mentally prepared a list of the places he wanted to visit and an order in which to see them.

By eleven o'clock he had been to four of the sites, and he stopped at a cafe in a small, unnamed village—the only place he saw open during the entire morning—for a coffee. There were five or six farming men in the room, and as he sat drinking he looked at their faces.

For some reason, all of them reminded him of the men of the Résistance who he knew had fought so bravely in the area. They were coarse-looking men, as silent to strangers as the fields in which they worked, and they continually glanced suspiciously at the stranger in their midst.

Max finished his coffee, paid and left. He could feel the men staring at his back as he climbed into the car, and slowly, deliberately, took his time looking at his Michelin map despite the fact that he knew exactly where he wanted to go next.

That next location was simply a field about six kilometres on from the cafe. He drove there unhurriedly along a long, straight road lined with tall poplar trees, and soon pulled off the road and parked close by. He left the car and sauntered slowly along a narrow dried-mud path through the trees until he saw an open glade off to his right, stopping for a moment to study it before walking thoughtfully forward.

The clearing led away from the path and went deep into the trees, which gave it lonely, silent protection. It was quite a long open space but not very wide, and as he looked at it, Max could almost hear in his imagination the low drone of an aircraft engine as a Westland Lysander, the "Lizzie", the "Flying Carrot", began to lose height. The pilot would have seen the inverted-L flickering of Résistance torches on the ground, received the coded letter flashed once, before coming into land, and Max pictured the scene as the small, high-winged light aircraft touched down, between torches now lit in twin rows to provide a runway flarepath.

He could visualise the aviator throttling back and rolling to the far end of the brief four-hundred-and-fifty-yard-long makeshift landing strip before swivelling the plane on its tail wheel to taxi back as near to the trees as he could.

As Max stood close to where the aircraft would have stopped, he could picture the dark clothed farm men running to it—their shadowy figures lit by a full moon because night operational landings like this could only took place at a time of the full moon. Max could almost feel the moment as the plane came to a halt, and the workers of the Résistance hustled two silent individuals down the fixed ladder by the rear seats without greeting before slamming the aircraft cockpit shut.

A strong suggestion of reality came to Max, and he virtually heard the full-throttled roar of the Lizzie's 870 hp Bristol Mercury engine as it bounced back along the clearing and took off back to RAF Tangmere in England, while on the ground a screech of tyres and brakes heralded the arrival of a troop of German soldiers. By instinct he looked across as if trying to see the men of the Maquis fading into the trees with their two new arrivals, disappearing and escaping to further the fight against the invader.

Max looked, and listened, but obviously did not see anything. He could picture it all in his mind though, and he stood there silently as the image play-acted in the empty clearing.

It seemed that he stood there for hours, but in reality it was only about fifteen minutes. In that time, Max recalled the bravery of those home-loving Frenchmen who had risked their lives to join the groups of provincial guerilla fighters, the secret Maquis.

As a wartime soldier he knew all about the French Résistance, the various underground movements of men and women fighting to free their country of the German invader. He knew about the official FFI, the French Forces of the Interior organised by de Gaulle in London, and he knew about the organised urban groups who could meet and hide in the houses and narrow streets of most of the major cities. But during the war, and even now, he was especially full of admiration for the clandestine gallantry of the maquisards, those simple, silent, faceless country folk who had taken their name from the Maquis, the rough scrubland in which they hid from their German pursuers.

Max went back to his car in quiet contemplation. He drove on, but throughout the day he kept the image of the Maquis in his mind, and that evening he dined alone in a small cafe before going back to the chateau.

There were four other guests sitting drinking the house beer with the hotel proprietor when he arrived, but he politely turned down their offer to join them and went to his room. The others simply noted the drawn expression on his face, and carried on with their carousing.

Once in his room, Max took off his clothes, again diligently hanging them up before turning off the lights and lying naked in the dark on top of the bed. In his brain he could still hear the roar of the Lysander's engine, hear the squeal of the German hunters' car brakes, see the Maquis fading into the trees. He fell asleep in a sweat.

The birds on the lake woke him again early in the morning, but this time, in need of company, he stayed longer over the communal breakfast, once again noting the disparity of the voices and accents of the other guests. For their part, they enjoyed a joking repartee over his rather clipped English tones of voice—an accent that had a certain inflection that made it almost too perfect to a trained ear almost as if he had come from immigrant stock at some time in the past. Once again, Max's tranquil, almost docile, manner and gracious dignity caught their attention.

As well as his age, it was the voice, they felt, that gave Max a rather superior air of authority, but he just accepted it and did not bother when people made comment about it. So the breakfast banter continued until the guests left one after the other and Max was left alone with a second cup of rich black coffee.

After a short while the proprietor, Henri Camet, came to clear the table, but seeing Max still there sat with him and chatted about the hotel. During the war, he said, it had been occupied successively by both German and British troops, the old brewing kettles used as a bath by the grubby soldiers marching to and from the front line fighting less than nine kilometres way. In his vivid mind's eye recollection, Max could imagine the tramp of first the jackboots then the sturdy ankle boots of the British marching along the road outside.

The hotel, continued Camet, had been used by both sides as a brigade headquarters, but visiting officers were allowed to sleep in its nine bedrooms, while the old brewery buildings were used not only as a bathing house but as a secondary first aid post and occasional operating theatre.

Later in the war, most of the outbuildings had been destroyed, but somehow the house itself had remained intact, its charm untouched. Max listened with interest, although it was a story he knew.

"And you were here then?" he asked casually.

"*Mais non*, I was just a little boy living in Paris. I came here three years ago and rebuilt it as it is today," said the owner. "It had been empty for many years; no one would take it because of its wartime secrets."

"Secrets?"

"I could not tell you, but the owner and all his family were executed by the Bosch. Taken out and bayonetted in the chest one after the other—in front of each other, father, mother and five children, the youngest just three years old. It was too terrible, I cannot speak of it…"

Max stood up, wiping a smear of jam from the corner of his lips with the thumb of his right hand. He said something appropriate and left to continue his tour.

He saw several more sights that day, most of them recalling events from the Résistance. There was the open garden that had once been the Hotel de Ville, the town hall of the small township, used during the war as a Nazi headquarters and blown up one night killing a hundred and seven of the dreaded Gestapo. There had been many killed in the reprisals for that.

In another location, Max visited a small market square where there had been an open gun fight between a German foot patrol and a dozen and a half maquisards. Max looked at the faded red, white and blue ribbons on a plastic wreath laid by present-day survivors and still recalling the event over half a century later.

His expression was imperturbable, his face set and impassive, but once again his mind's eye fancied that it could see the battle— the soldiers approaching the square from a side street and beginning to spread out on either side of the square, the faceless men, women, boys and girls of the Maquis suddenly appearing ghost-like to open fire.

The soldiers would have been half-prepared for an attack, and Max's mind thought of their swift response and the massacre of the civilians, many innocent bystanders, that inevitably followed.

Yet one more place Max visited was a hollow in the woods where five more French Résistance fighters had been executed by one black-uniformed SS stormtrooper, each having a single pistol shot neatly into the back of the skull.

That evening Max returned to the hotel late, after all the other guests had gone to bed. He climbed the stairs and went into his bedroom, and that night he deliberately left the bathroom lights on—the aura in the main room was such that he could not face being in the dark with the night-time images of all the wasted lives and especially those of the chateau's wartime family being bayonetted to death outside. His mind was twisted, as a well-coiled wire will twist when unwound.

Max sighed. *Yes*, he thought, *I've stayed here before.*

They found his naked body the next morning, sprawled in a ditch near the field where he had relived the landing of the Lysander. He had a large gunshot wound on the left side of his chest just above the heart, and death must have been slow and painful.

The police called all the hotels in the area until Henri Camet of the Deux Bières said Max had been staying with him. After the call, he hurried to Max's bedroom and found a note by his bed, on the side table propped up neatly against an unset alarm clock. Henri had no compunction about reading it to learn that Max was going out to take his own life.

Over breakfast, Camet told the other guests about Max's death, and recounted the details of what he had read in the note.

Max, said Henri Camet, had explained in his suicide note that he was not English at all, but a German whose real name was Max Falkenstein. He had apparently joined the Hitler Youth before the war and had helped the Nazis to power as a young member of the feared *Sturmabteilung*, the Storm Division, the Brownshirts.

When war broke out, he had graduated to the Waffen-SS and been posted to one of the many concentration camps in Poland as a guard before persuading his superiors to transfer him into the dreaded *Totenkopf*, the Death's Head brigade with its skull-and-crossbones cap badge. He had been a leading figure with its Second Regiment after the battle at Merville, when he had willingly helped execute some one hundred captive British soldiers forced to surrender after some bitter fighting.

Camet told his stunned guests that Max had been posted to what was then the Chateau de la Paix—the hotel of the peace— as *Hauptsturmführer* (captain) in charge of a *Zug*, a small platoon of some twenty-five men given the task of ridding the area of its French Résistance workers. It was a job he had done with enthusiasm, efficiency and enjoyment.

The proprietor poured himself a cup of coffee before continuing. He said that in his letter, Max had described how his *Zug* had sought out and executed the young men and women, some no more than fifteen years old, who had blown up a Gestapo headquarters in a nearby township, and just days later had killed a number of the insidious Maquis in an open gun fight.

His voice lowered as he recounted Max's detailed account of how he and his men had captured five maquisards in a wood, and how he had then—rather than take them back to jail—pulled out his Luger pistol and personally shot each one in the back of the skull.

But Max had written that what he had then regarded as his biggest success was in turning the then landlord of the chateau into an informer. The proprietor had eventually told Max about the planned arrival of two SOE agents trained in England to unite the many Résistance groups in the area. He had given Max full details of when and where they were to arrive, but unfortunately (according to the note) his timing had not been all that good and the SS men had arrived just too late to capture them all at the wooded landing strip nearby.

Max had been furious and, knowing that his brigade commander would need a scapegoat, had returned to the hotel, where he lined up the proprietor and his family and—just to show his men what kind of leader he was—had again personally bayonetted them to death one after the other… the five children first, then the mother, and finally the father. Before killing him, he had looked the man in the eye and said just one word, "*Verräter.*" Traitor.

Henri Camet came to the end of the story. "Max Falkenstein, Falke, managed to escape when the British arrived to free us. He got away from the vengeance of the local people and managed to get to England, where he found himself a new personage and began a new life. But he said he somehow felt compelled to return to the scenes of his crimes. That is why he was here again, here in the Auberge des Deux Bières."

The proprietor stood and began to gather the breakfast things together. The other guests left him to it, mumbling quietly among themselves before disappearing to their rooms to prepare for the day ahead.

Soon after, the police arrived and went to Max's bedroom to see the note for themselves. They found all Max's possessions neatly stacked and put away, and there was an aura of lightness about the room—a clean, airy, untainted feeling although the windows were closed tight.

A CORNISH HONEYMOON

Harry and Bessie Edwards first went into the hotel bar on the first evening of their arrival in Cornwall. It was a Thursday evening and business had been slack, and they were the only customers to go into the bar of that hotel in St. Ives that evening. They went to the bar at about nine o'clock and went to a corner seat and sat gazing into each other's eyes. Eventually, Harry stood up and went to get two drinks, then he sat down again and the two of them continued to gaze at each other lovingly. They were just about the most loving couple you ever saw. They sat close to each other, and they almost breathed as one person. Long, steady, unmoving breaths of air. In and out. In and out.

It was sweet, but just a little embarrassing for the bartender, who polished away at his glasses trying his hardest not to watch the pair of them.

After a while they picked up their drinks—a sweet martini for her, a dry sherry for him—sipping them lightly and in perfect unison. Their eyes never left each other for a second, and when they had finished their drinks they left the bar and made for the lift to their bedroom. The clock in the hotel hall struck half past nine as the lift doors closed behind them, and within minutes of their leaving the bartender closed down for the night and wandered to the hotel kitchen for a coffee where he sat chatting to the waiters and housemaids, moaning that his only customers of the evening were "that honeymoon couple".

The next day, Harry and Bessie were last down to breakfast. They walked hand in hand into the dining room of the small hotel, crossing to a corner seat where knives and forks and plates had been set out. Everyone watched them cross to the table, but neither Harry nor Bessie took any notice. They held hands tightly right up to the moment he helped her into her seat.

After breakfast, Harry and Bessie went out for a walk around the town. They ambled hand in hand through the narrow and quaint street. They stopped to look in shop windows and they pointed out pretty views between tumble-down houses to each other. And later, they stopped for coffee in one of the small cafes on the harbour front and sat drinking while looking out across the bay towards the far point.

After their coffees, the pair of them strolled around the harbour and got lost in the back streets as they made their way back to the hotel for lunch.

The afternoon wore on, and the temperature soared up into the high seventies. There wasn't a cloud anywhere in sight, and the heavens were a rich perfect-blue, washing down to a green-blue sea that stretched into the horizon far beyond.

Harry and Bessie went down to the beach during the afternoon, spending the time there building a huge castle in the sand, then watching the seas come in, knowing that the sandy moat would soon be filled and then its bulwarks broken.

That evening, they disappeared to their room for a while, and then they went back to the bar and had one small drink each as they sat in the same seat by the corner before they went back to the lift and back up to their room. The time, again, was just on half past nine as the lift doors shut behind them.

The third day of their holiday was spent much as the second. And the fourth and fifth. Then on the sixth day, Harry and Bessie booked up to go for a small trip around Seal Island. They went down to the small beach just behind the harbour bar and waited anxiously with about thirty other people as they watched for the boats to come back from the trip before.

When the boats did get back and had unloaded their cargoes of land-locked sailors, they waited to find out which was theirs and then climbed on board the small rowboat that was to take them out to the larger sea craft bobbing gently on the lapping waves.

Harry stiffened his forearm as Bessie leant on it to climb aboard the motor cruiser, and then jumped nimbly up behind her and they sat down in the stern of the boat. They held hands and gazed into each other's eyes as the captain, a bluff red-necked man, steered a course around the five points of the headland and out to sea, but just a little way.

They looked up dutifully as the captain pointed out the sights on the land as they passed. At the waterfall dropping down from Zennor. At the rocks that seemed to have been slung down in some haphazard heap.

As the land dropped away slightly, they looked back into each other's eyes until finally the captain stopped the boat off the small clump of stone called Seal Island. Then they looked with the others to try to pick out the small black heads juggling about on the surface of the water, and laughed amused at the two old bull seals stretched, seemingly helpless, on top of the rocks.

On the way back, Bessie's shoulders were cold, and Harry put his jacket around her and held his arm over her to protect her from the flying spray.

Back in the town, they walked hand in hand as usual straight to their hotel, stopping just once to peck lightly on each other's lips. They went straight to their room that evening, and didn't even come down for dinner.

The seventh day of their holiday, the last, Harry and Bessie each went out on their own for a while. They seemed broken-hearted as they kissed goodbye on the front lawn of the hotel, and Harry watched with moistening eyes as Bessie walked away down the road to the village. He went off in the other direction, but was back before her and was waiting on the same spot when she eventually returned. They kissed, and Harry helped Bessie carry the parcels she had gone to buy in the village.

During the afternoon they took a coach trip to Land's End, passing through the landward side of the huddle of Zennor, and then going around the curve of the mainland to Mousehole and Penzance, stopping to walk over the rough, hardened fields to Logan's Rock, then back over the roaring downs to the quaintness of St. Ives. In the coach they sat at the back hand in hand, pointing out views to each other, smiling and happy in some faraway manner of their own.

In the evening, they packed and then, laughing, handed over the presents they had bought during the day before going down to dinner. Afterwards, they went into the bar at nine o'clock to sit in the same two seats they had used on their first night in the hotel. Eventually, they drank the same drinks, and they gazed at each other in the same loving way. They sat close, breathing as one, and the bartender was embarrassed once more. They sipped their drinks in unison again, and then they went to the lift and back up to their room on the second floor. As the lift gates shut behind them, the clock in the hall struck its usual half hour—it was just half past nine.

The next morning was overcast as Harry and Bessie silently ate their breakfasts. Their eyes were downcast for a while, but over the second cups of tea Bessie smiled slowly, and their world was all right yet again. They were back in their own world, alone and unmindful of others as they feasted on each other's appearance and gave happiness one to the other. They were accepted in that dining room now, and people only thought that they were happy—and that made some of them happy too, in their own way.

Harry and Bessie left for the station at about eleven, and when they had gone the maids moved into the room that they had used and cleaned it clinically. They changed the sheets and dusted the dressing table, washed the hand basin and wiped the mirrors, shook out the curtains and opened the windows wide to let the sea air cleanse the room of all memories of Harry and Bessie Edwards.

And when they had finished, the maids went down to the kitchen and drank tea with the others of the staff, and somehow the subject of the loving couple came up.

"I think it was rather nice," said the waitress who had served them in the dining room.

"It's unnatural," said the barman who had watched them for a half hour an evening every night during their stay. "A couple like that."

"No," said the receptionist deliberately, "It is rather touching to be like that—at their age.

"Sixty-five years old the pair, they say. And married for forty years of 'em."

GUTSACHE

The scheme was simple and obvious and it came to Gordon Lafferty between the duck pate hors d'oeuvre and his main course, Peruvian quinoa-crusted salmon with a spicy orange miso sauce.

Gordon liked fine dining, but he also had a huge hunger for money, and as the plan struck his mind he grabbed at a menu sitting in the middle of the table and there it was. The very first item: "the best steaks in town".

Every menu in every restaurant said that—"the best". They all said that; none of them owned that their food was actually bad.

But what if… what if he said the opposite? Nobody would believe it. What if he admitted that his steaks were leathery and over cooked and his fillet of sea bream was riddled with bones and had a raw skin that was actually inedible.

It would be different—and people are gullible.

A man of swift action where money was concerned, Gordon wasted no time, and within a month had opened his own restaurant advertising the worst food in town: "We sell the worst smoked salmon, terrible steaks and horrid hotpots."

He called it Gutsache.

He offered the worst wurst, bad burgers, turgid trout and venomous venison at ridiculously high, overpriced prices—although the dishes he actually served with an ingratiating smile were really slightly above average—and the diners-who-know quickly loved the idea that they were being offered the exact opposite to their normal gastronomic favourites.

With dishes like Mona Pizza (with small pieces of Parma ham arranged as a woman's face on a cheese base), it was a gimmick, and although the food was a long way from Michelin-star standard it was better than its description on the menu. With Gordon's sparkling personality as maître d' greeting and personally serving them, the idea somehow, quickly, caught on as the dining *hoi poloi* felt nobody could possibly serve food as bad as it advertised and they flocked to the new restaurant.

"It's a good looking menu," said one supercilious food writer on opening night.

"Yes," replied Gordon, "The menu looks good, but the food's awful."

As word spread, bookings were hard to make and there were daily queues of diners outside the modest front door hoping for cancellations. It was so successful that Gordon quickly set up an extra kitchen catering for weddings after he had attended an expensive and over-publicised society soiree in Mayfair. It was a novelty and he was soon servicing all the big society weddings (bare shoulders and near bare breasts under stupidly wide hats that hid the wrinkles on the face) and Gordon began to expand the restaurant into a chain.

The success continued, and as the popularity of the chain's unusual menus grew, so its descriptions of the food grew ever worse. And the dining public literally lapped it up. Sour stews, mouldy melon, rubbish risotto, and charred chops became bestsellers along with heartburn hummus and gangrenous grub, and Gordon's reputation soared. Soon Gutsache's disgusting diets topped every fashionable list of "in" places to dine and was casually dropped into conversations by TV personalities showing they were "with it".

Things were so rapidly and financially successful that Gordon was quickly able to expand even further. He hired more staff, invested in buying up closed restaurant buildings, and in next to no time opened branches serving Thai food (poor pad noodles, lousy laab salads, greasy gaeng daeng curries and tummy turning tom yum goong, soggy sweet and sour chicken, cringy Cantonese dim sum) and Mexican dishes like terrible tortillas and toe-turning tamales.

He also opened a sumptuous and all-embracing Asian restaurant in the heart of London's super-select Mayfair serving the best of the rest along with such delicacies as chow mean (very small portions of the Chinese delicacy) and Mumbai duck (an updated downbeat version of Bombay duck). A particular favourite there was his "daily traditional poi"—which always raised a smile when the straight-faced reply when asked what that day's poi was… "Chicken, beef or pork poi!" It sold by the dozen.

The rich and the famous—and those who were merely telly "personalities"—were joined by people who saved for weeks to try the food belittled in the Gutsache chain of restaurants. Gordon quickly had a million pounds spare cash in the bank, and soon his perverse idea was copied by others who started to imitate the menus. But Gordon had been cute enough to legally patent the idea, and with some rather smart pay-as-you-win lawyers threatened (and won) copyright lawsuits and compensation poured in.

Eventually his million in the bank had added many extra noughts that eventually turned him into a billionaire. The whole basis of his original thought that people were gullible proved an unprecedented success. Every day seemed to bring more plaudits, more customers… and more money.

It was a complete gimmick, of course, but the fine diners who couldn't tell a soufflé from a timbale fell for it hook, line and fish fork.

It was hard work, continually dreaming up derogatory descriptions for his ever-popular menus, and one day at a late morning breakfast when he had managed to wangle a rare night off from his work in the original Gutsache restaurant he was sitting grumpily on a high stool at the fashionable built-in kitchen top table in the flat he temporarily shared with his latest girlfriend, a prominent (in every way) model, with his mind on a new description for roast beef.

She was eating a breakfast croissant tearing it into small chunks with both hands then delicately, refinedly, picking up each piece in turn with her little finger extended to dunk it in an espresso coffee poured from a De'Longhi La Specialista Maestro coffee maker and could see that he was getting het up, so she suggested that they go out that night.

"We could try that new upmarket eating house round the corner for a quick meal then come back here to relax," she said. "It's all the rage. Lots of paparazzi lurk there."

Gordon was a bit taken aback at her talking about another restaurant being "all the rage", but noting her half-exposed figure he bit back a reply and agreed, then went back to his thoughts about the burning beef.

The restaurant had a trendy low-key exterior, its plain green painted front door with a simple silver name across its top being the only thing distinguishing it from looking exactly like all the other houses in the side street where it sat demurely.

But inside it looked and smelt opulent. It smelt of money and success, and as they walked in Gordon knew the bill was going to be fashionably overpriced and somewhat stupid.

A smarmy head waiter, all hand rubbing, greased hair, mustachio—and from Acton—gushed them to a favourable table, wafted away, then reappeared with two glasses of Dom Perignon champagne.

"On the house as a tribute to the king of London restaurants," he said with a Cockney accent on top of which he had planted a heavy Italianate tone.

A smartly dressed waitress produced menus, and Gordon casually cast his professional eye through it. Cordon Blimey cabbage, reluctant ravioli and pongy pizza. "Or you could have the stale steak," she purred.

Gordon was furious. "I wouldn't eat that muck," he shouted.

He stormed out of the restaurant in a rage, followed closely by his girlfriend tottering slightly on eight-inch heels and they ended up in a nearby greasy spoon caff enjoying a satisfying full English fry-up. With baked beans.

"Ah, the best grub going," said Gordon, belching and with a satisfied grin on his face. "I wonder if over greased sausage, bacon, egg and soggy chips would catch on…"

THE BATTLE

The first thing they heard was an eerie whine. Then the bang.

Ernie, the third man in the line, was flung to the ground, and as he lay there stunned he heard a voice calling out, "Incoming… incoming… watch out."

A bit late, he thought.

Then another frenzied voice echoed in his mind. "Attack, attack."

Slowly he struggled to his feet, groped around to find his weapon, and shook his head to try to bring reality back into line, The patrol was spread round him in a wide defensive ring, and he crawled forward to join them.

"Nasties over there in that gully," said his partner on the right, not taking his eye away from the front sight of his weapon aiming into the near distance.

Ernie looked, and joined in with the battle. Shots were being fired from both sides, the bullets wanging their way over the heads of the soldiers but not really affecting them.

Suddenly two of the attacking terrorists stood—one at either end of the gully—and began charging forward. The soldiers turned their attentions to them, volleying fire but somehow missing the bearded enemy as they weaved around the open ground.

It distracted them, and then a third terrorist stood, unmarked, in the centre of the enemy position and lobbed a hand grenade. Ernie saw it leave his hand, and almost in slow motion watched it arc over the space between the two groups until it landed just a few feet in front of him.

In an almost surreal way, he watched the grenade explode, a sharp bang, then he saw earth shoot up and a blast of hot air hit him and for a second time threw him upwards and back. He vaguely heard voices. "Man down… man down…"

Ernie lay there, and from seemingly a long way away he heard guns shooting, the rattle of a sub-machine gun, the ker-thump of another grenade landing nearby. After a while he passed out and the battle raged around him.

Ernie had been part of a regular army foot patrol in the opium-producing low hills around the mainly desert region of Helmand province in southwest Afghanistan, and this time the men had come under several attacks since leaving the security of the base. This latest skirmish was the strongest so far, and unknown to Ernie as he lay unconscious, his mates fought off the raid by unseen attackers with a grim reality.

He did not know anything about it, nor the fact that a daring Chinook helicopter crew landed soon after to evacuate him and the others of his patrol from the firing line. The whole withdrawal was under intense fire from the marauding terrorist attackers, but Ernie was unaware of it.

Ernie knew nothing about the fact that a team of brave doctors and nurses operated on him on board the twin-rotored Chinook on its way back to base, literally plugging the shrapnel holes that splattered his body and sewing up veins in his legs rendered by the blast of whatever had first hit the patrol.

When he got back to camp, Lance Corporal Ernie Morrett of the Parachute Regiment was still unconscious, but he was alive and more or less stable. He was rushed to the base's main hospital, where more doctors and nurses performed miracles to help him get over the initial shock of being hit.

And he was still asleep getting over the traumas when TV news announcers at home told the public he served simply that "a soldier was wounded in a raid on British forces today." He did not, in fact, wake up for three days.

For many, many months afterwards, Ernie Morrett lapsed in and out of comas lasting anything from a couple of minutes to quite a few days at a time. While it was happening, he was evacuated from Afghanistan to an army-run hospital in England's central heartland for a series of operations on various parts of his body.

For much of the time he was in agony, but he never complained—never let anyone know what physical pain he was subjected to. He was a good, but wounded, soldier.

Two years later, a young night-shift nurse was on lone duty in the hospital's main ward, with Ernie in one of three single room wards just off to one side. It was in the early hours of the morning on one of her first days in the hospital and she was still trying to find her way round, but she was bright, intelligent and had a natural care for her patients.

She had seen all the other patients in the main ward asleep, and although she kept an eye on them decided to keep a special one-to-one watch on Ernie, who, as always, was still regularly slipping in and out of a coma. A pale night light shone down on both of them.

She was looking at his scarred face, then suddenly, as she sat there, he opened his eyes and smiled at her.

"What's your name?" His voice was soft. Gentle.

"Kate Watkins."

"Kate. You're so pretty."

The nurse wondered whether she should call for help, but as she started to move Ernie held out his hand and touched her arm. She stopped.

"I've been dreaming of the fight," he slowly muttered, then began to tell her the story of that battle and how he got wounded.

"But there's something strange I want to tell you," he continued after a long while. "I've always had a picture of a girl in my mind. I knew she was the right girl for me.

"I never met her, but then all the way through the battle I was thinking about her. Beautiful, she was. Looked like you. I wanted to survive—to meet her. I knew I would, and that I would get to know her. To let her know how I felt. The thought helped me all the way through."

Kate looked at him, her eyes filling.

Ernie lifted his arm, just an inch or two. "Hold my hand," he said.

Kate took it. The hand felt cold and somehow clammy.

"Funny to think I've found you at last. Weird," said Ernie. "But I think you really are the girl of my dreams."

He closed his eyes again, his hand dropping to his side as he seemed to slip back into his coma. Kate again wondered whether to call for help, but before she had time to do anything a doctor came into the room.

"What…?" he began to ask.

Kate looked up at him.

"What are you doing in here?"

"It's been quiet tonight so I decided to stay in here with him," Kate replied. "Lucky I did because he came out of the coma for a while."

The doctor did not say anything, and to fill the silence Kate went over the conversation she'd had with Ernie.

"He told me the attack when he was wounded was the fourth on that patrol," she said. "They'd come under fire earlier, and there was a stand-up battle even before they got out of the town. It sounded horrendous, but he just laughed about it and said it was all part of a day's work. Work! You wouldn't catch me doing it!"

Kate babbled on, telling the doctor everything Ernie had said, although she did not mention anything he'd said about his possible feelings for her.

As always, Kate was very precise and methodical in her reporting of what had happened. The doctor listened, but he was taken aback by what he had heard. He knew Kate, and knew she was honest and unusually accurate in her reporting of patients' facts, but now he looked at her in surprise.

"Are you sure?" he asked her. "He really held your hand and told you all that?"

"Yes," replied Kate. "It's just what happened."

The doctor knew the nurse was honest, and that she was so capable that from here earliest days in training school she had been fast-tracked for quick promotion through the ranks. She did not normally give wrong information about patients. He shook his head as he tried to understand her.

"Peculiar," he said eventually. "This soldier not only lost both arms in the battle, but he was wounded with several machine gun bullets through the brain. He went into a persistent vegetative state when he came here—a deep, deep coma. What was it, two years ago? He never came round in all that time and he died half an hour before you came on duty."

ESTELLE

Estelle is a prostitute—let there be no mistake about that. She is well known around the steamier districts of the West End of London, where she does a considerable amount of business owing to the fact that, while she is no raving beauty, she is passably good looking. An innocent look. There are signs of wear and tear around her eyes and mouth, it's true, but there is still something of the attractive about her.

It was about two months ago that Estelle, tiring of her daily routine, told her minder she was going to take a holiday, and that's where the story really began. So let's take a look back at that holiday: four days in the pleasant, phony Regency styling of a mid-autumn out-of-season Brighton.

Gone were the jolly, jolly types. Gone were the mums and dads and their jellied eels and Kiss-Me-Quick hats. Gone were the young men and girls out for a vicarious thrill down by Black Rock. Gone were the tourists, the holidaymakers, the two-weeks-by-the-sea types. Only the residents remained, and a few latecomers like Estelle.

When Estelle arrived at Central Station it was raining. Hurrying to a taxi, she first of all trod in a puddle, then carelessly let her shabby suitcase drop on the slippery surface of the pavement. But inside the taxi she relaxed, sitting back as the vehicle took her at almost frightening speed to her bed-sitter down by Queen's Park ("only two minutes from the sea, love").

In the grimy, dusty and stained room, like so many she had known in her working life, she permitted herself a few busy, womanish moments arranging her hair and make up, then threw herself on the bed, finally revelling in the unaccustomed feeling of freedom. Four days and nothing to do, no one to see.

But like all holidaymakers Estelle soon grew tired of doing nothing. She wanted to see the town, and as it had stopped raining by then she went out, telling Mrs Entwhistle ("I know it's a funny name for a landlady outside of Blackpool, dearie") she wouldn't be in for an evening meal and, please, not to wait up as she might be going to the pictures or a dance or something.

Estelle walked down the steep steps from Marine Parade to Madeira Drive ("a bloody long two-minute walk") and then sauntered casually along the front, looking at the darkening horizon over a frothy, whipped-cream sea. Everything was so quiet she felt she could sing aloud, but she didn't, although she hummed softly as she walked towards the centre of the town.

That night, Estelle ate spaghetti and a rum baba in a small cafe inhabited by students and dirty-looking girls. She studied the girls particularly thinking, possibly, of her own youth a few years back.

And that night she slept between clean sheets, slept the deep uninterrupted sleep of the not-so-innocent at peace with the world.

The next day was Sunday, and the sun was shining. Estelle breakfasted well, then walked down to Madeira Drive again and followed her path of the night before towards the now derelict Palace Pier. It was a glorious day—the slight breeze played in her hair, the sun made her feel good to be alive. It was a different world to Soho, but still she couldn't help noticing that the men eyed her as she walked, no doubt appraising her and weighing up their chances of a pick-up.

But Estelle took no notice. Men were "out" for the next few days. She was on holiday.

Instead, she spent that first morning sitting in a deck chair by the pier. Around her, the few remaining holidaymakers busied themselves with frantic pursuits in search of relaxation, and the town folk hurried along going about their business unmindful of the guests their town still harboured.

After lunch—in the same cafe, again with students and dirty-looking girlfriends—she ambled down onto the expanse of stone that Brighton calls a beach. There she sat, watching the comings and goings of the sea and wondering where it flowed, what was on the other side of the horizon.

And it was there that a large, red, yellow and blue beachball landed on Estelle's lap—a particularly vicious-looking eye painted on it seeming to stare her in the face as if defying her to complain.

Estelle sat with the ball on her lap.

"I'm sorry. I hope you're all right."

The voice was soft, well mannered, only a trace of Cockney about it. Estelle looked up and saw the owner of the voice was of medium height, medium build, medium looking. He had a trace of a medium moustache, his medium coloured eyes were fixed on her—and the beachball on her lap—and he smiled.

It was the smile, Estelle thought later, that had caught her attention. Everything else was so darned ordinary, so sort of… medium.

"Oh, yes." Her own voice, softish, was almost lost as a bus rumbled by on the Parade just above them.

"We were playing with the ball. I couldn't catch it."

"It's all right. It didn't hurt me none."

"Well, I'm sorry it happened."

"It's all right. I don't mind, really."

And so a love was born. There was no frightening flash of lightening. No roaring noises in the head. No miraculous parting of the waves. It was just a simple, everyday event. And it happened to Estelle, the prostitute.

Thinking back on it all, Estelle couldn't quite remember how she came to be playing with the beachball, Bill (for that was the medium man's name) and two other men whose names she hadn't really listened to. What was important was that she did play. And Bill did ask her to have a coffee with them. And she had. And then Bill had got rid of the other two men. And they had gone. And then he'd invited her to the cinema. And the film was a repeat of that one all about the man with no hair dancing with all his thousands of children and that beautiful English teacher who sang to her school pupils. And she'd cried. And Bill had given her a large handkerchief to wipe her eyes and to blow her nose. And when she'd blown her nose loudly and obviously, the teenagers around them in the back row had laughed. And she and Bill had laughed too.

Then all of a sudden it was time to go home and Bill had walked her to the front door of the bed-sit and seen her safely in. He'd been quite a proper gent about it all, not like some of the men she'd known who'd have pawed her about from the word go. A real gentleman.

And then it was time to sleep again between clean sheets, once more with that deep uninterrupted sleep. But this time there was a mental picture in her mind. A mental picture of Bill turning to wave goodbye as he left her to go to her small, untidy room with its grime, its stains and its dusty floor.

Monday was sunny again. When Estelle met Bill as planned, the sun seemed determined never to go away again. All that day and well past the public lighting up time it shone bright in a sky blown clear of all clouds. It was the sort of day on which people enjoy themselves, and that's just what Estelle and Bill did.

Tuesday, too, was a good day. Estelle and Bill met early and spent the day enjoying themselves together once more. Only this time they were more relaxed with each other, felt at home in each other's company. They laughed a lot, and the day was good.

In an amusement arcade near the pier they looked to see what the butler saw. In a fairground at Preston Park (barely a person in sight, and the stall holders almost polite as it was near to the end of the year's work). Paddling in a sea that wasn't quite as hot as the sun should have made it. Eating slippery, slimy little things from the stalls on the sea front. It was a day for fun and that's just what Estelle had. Bill made her dreams come true.

All too soon it was night again. But still Bill kept the party spirit alive taking her to ice hockey at the Brighton Stadium, buying her gin and tonics in a small pub round the back streets while he drank beer, dancing in the Mecca till the small hours.

Then the long walk home. *I'm glad it's more than two minutes,* she thought.

At the front door Bill's hand reached out to shake Estelle's goodnight. A gentlemanly gesture. There was a momentary fumbling as their fingers tried to grip. Then a kiss. Not the Soho kind—all wet and cheap and lipstick. A gentle kiss such as Estelle had hardly known since leaving school.

"I've never been kissed like that, not for simply ages."

"Nor me."

"It makes me feel all sort of funny inside."

"Me too."

"You're not like any man I've ever met."

"I don't know how you describe this funny feeling I've got."

"It couldn't be…"

"Don't know."

"I won't sleep a wink tonight."

"Nor me."

They kissed again. And then, without a word, they started to walk. Back down to the pebbled beach. Along the rough surface of stones under a pale, watery moon. Hardly a word. An occasional pause to look at the sea. And at each other. Arms around waists, backwards and forwards along the deserted beach.

Neither had ever known the feeling before. Neither could describe it. But it was love. Real love.

Soon it was dawn, and they were sitting on a hard, wooden seat watching the sea when the first shafts of sunlight came filtering over the horizon. And finally Estelle broke the silence.

"I've got to go home today."

"Me too."

"Will you be here again?"

"Next year."

"I'll remember you."

"If I'm ever in London…"

"Perhaps you'd better not."

"I'd like to see you though."

"I'll be back next year as well."

Around them, Brighton was waking up. The buses started their purposeful meanderings up and down Marine Parade. People began to appear about the town.

Life was going on and Estelle had to go back to work. But she knew, absolutely knew, that both she and Bill would meet again next year.

HALF PAST ONE

E d Murchison didn't need to look at the green-glowing radio alarm clock on the dressing table when he woke with a start in the middle of the night. He was bursting to go to the loo, and he knew the time would be half past one. It was always half past one when he first woke at night.

Ed was at an age when waking up was a normal way of things. He would be in the middle of a deep sleep when he woke, to get out of bed and go to the lavatory, to then creep back and slide back into a deep sleep again. It happened night after night, and he knew from talking to friends of a similar age that it happened to plenty of men of more mature years.

This time, he eased himself from under the lightweight duvet, slid his feet to the floor, sat for a moment or two listening to the sound of his wife's deep breathing—almost a snore—then stood and went to the en-suite bathroom. As always he did not look at the clock, but while about his toiletry he estimated what the time actually was. Half past one or thereabout was a starting point; it could be five or ten minutes either way. He settled for one thirty-four.

It was his only conscious thought—part of his brain was still asleep and cutting out the rest of life—and when he returned to the bedroom and slid back onto the bed he had a sip of the night-time drink he kept on a bedside table, but still did not look at the alarm clock.

Apart from the fact that he couldn't quite focus on it without his glasses, he knew what it would read. It was always around half past one when he first woke up.

He had a feeling something was not quite right, but he put it down to tiredness and the fact that a week or so before he had learnt through a phone call from the bank that his wife had opened a private bank account with a rather large sum of money. He wondered where it had come from. He had suspected some sort of annoying meddling by his best friend and business partner—his wife's latest boyfriend—but he could not think she was part of it.

He had always preached the doctrine of free enterprise and was rich enough to recognise greed both in himself and others. After years in which his wife had spent his money in a way he considered frivolous, he was rather delighted that she was at last doing something in her own right and decided to keep quiet about it all, determined to wait it out to see what she was up to.

Eventually—it seemed a long time but was probably only minutes—Ed put his head down and slept solidly for an hour, then went through the whole procedure again at around half past two, and yet again at half past three. Each time he sighed as he got out of bed, shivered when he returned, and tried unsuccessfully to look at the clock in the growing darkness, screwing his eyes to try to see the time figures without his glasses.

It was not until he woke in the pre-dawn twilight at four thirty-three that he glanced at his wife in bed next to him. With the slow look of dawn lighting the room he saw that she had a ghastly grin on her face. He was, for some reason, immediately afraid, but he still went back to sleep again.

It was not until five thirty that he woke to look at his wife again. And this time he knew that she was dead. He reached across for a telephone and called for an ambulance to report the mystery death. The paramedics, in turn, called the police, and an hour later Ed was sitting in his bedroom, clad in a thin silk dressing gown and surrounded by a whole host of police and medical people.

"I don't know when she died," he kept repeating by mantra. "I woke around half past one and I think she was still alive, but I don't know. It wasn't until later that I realised she was dead. I don't know anything more…"

As the ambulance crew removed the body, detectives continued to ask Ed questions about his wife.

"Yeah, we had arguments. Who doesn't?" he told them. "But they were friendly arguments. The usual thing between husband and wife."

More questions, and eventually Ed began to wonder if he had, in fact, done something wrong. By the time he was left alone he felt he had been dragged through a wringer, and as he shaved and prepared for the day ahead, he tried to make sense of what had happened.

Did he want his wife dead? No was the inevitable answer, although there was the suspicious new bank account she had set up. Did he have any thoughts about her surprising demise? No. Did he need the money from her new personal bank account or from the sale of jewellery and other expensive possessions she had owned? Again, he didn't need the money; he was wealthy enough in his own right.

The questions went round endlessly in his mind, and he began to feel guilty, as though he was responsible for the death. Was he in love with her? Of course, she was his wife. Had he ever had a relationship with someone else? Ed was aghast at the thought. Had his wife? Ed knew she had, but as he grew older and was unable to cope, he was ambivalent about it all. Had she been ill? No. Had she been complaining about feeling unwell? Once more, he had to answer "no".

When the detectives returned later that day, they told Ed they could find no reason for his wife's death. In fact, it seemed to them she had just stopped breathing in her sleep.

"The pathologist has given a rough estimate of the time of her death. Seems that just past twelve—perhaps half past—she just passed away," they reported. "Doesn't seem to be anything suspicious, but the final decision is up to the coroner, of course."

"I hope you don't mind, but you realise we have to ask the question, do you know anything about what happened just after twelve o'clock?"

"No. I was asleep. I always wake at half past one—almost every night—but I sleep deeply until then. But it's always around half past one when I wake for the first time any night. Then I sleep on, perhaps waking every hour after that. But nothing until half past one. Every night, half past one."

Ed was devastated by the death—in one moment he had lost his wife, occasional lover and housekeeper. The doubts remained—locked in his mind—and over the next couple of weeks he worried and fretted, continually asking himself the same questions about his wife's passing. He could find no answers. But as no one else seemed at all interested he soon got over the feeling and began to settle down again.

It took eight months for the full details of his wife's will to come to light, and everything was detailed to the last penny. Because there were no children, everything she possessed was left to him, even the cash left in her new financial set-up. The solicitor had worked hard and had finally got to grips with that, and the details were laid out for Ed. It appeared he had been right, and she and her partner (Ed's friend and *his* partner too) had been systematically taking stock from Ed's company and selling it on through their new venture.

From then on, there were moments when Ed wondered what on earth had been happening to his marriage. He discovered evidence that his wife had opened bank accounts in various islands around the world, amassed a huge amount of money, taken on company directorships galore based on using goods from his own various companies. She had become, he discovered, quite a tycoon in her own right.

It should have worried him, but in a practical business-like sort of way he put it down to the fact that her new boyfriend had advised her well and given her financial stability in her own right. Despite the financial hoo-ha it caused, it was not, he felt, too big a deal… although he was a bit upset at her apparent duplicity.

Eventually, about a month later, Ed woke up in the jet-dark of the night. He tried to get his thoughts together, but as he wanted to go to the loo he eased himself from under the lightweight duvet, slid his feet to the floor as usual, then stood and went to the toilet. He did not look at the alarm clock glowing on the other side of the room, but he knew it must say somewhere in the region of half past one. It always did.

Soon he was back in bed, pulling the duvet around his now shivering body, but instead of going off into his usual deep catatonic sleep his mind was awhirl. He had a mental picture of his wife in bed, on her back, and breathing so deeply it was almost a snore.

He had a swift mental picture of a body looming over her, a pillow in its hand. The pillow was pushed over his sleeping wife's face. He had a picture of the green alarm clock figures brought into sight by narrowed eyes.

Ed sat up with a start. It couldn't be. He had no reason. Well, apart from her apparent new boyfriend and the comprehensive fortune she had been stealing from him.

He reached for his glasses and looked at the radio clock. It was bound to be half past one (it always was) but as he looked the digital figures clicked over—twelve thirty-seven—and he suddenly realised that on the night of his wife's death the clocks had gone back at the end of summertime. He screwed his eyes up and looked again at the clock: twelve thirty-seven. He had still not altered the clock, and he realised that on the night of his wife's death, what had been half past one was really half past twelve.

That was the time the detectives said she had died and he burst into tears.

"But I always wake up at half past one," he said to himself.

ADOPTED

PART ONE

It was a grey day although a weak sun was shining in a cloudy sky and there was a small bird singing his heart out loud in a tree above the bedroom window. It was the day on which Austin Fowler got a letter telling him he had been adopted as a baby and asking if he wanted to meet his real-life mother. It was the first time Austin had heard he had been adopted, and it was a shock.

The letter from the adoption agency dropped on his door mat with a pile of advertising material, and Austin was at first slow to pick it out. He had buttered and marmaladed his morning slice of toast to have with his first cup of coffee of the day before he picked it out and opened it, but as he read the apparently photocopied words the toast and the coffee remained on the table growing cold. The letter said that Austin's natural mother had written to the agency asking if there was any way in which she could find out how he was getting on, and the agency said that, as was its custom, it first of all wanted to know how Austin felt about the request.

Reading the letter, Austin was not at all sure how he did feel. It was as if the bottom had fallen out of his orderly, safe, secure world, and he just wanted to throw the letter in the waste bin and pretend it did not exist.

All that day, as he went about the movements of his job in an accountancy office, Austin had the shock contents of the letter at the back of his mind, and he knew that, as much as he wanted to, he could not just forget it. His mind was in a disturbed state of agitation throughout the day, and several times the office secretary asked if he was feeling unwell.

That night, he went to bed early but lay awake into the small hours of darkness with his mind still disorganised and confused by the content of the letter, but eventually he did fall into a tormented sleep during which he tossed and turned and did not really relax.

In the morning, Austin's mind was still just as confused, and once again the early morning cup of coffee grew cold and went undrunk. During the whole of the day he wondered what his best course of action should be, and this time it was not only the secretary who asked about his state of health but his boss as well. Austin covered his strange behaviour by saying he had some sort of stomach upset that would soon clear up.

During the day, his mind would not settle on the various jobs he tried to do, and his mind kept wandering back to the problem presented by the suddenness of the letter.

Apart from his own feelings, he wondered how his adoptive mother—who had died less than a year before—would have reacted if she were to hear of the letter. She was the only real mother he had ever known, and he still cherished her memory dearly, and although she had never mentioned anything about his having been adopted in all his thirty-six years before her death he knew she would have been distraught.

By the end of that second day he had decided on what course of action he should take.

He knew it would involve a bit of contrivance, but he was not too bothered about that as he now felt that the whole of his life until receipt of that letter had been a subterfuge as well.

The next day he drank his early coffee and had a piece of toast and marmalade before going to work with a more normal step than in the previous couple of days. At the office, he kissed the secretary on the cheek, making her blush, and sat down at his desk as if he did not have a care in the world.

During the morning though, he quietly took the telephone number of the adoption agency from the top of its letter and rang through when the office was quiet, telling the girl who answered that he felt he might like to see his natural mother as she had requested. When the girl on the phone told him the policy was for the agency to book the meeting, he said he was going away on business for a month and simply wanted to write to the woman— his birth mother—to explain the delay.

The girl, a junior manning the telephones at lunchtime, believed him and, although she should not have done so, gave him the address. Austin jotted it down on a piece of office-headed notepaper, which he folded carefully into four, and put in his jacket pocket.

Some time that evening, he took out the note, unfolded it slowly, and studied it with care, sitting in an armchair and holding it up in front of his face as he reflected on it.

After half an hour or so, he slowly stood, went to a bookcase, and got a road map of the district to look up the address.

PART TWO

Austin stood opposite the house, standing on the other side of what was a slightly shabby tree-lined street long past its best. He was wearing a dark grey suit, but with an open-necked shirt, although he had a sober blue tie in his pocket.

A slight breeze ruffled his fair, curly hair, but he just stood with his arms down by his side studying the home of the woman who claimed to be his natural mother. He did not know what his feelings were—or should have been.

He stood there for maybe five or six minutes without moving, without anyone noticing him, then without any reason he began to walk slowly along the pavement looking at the other houses in this street.

The street was one of many residential streets in the area, all similar. Like all the others it was lined with plaster-fronted semi-detached houses, some painted others still a dark grey, but all now looking in urgent need of decorating. The windows, too, looked as if a lick of fresh paint would not come amiss, and to

Austin it seemed that the street had somehow taken him back ten or fifteen years. He could not have said why he had that feeling.

At the far end of the street he crossed over, and began to walk back the way he had just come, slowing down almost to a standstill as he neared the home of his birth mother.

His mind was still a blank; he still had no real idea why he was there and what he wanted to do.

But his mind was starting to kick into action now. It pondered why the woman from this house, his mother (although he could not think of her with that title) should want to meet him now, after all these years. It wondered what she looked like; what she thought, felt, considered, anticipated. His mind gave him no answers.

Austin stopped in front of the house. The front garden was immaculate, although in the now late autumn sunlight it was starting to look faded and dying. It was quite deep to the house, but not very wide, and there were flower-bare rose bushes off to one side, a large clump of some still flowering yellow flowers to the right. Austin saw at a glance that it was in far better condition than its counterpart in the other half of the semi-detached.

On an impulse, he turned into the front path, pushing the gate open and letting it swing shut on slightly rusting hinges behind him. He noticed, for some obscure reason, that the curtain in one of the upstairs windows was still drawn closed, although its partner was pulled back. They were golden coloured curtains, matching those in the front room downstairs.

Austin walked down the path and knocked on the front door. It was a dark blue door, with a golden letter box—*golden like the curtains*, he thought. He stood there, biting the inside of his top lip with his lower teeth.

He heard a noise from inside, then footsteps. A bolt was drawn, a key turned in the lock, then the door opened.

The woman standing there was short, grey-haired, and with a kind, if elderly, pixie face. Her hair was curly like Austin's, and bobbed, and there were unruly locks sticking out at one side and at the back. The woman's eyes were the same pale blue as his, and looking closely Austin could recognise a slight similarity between them. Now though, she looked a little anxious because of the strange man standing on her doorstep.

"Yes?" she asked, her voice a little frail and hesitant. "Can I help you?"

Austin swallowed. He wished he had put on the tie in his jacket pocket. "You are…" He paused, and the old lady nodded as if she was agreeing with the sentence he had not finished.

"Mrs Grenfell," she said.

"Ah yes, Mrs Grenfell. I believe you wrote to the adoption agency about the son you offered some years back."

"That's right."

"Well, I wonder… can I have a chat about it?"

"Of course. But the woman I spoke to said—"

"It's just a formality. I'd really like to speak about your son and everything."

"Right. You'd better come in then."

The woman stood back to make way, and Austin stepped into the house. She turned to lead the way to the front room, and he followed.

"Would you like a cup of tea?"

"No thanks." Then he thought again. A cup of tea might help the woman relax and be less restrained. "Well, on second thoughts, perhaps, yes. It would be rather nice."

"And a biscuit?"

"Ah, no. No biscuits. I have to think of my figure."

They both smiled.

"Well, sit down. I won't be many minutes. I'd just boiled the kettle when you came."

She went to the door of the room, and Austin thought he had been clever to think of the tea after all.

He watched as the woman opened the door, then on another impulse asked, "Could I, perhaps, use your... your toilet?" He wondered why he had hesitated about using the word.

"Oh yes, it's upstairs. In the bathroom opposite, you can't miss it."

She went out of the room, and after a moment Austin followed, but as she went to the kitchen he went upstairs. At the top he glanced behind him down to the ground floor before he had a cautious peep through the two bedroom doors he could see. Then he went to the bathroom and saw the first thing that looked out of place in what seemed a very orderly house: a framed painting of a cheeky lady doing a can-can, her skirt held high to reveal frilly underwear beneath the garish skirt. Austin guessed it had been given to her as a present and put in what she perceived as the only decent place a painting like that could hang.

For some reason he spotted that the print was signed simply "T. Lautrec 93", with an address at 8 rue de la Victoire. He smiled to himself as he wondered if T. Lautrec could possibly have had a matching picture of a sedate old English woman hanging in his own bathroom in the rue de la Victoire and whether the *rue* itself was anything like an English suburban street in any case.

Austin glanced around the bathroom, saw soap in a dish, shampoo and some talc in a bowl. He looked out of the window at a back garden as immaculate as that in the front of the house, then he pulled the toilet chain for effect and went back to the stairs.

As he went downstairs again Austin thought he had seen houses like this one everywhere he had ever travelled. It was neat and, the one "naughty" painting apart, there was nothing at all surprising or unusual about it. It was the home of someone for whom everything had its place, and where everything was in that place. He guessed that Mrs Grenfell was an overly tidy person, a woman who would never leave the washing up until the next meal or next day, who would always cover her mouth when she yawned no matter that there was no one else in the room, would always systematically clear up behind her.

When he got back to the front room Mrs Grenfell had not yet returned, so he walked round giving fairly casual glances at everything. It was a typical suburban front parlour, pictures of elderly men, middle-aged children, and babies on the mantlepiece and on a sideboard to one side. The wallpaper was patterned, and there were a few odd ornaments littered around. He went over to the mantlepiece and started looking at the photographs. On each end there were matching silver framed pictures: one of a woman obviously Mrs Grenfell herself, the other of a rather stern-looking man whom Austin thought must have been her husband. He wondered if the man was his father.

While he was looking at the man and wondering, Mrs Grenfell came back into the room carrying a tray. There were two cups and a teapot on it, with a small china jug containing the milk and a bowl with sugar. Austin saw that there was also a plate with some sweet biscuits on it.

Mrs Grenfell put the tray on a small table, and Austin went back across the room to sit in one of the easy chairs close to it.

"Milk and sugar?"

"Yes please. Two spoons."

Mrs Grenfell poured the tea, and as she did so Austin studied her closely.

She was wearing a simple grey skirt with a blue cotton blouse that went to her neck. She had no jewellery apart from a simple gold wedding band, and Austin noted that she had eased the stray locks of hair back into position.

Mrs Grenfell handed one of the cups across, and Austin stirred it without thinking. She offered the plate of biscuits, but he shook his head and she put the plate back on the tray.

They sat there for a moment, and as Mrs Grenfell sipped her tea, not quite sure what to do, Austin looked at her face—this woman, this stranger, his mother.

"Look," he said as he took a sip of his own tea, "Why is it you want to meet your son after all these years?"

Mrs Grenfell looked back at Austin over the top of her cup, now held unmoving in her right hand just a few inches below her mouth. It seemed to him that for a brief moment her lips held a slight tremor, but her eyes never left his.

Mrs Grenfell put the cup back on its saucer held in her other hand and bent forward to put the saucer back on the table by her side. "I can't explain it," she finally said. "It's just something I felt I wanted to do. Needed to do."

Austin's eyes were still fixed in a stare, and he waited for more. After another moment or two Mrs Grenfell gave it to him.

PART THREE

"When I had my so—my baby… I was a little bit of a tearaway," she continued, "You know, a sort of good time girl. I used to go around with all the wrong sort, and all we wanted to do was to have fun—all the time. It all seems so long ago that I don't know how I could have, but somehow I got caught up with the wrong people and just let things flow along.

"You know, in those days we didn't know all about contraception—it was something we left to the boys—and I didn't think too much about the consequences. The result was that I suddenly found myself pregnant." She paused, and Austin turned his eyes away for a moment.

When his gaze returned, Mrs Grenfell looked down at her cup. "No one wanted to know me when they heard I was having a baby. Nice girls didn't get like that in those days," she went on. "None of the old crowd would even talk to me. Even my parents used to give me disgusted looks. It was awful. I didn't know what to do."

She looked up at Austin again, her eyes moist but now steady as she tried to look him straight in the eye.

"The doctor sent me along to see some people from the council, but I could tell they thought I was awful as well. I felt all alone; no one was there to help me."

Austin thought there were tears starting to form in her eyes. "Have a sip of tea," he said quietly.

Mrs Grenfell picked up her cup, holding it this time in both hands. She did not drink from it. "I went to see the baby's father one evening, but he slammed the door in my face. I waited for a while, thinking he might open it up again, but all I heard was him laughing inside the house. At least, I can remember that I thought I heard him," she went on.

"When the baby was eventually born, a lovely sweet little lad he was, I tried to get in to see the boy several more times, but he wouldn't even open the door at the end. There was nothing else I could do. My parents wouldn't help, and I couldn't look after him on my own."

The tears were still in her eyes, but Austin could tell that she was now trying to get control of herself; to be, well, very stoical and English about it. "He was a lovely little boy, a real delight.

Such small fingers and toes," she said eventually. "But I honestly felt it was for the best to give him away. I felt it would have to be a better life for him with someone who not only wanted him but who could look after him."

Austin recognised she was giving him all the usual old excuses, but as his mind wandered on he realised that throughout the whole saga, Mrs Grenfell had only spoken about "my baby" or "my little boy", she had not, as he might have expected after all the time that had gone by, referred to "it" or "the baby".

His mind jerked back as he suddenly thought Mrs Grenfell had said something about "his sister". He did not know if he was mistaken, and he didn't like, or dare, to ask her to repeat the sentence. He blinked rapidly a few times.

Mrs Grenfell paused, and drank her tea impatiently, as if she not only wanted to clear her throat after talking a lot but wanted to cleanse something inside herself.

"It was a long time before I finally met Mr Grenfell," she said when she had finished drinking and put the cup back on the saucer on the small table beside her. "He was a nice man, a steady man, and although I told him about having had the little boy he was not worried. He was a proper gentleman, and we fell in love."

Mrs Grenfell started to talk about her marriage, and the story came out in Austin's mind that Mr Grenfell had helped change and completely reform her character. Over the years of their marriage he had given her a cosy, safe suburban life, a serene life. He felt quite pleased at that, and the thought struck him as Mrs Grenfell spoke that perhaps he should have put on his tie before knocking on her front door. He felt in his pocket to reassure himself that it was still there, neatly folded as he believed she would have wished it.

"But why do you want to see your son now? After all these years," he asked, his voice sympathetic as he tried to hide the secret confusion in his brain.

Mrs Grenfell smiled, a rather sad smile he thought. "There's been so many times in the past when I've wanted to see him but didn't dare," she said without pausing to think. "I thought he was probably part of a happy family. Could even have a family of his own, children perhaps. I didn't want to upset any of that."

The smile was still there. "But there have been so many times when I missed him; I can still see him as a little darling, my small baby son. There were times when I wanted so much to know that he was happy, just as I wanted him to be when I had to give him up all those years ago."

She suddenly stopped speaking, as if she had no more words to explain.

"But why now?" persisted Austin.

Mrs Grenfell tipped her head slightly to one side, the right. "I suddenly thought, *Well, he's old enough to cope now.* I've been so lonely since my husband died, and I just wanted some sort of guarantee that he's happy and well… I want to know that he's grown up happy."

She sat up straight in the chair, seeming to force her head upright again. "I suppose it sounds a bit silly to say I simply want to try and make amends," she said.

Austin nodded. It did sound trite, overused, to him. *Just another of the regular excuses,* he thought.

He did not say anything, and for a moment or two there was a silence between them. Despite the list of conforming justifications befuddling his mind, he felt quite a bit of sympathy towards the ageing woman in front of him.

"What's he like?" asked Mrs Grenfell.

Austin remembered that she thought he was from the adoption agency and managed to evade the issue. But as he did so, it made him wonder what he *was* like; if he was at all like her—a woman he had to force himself to think of as his natural mother—and his sister if there was one… or if he was more like his real mother and father, his adoptive parents.

Soon after, he was ready to leave, but as he stood he picked up the tea tray from the small table and carried it into the kitchen for Mrs Grenfell. This time he noticed a cat flap in the back door, and he wondered about that. She seemed to him far too tidy a person to keep a cat, not the sort to be prepared to give love to any animal.

It struck him that a cat flap would be too messy for her— having a cat would require emotion, a bit of giving. He had an inner sardonic smile as he tried to match that thought with her giving up both him, and possibly a sister too when they were babies. Back at the front door, Austin shook Mrs Grenfell's hand and said someone would soon be in touch. He walked out into the dying sunshine, feeling the breeze blowing and a chill around his ankles and face. He got to the end of the garden pathway, opened the squeaking gate, and stepped into the suburban street again. He took a deep, obvious breath, two deep breaths, and turned to look back at the house.

Mrs Grenfell was still standing, small and seemingly lonely, by the dark blue front door, and Austin noticed once more that the one golden coloured curtain in the upstairs window was still drawn closed. It was exactly as it had been when he arrived, but to Austin it was somehow different.

PART FOUR

The next few days saw Austin's mind in a natural turmoil. He did not understand the inner feelings that had grown in his memory towards Mrs Grenfell, and neither did he know what he should, or was supposed to, think about his subterfuge meeting her.

He liked the woman and had a certain respect and compassion for her as a lonely old person, sure, but there was a hard-to-forget suspicion nagging away in his mind that she was also the woman had had thrown him away as a baby—possibly along with an unknown sister.

That last was a thought that would not go away, and he knew now that his life would never be exactly the same because of it.

On the outside, to the other people he knew, Austin was his normal self; inwardly he was a bundle of bewilderment, his brain befuddled by doubt. During the darkness of the nights that followed the days after his visit to Mrs Grenfell, Austin would lie awake with his mind trying to sort out the unbidden dilemma he had been handed. Although she had explained herself in the trite, customary excuses of those others he had often read about in the same situation, Austin felt a sympathy for Mrs Grenfell. He could, he felt in the snug blackness of his bed, believe that in the age when she had grown up she would have been shunned by her peers and parents when she discovered her unwanted pregnancy, might have felt the need to give away an unbidden baby, could have felt that it would be better for the child to be given a home with someone in a better position than she had herself been.

At the same time, he knew that she had deliberately given him away. Had banished him, cast him out of her life, discarded him. It was that incessant, nagging, recurrent, obsessive thought that held sway in the darkness of the night.

The more he thought about it, the less Austin could make sense of the unhappy twist that had taken over his life. From their meeting, he knew Mrs Grenfell genuinely felt she now wanted him back as a son, but he was someone else's son. He realised she wanted to be his mother, but he already had a mother, the mother he had grown up with.

Did he, he wondered, want to suddenly become a different person? Did he need a new family in a life that had, until the arrival of the adoption agency letter, been settled and reasonably happy?

Austin thought about it continually. But the more he thought, the less he answered the agonising questions that clouded his mind. It was a continual enigma. He felt instinctively that, although Mrs Grenfell was lonely, it would be wrong to mess up his own life with its happy family background, but perversely it continually occurred to him that no matter what, she was his natural mother.

Then one morning he woke with a clear answer. He went to the office as usual, kissed the blushing secretary on the cheek as usual, and sat down to a morning's work as usual. But at lunchtime, he made an excuse that he had a meeting to attend—although his secretary knew he had not—and left the office to go home.

Once there, for a reason even he could not understand, he went to his bedroom, shut and locked the door, and sat down on the bed to hand write a letter to Mrs Grenfell. He began by telling her who he was, and that he was the tieless man who had called on her. He said it had been lovely meeting her, and insisted that he had enjoyed their rather short conversation. He apologised, in a strictly formal way, for his subterfuge, and added that he liked her and hoped she did not hold it against him that he had used the intrigue.

The words flowed, seemingly effortlessly, as Austin wrote. He told Mrs Grenfell that despite the turmoil of the last few weeks, his life had turned out just the way she had hoped; he had been raised by a caring family who had the wealth and the love to give him a happy childhood and start in life.

That life, he explained, now seemed to him to have been far better than he might have had if he had not been adopted.

Austin paused in the letter writing. He read, then re-read, the last few sentences, and as he did so he realised that he was using the same words and phrases that Mrs Grenfell had used to explain herself and the adoption to him. He thought he was being a hypocrite for using the same excuses to cover her action as she had given him.

"But I am afraid that we mustn't meet again," he added at the end of the letter. "The shock would, I feel, be too disloyal to my mother's memory."

He read that sentence again too. "My mother."

Then he sat there, looking at the letter with blank eyes that didn't really see the two words shouting back at him from the notepaper. In his mind's eye he could picture Mrs Grenfell standing at the door of her house, the dark blue door with the golden letter box, and he wondered why the golden yellow curtain that matched that letter box had still been drawn.

Then it struck him. He remembered the day, a Saturday when Rovers were at home, when he had been called to his adoptive mother's bedside. The football crowd had held him up, and she had died ten minutes before he arrived. He recalled the devastated feelings he had felt then.

He remembered the feeling of doom that seemed to envelop him as he approached the house, and he remembered seeing his mother's bedroom curtain drawn then too. A golden curtain. It had still been drawn shut to hide her lifeless body when he left the house hours later.

Austin sat there looking at the letter for many minutes, while outside it was once more a grey day although the sun was again shining bright in a blue sky and there was a small bird singing his heart out loud in a tree above the bedroom window.

Then all of a sudden, Austin Fowler, a motherless child, burst into tears.

KWAN-TIN'S WAR

t was only a small war in a small place, and it seemed quite unrealistic to the rest of the world. The bullet that shot Kwan-Tin in the middle of the forehead, however, was quite realistic, and very deadly.

Because Kwan-Tin was killed by that bullet in the forehead, his wife San H'uang fell to grieving and wept tears of sorrow. She spent most of her time in prayer before the household Buddha, her own private god, and she never had time to give her orders to the men who worked on the Kwan-Tin farm.

Because San H'uang failed to give them orders and instructions about the sowing and tilling and feeding of the meagre twelve and a half acres of farmland, the workers took to resting and lazed about in the hot daytime sun gossiping.

Because the farmhands failed to work the land, the ground grew hard and cracked under the heat of the sun and the dust blew up and killed the crops and the beasts in the farm died. The farm fell into disrepair and looked sad.

Because the farm went into ruin, San H'uang lost the money that was left to her by Kwan-Tin, and soon she could not afford to pay the wages of the workmen who lazed their days in the sun in her fields. Her family starved, and she had to tell the farmhands to leave.

Because they had to leave San H'uang and the farm left by Kwan-Tin, the farm workers had to scrape and save and had to spend their days in search of work.

Because there was a war, the farmhands could find no jobs and had to spend their days bemoaning their fate to their families, and had to ration out their food. Their children did not have enough to eat and they, too, starved and fell sick.

Because the farm workers' children grew ill, the rest of the province protested, and it spread throughout the country and under workers' leader Hu Yat-San the people turned on the government in the capital. The government could do nothing about the trouble, and so the workers took action and went on strike and marched on the capital.

Because of the strike, the government faced ruin and had to seek appeasement and go to the opposition for advice and help. With the "help" they received, the government fell and there were riots in the country.

Because the government fell, the country had no leadership and soon the treasury announced that there was no money left to run the country.

Because there was no money, the country could not afford international barter, and so the to-and-fro business of world trade fell off and supplies grew low until gradually more people starved.

Because the people starved, they grew weak and their muscles slowly wasted and their ribs showed through and their bellies distended and disease riddled the country. People like that, of course, they could not work.

Because the people could not work, the supplies of the nation dwindled and vast plants and factories grew idle and there were no goods delivered, no arms or ammunition, and so the war was lost.

It was only a small war in a small place, and it seemed quite unrealistic to the rest of the world.

THE UGLY COUPLE

A small jagged scar cut down her cheek. There was another below her right eye, and her forehead was also marked. A thin puckering of her lower lip indicated another old wound, while her hair was clipped short and stuck up in a tangle. There was a permanent bruising on both her upper cheekbones.

I found out later that her name was Anna, and that she had spent four of her formative years in Dachau.

The man—his name was Carl—was short and fat. He had unruly, ugly jowls, and his lips were parted and pouted out thickly. He was a stumpy man and incredibly ugly.

They came into the restaurant together, and for a moment they paused at the end of the short self-service counter. There was a small queue, so they came over to my table—Carl in front and Anna following meekly behind. Carl sat opposite me without a word. Anna looked down at him, then across to me.

"Do you mind if we sit at your table?" Her voice had a European accent that I found difficult to place at the time, and there was an apology in her expression.

"Not at all. Please do." I tried to make my own voice as friendly as I could.

Carl glowered at me, then turned away.

Anna was still standing meekly and looking down at him. "Shall I get the food?" Her accent still puzzled me.

"Go get it. You know what I want."

Anna waited, and Carl reached in his pocket and brought out some money. He slapped it down on the table. There were three pound coins, two fifty pence pieces, twenty and ten pence coins and about six pennies. Anna picked it all up and went to the counter. The restaurant seemed quiet while she was away, then she came back with two plates and set them down. She sat.

Carl ate ferociously from the fuller plate, cramming his mouth until the food overflowed and sprinkled his chin.

"Do you want some bread?" Her voice was soft, and still the accent puzzled.

"Yes. Get me a roll." As Anna stood, Carl added as an afterthought, "And butter."

He hardly looked up from his plate, and as he spoke I could see the partly chewed food in his mouth. I noticed his teeth were badly stained.

Anna stood up again and squeezed past Carl's seat. She was gone only a few moments, but already the fat was beginning to congeal on her plate. She put the roll and butter down in front of Carl, then sat and picked up her own knife and fork.

"Have you got the coffee yet?" Carl had finished the main meal and was mopping his plate with the roll. The butter was left on the side of the bread plate untouched.

"I'll get it." Anna put down her knife and fork and stood again. There was no expression in her voice. The accent worried me.

Once more she came back quickly, this time with two cups of coffee, taking care to put the cup that had slopped over onto the saucer on her own side of the table. Carl belched with his mouth closed, then he held out his hand and Anna put the change into it. There was the ten-penny piece and three pennies.

Anna finally started to eat her meal. Although it was cold she cut it into small pieces and chewed nervously. Carl drank his coffee with a great amount of noise, then he wiped his mouth with the back of his hand and belched again, noisily.

"Eat up, we don't have all day," he said.

Anna was about to put cold potato into her mouth, but she stopped the fork in mid-air. "I won't be more than a few minutes." She put the potato in her mouth apologetically.

"Then I'll go and pay a visit." Carl looked me in the eye for the first time, and there seemed to be a wink between us although his eyes did not move. "A call of nature, you say!"

He stood up and went off chuckling. Anna put her knife and fork down although there was still food on the plate. I saw a tear building up in her eye, and she put a hand to the scar on her cheek.

"Does he hit you?" I don't know why I asked the question, but it did not seem out of place although we had never met before.

She nodded, but did not lift her eyes from her plate.

"Often?"

She nodded again.

"Then why?" My hand reached out automatically across the table, although I did not touch her. "Why do you stay with him? Why?"

A smile crossed her face for the first time. A vague smile. Beautiful in her scarred, ugly face.

"Because I love him. Since the camp. A guard. That's why."

The accent was German. *Bavarian*, I thought.

BURIED ALIVE

It was at three fifty-three in the afternoon of Thursday that the explosion ripped the heart out of the massive office block on the edge of the city. Something triggered it off, a gas explosion maybe, but within seconds the thirty-two storeys had fallen on top of themselves in a gigantic pile of rubble standing only as high as the original lower two floors. Part of the tower block next door also collapsed as the weight of the office block fell against it.

The two buildings were filled with dozens of small offices on their lower twenty-seven storeys, and above the offices were many reputation-seductive, highly prestigious, highly desirable, highly expensive apartments.

Many people who had been in the two blocks working or at home preparing for an evening with friends were buried under that mound of broken bricks, steel girders, plaster and glass, and rapidly though the emergency services screamed to the scene, blue lights flashing and sirens wailing, there was no way of knowing how many there were and if any were alive—if any were, indeed, still able to live under that horrific framework of building slabs.

As many small fires were doused, some of the rescuers began tearing at the rubble with their bare hands. Further helpers turned off the gas main. Yet more tried to organise proper clearance methods. Others began to painstakingly prepare a possible list of those who had been in the building at the height of a working day.

As daylight turned to gloom, huge banks of spotlights were focused onto the wreckage, and the work continued. The digging teams slowly organised, the list of potential victims grew larger seemingly by the minute, and by the time the first politician appeared on the scene to face the television cameras, it had been fairly accurately estimated that there could be as many as two to three thousand people buried by the disaster.

By eight o'clock, forty dead bodies had been recovered, but the industrious helpers diligently continued with the gruesome task of sifting and digging, digging and sifting, trying to get as many more out as possible. By morning, a steady flow of hearses and ambulances had removed a further two hundred and twenty.

Beneath the rubble was Joe Cosway. A fifty-five-year-old devoted father of two fine sons in their early teens and the romantically minded husband of a pretty wife Shula, he had been working on a sales report on the seventeenth floor when the building collapsed, and as he recovered consciousness in the depths of the debris he vaguely recalled suddenly dropping as though over a waterfall. The noise, he remembered, had been much the same.

Now he gradually came to his senses, and slowly began to realise what had happened. He was caught in a small pocket between two huge girders that he could just vaguely make out in the almost unbearable gloom filtering through; two thick steel bars that seemed to be holding the building steady above and around him.

Joe felt himself as well as he could, touching his ribs and his arms, his shoulders, neck and legs, and there did not seem to be too much physically wrong with him, although he could not move his right leg. He realised it was trapped by one of the girders. Luckily, there seemed to be air to breathe, and he knew instinctively that he should not move too violently despite the feeling that he should try to claw his way to freedom. Fighting off the instinctive panic, he lay back and tried to figure out what to do.

Joe knew that helpers would soon be digging, maybe they had even now started, and he knew, too, that he could not move to help them. His trapped right leg would see to that. He reasoned, carefully, that he should wait until he heard some sound before even trying to call for help, but he could not control himself.

"Help. Please, someone, help me," he shouted. It was a panic call, and Joe knew it. He settled back to wait.

It seemed to him that he lay there for several hours, although in reality it was only about forty-five minutes. Joe's mind whirred with a mixture of thoughts; what he had been doing before the explosion, what was on the cards for the evening, who might miss him… Would anyone miss him?

He wondered how the rescuers were getting on, and fought back the urge to again scream for help. He listened carefully but could hear nothing. He tried to work out what the time might be. If it was night-time, he might see floodlighting seeping through cracks in the mound of rubble above him. How much rubble? He tried not to think of that.

Above him, teams of emergency workers had been drawn to the scene both officially and unofficially. While experts sought out and examined plans of the building, others had already started to climb on top of the piled-high ruins to try to hand-claw their way through it. There was noise and dust and debris everywhere. Wreckage. Fright. Confusion.

By eight o'clock, the rescue operation had settled down to something almost akin to normal. Huge digging machines had arrived, and their workers were hacking away at the horrific heap of rubble. Individuals were still on their hands and knees tearing at the piles of masonry, stone and metal.

Every now and then, the movement of a pile of fragments made them all jerk back, frightened that the whole lot might tip down on them. It was almost, as one scavenging television reporter described it, like working on a moving man-made avalanche of bricks and mortar. He smiled at the description. A bonus, perhaps. It was good for the career.

Down deep in the pile of litter, Joe could feel the moving mass around him. He felt the occasional shift in the walls holding him captive, and once he thought it might even lead to his leg being freed. He wondered what he would do if it did. Would he be able to dig his way out? Could he reach the helpers he knew must be working frantically above him?

He tried to relax. He lay there, waiting, waiting and it seemed several more hours before he worked out that it must be morning. Daylight would be back. Rescue work would double up now. It would not be long.

Above him, it was indeed early morning. Dawn. The first light of a new day had crept over the horizon to show that the huge pile that was once a living, breathing, working building was still pretty much as it had been the night before. Workers who had torn at it throughout the night stood and wiped torn, bleeding hands over dirty, sweatwrapped faces. Then they bent down and carried on digging.

Joe could see the glimmer of light seeping through, and he began to hope that the rescuers might be closer than he had thought. He began trying to draw deep breaths, panting a little with excitement and anticipation. But it was hard to breathe. The air coming through to him was slowly running out. He felt, rather than saw, that it was getting darker. Could it be night already? So soon after the dawn?

What had happened was that the rescuers above him had been moving the rubble around. They threw it to one side, and the pieces slowly began to block the passages through which the air and light had been seeping down to Joe in the bowels of the heap.

Joe's eyes began to fill with tears. *I must not cry*, he said to himself over and over as the tears started to roll down his cheeks. He lay still, forcing himself to reason out the situation. Half an hour later he still had the tears... and no answers. It seemed like days later, although it was in reality just another forty minutes on, before Joe managed to calm himself down. He consciously forced himself to control his breathing; slow, steady, slow, steady, slow. It would help conserve the air. And surely, soon, someone would reach him.

Although he could not help wondering what was happening, Joe gradually began to get control of his feelings, and to help him forget the situation and pass time until he was rescued he started forcing his mind to think over things from his past.

He remembered his school days, and wondered if he should, perhaps, have worked harder at the subjects he did not like.

He thought of the others in the class of his old co-ed school. There was Pete Waters, Mike Abbott and that pretty brunette, what's-her-name? What had happened to them? Where were they now? Perhaps Betty, yes that was her name, perhaps she was a paramedic helping dig him out.

He thought of the jobs he had taken. Shopkeeper. Insurance rep. Salesman.

He thought of many others he had known over the years. People he had worked with, befriended, drunk with, dealt with in the line of business.

Then he thought of his wife Shula, such a pretty girl, so beautiful in her pristine white wedding dress with her cheeks shiny and scrubbed and a sort of new look about her.

He thought of their life together, how they had met at a friend's house. Then he thought of their two sons, Ben and Adie, both now in their early teens. He hoped that if anything went wrong they would look after Shula.

Nothing will go wrong, he told himself sharply. *But what if...?*

Joe forced himself to think of Shula and the boys again. Had he treated them right? Had he done everything he could to make their lives easy, happy? He thought he had; he hoped he had.

"If I didn't, forgive me," he shouted in the cold, dark coffin of space under the pile of rubble that was once a majestic, modem, thirty-two-floor tower block.

Joe's thoughts moved headlong forward and he smiled to himself. He wondered what had happened to the sales report he had been working on. Old Mr Clive would want that in the morning. Oh yes, it was morning. Sorry, guv, got held up.

Where are you, rescuers? Joe tried to imagine his rescuers. They would soon be there. He wondered who they were. Policemen, firemen, paramedics. And women. There would be demolition experts too. Demolition experts? Joe laughed inwardly, quietly gruesome and sardonic.

They would all be handsome, good looking. Eager, helpful. But they'd be tired. He'd get them all a cup of tea and a biscuit. Or a creamy cake. Every one of them.

Perhaps Betty would be one of them. Would she want a cake? Or would she now be fat and jolly and on a diet? And would Mr Clive be there, looking for his overdue sales report?

Joe tried to focus his thoughts on the rescue, but suddenly all he could think about was the dark and the cold and the time passing oh so slowly.

He slept, and when he woke up it was to a feeling of complete, stark terror. As Joe opened his eyes he could not at first remember where he was, then when memory kicked back in, he screamed. He had no way of knowing what time it was, but his brain now had the unproven impression that it was at least six hours since the explosion. It was, in fact, a full twenty-four hours.

Joe lay there for a moment trying to sort out his thoughts. He tried to move his foot, but it was still jammed, and now he had a feeling of cramp in the other leg. He was in a fit of despair, unable to move, unable to do anything but guess at the time.

A low whine crept from his throat, and tears again began to trickle from his eyes, settling wet on his cheeks. This time though, the tears were tears of frustration. And panic.

Joe lay there and tried to figure how long it would take the rescuers to dig through thirty-two storeys of rubble to get to him. His mind tried to approach the problem logically. Like the sales report he had been working on when the explosion happened. One hour? Five hours? Twenty hours?

In his mind, too, he was adding together the time he supposed he had been buried, and time started to get longer and longer. Still nothing happened to free him. Not a sound. Not a light. Not a hope. He screamed again.

Above him, statements were being made about the complete loss of life. Over twenty-five hours, and just eleven bodies had been found. They now reckoned two thousand had been inside the two shattered buildings. Politicians and the senior executives and officers behind the rescue squads all tried to put a good light on their activities. No more could have been done. We'll keep trying until there is no hope. There is no hope left.

Although Joe could not hear the pontificating speeches, he, too, was starting to feel there could be no hope. Time had ceased to exist in his small, cold, dark chasm. And now he thought he felt damp rising from under his shoulders. It reminded him that he had drunk nothing, eaten nothing, since the explosion.

His mind began to dwell on it. No hope. No life. Forsaken despair.

In actual time, almost exactly twenty-six hours had gone by when Joe first heard sounds from somewhere above him. Hope which had long since disappeared returned and began to grow. He tried to cry out for help, but he found that he could not. His throat was dry and restricted and he did not have the energy.

He blinked rapidly as he tried not to cry, and he struggled to try to help with a body he could not control.

Then he saw a small chink of light above his head, and minutes later heard voices. They seemed to be getting close, and he dared, for a moment, to think that he might be freed. A small trickle of rubble fell around his neck, and he hoped the so-close rescuers would be careful. They seemed to be getting closer by the moment, and now he could hear them talking. Vague voices without words. But voices—voices talking.

After an hour or more there was quite a large splinter of daylight above him. He heard the rescuers calling for more help as they realised there was something showing itself on their infra-red device.

"There seems to be something down here," called one.

It must be me, thought Joe. So close. Hope began to build.

Then a voice above him shouted back over its shoulder. "There is a body down here. Must be dead though, after all this time under this pile. Is it worth digging on?"

Of course it is, thought Joe. *What are they talking about? I'm here. Can't they tell I'm alive?*

He felt he should shout out to tell them, but his mind told him they must know so he did not bother. *I'm here. I'm here. Just dig on.* The voices disappeared, and hope seemed to shut off as suddenly as if it had been cut with a knife. *They can't just leave me. I'm alive.*

Then the voices came back, muffled now, and he heard sounds of digging again. Soon the small shaft of light above his head began to get bigger.

"Anyone down there?" called a voice.

Yes, I'm here, thought Joe, but he couldn't find a voice to say it out loud.

"Anyone there?"

Joe tried to take a deep breath, but it hurt his chest. "Yes," he managed to croak faintly, as if whispering into the ears of his young sons.

Then the hole grew bigger and he saw the sun high above it. A face appeared in the hole. "Anyone there?"

Joe smiled at last. "Yes, I'm here," he muttered hoarsely. The effort hurt his throat and deep inside him.

The face disappeared, and then he heard another voice. A deeper, older sounding voice.

Joe murmured again.

"I think you're right. I'm sure I heard something. I think we've got a live one."

Joe's eyes filled, and he had to swallow several times. Suddenly, unexpectedly, although they had been coming for some time they were there. Five rescuers with hard hats and soft faces.

"My leg," said Joe.

"OK, we'll get it," said a voice.

Joe relaxed.

Soon the liberators had dug him free. He was carried out into the bright sunshine, two men holding him as they scrambled down the side of the devastation. Soon he was put down on a stretcher.

"God, you're lucky," said a young girl. Was it Betty? Shula? He couldn't see, the sun was in his eyes. "Only twelve of you have got out. Just twelve survivors." She knew the estimate of two thousand people buried in the rubble of the ruined office towers.

Joe tried to sit up.

Soft hands pushed him back.

"How many rescuers are there?" he asked. "How many cream cakes do I have to buy?"

WATER TAXI

Bill Martin eased the twin throttles forward, and the two powerful outboard engines surged his ten-seat water taxi away from its mooring at the side of the lake. Five passengers were behind him: one with her feet up and spread out across the bench at the rear of the small cabin, the others grouped on one side of the twin row of plastic seats running forward and aft.

The sun was now brilliant on the waters of Lake Macquarie after an overcast early morning, its light bouncing off the shimmering surface like the flashing lights in an amusement arcade. Everyone was happy.

Bill set the throttles back to give the boat a half-speed course down the edge of the lake, leaving a trail of semi-circular ripples across the placid water as he steered surely away from the narrow wooden pier of the township of Toronto, and aimed south towards Coal Point, Rathmines and Wangi Wangi. It was part of his almost daily trip taking tourists around for an outing they rarely appreciated.

Bill ran a water taxi for visitors to the lake, and as he settled into the rhythm of the trip he pointed out the various sights. "Did you know, this is the largest saltwater lake in the whole southern hemisphere?" he said. *Everything in Australia is the biggest this or that,* he thought as he said it.

"It's named after some guy called Macquarie, naturally. He was once the governor of New South Wales back in the 1800s sometime. Some folk say he even gave Australia its name."

As he repeated the oft-told piece of history, the passengers—as always—seemed disinterested.

A few minutes out of Toronto though, Bill's mind suddenly switched from the passengers as he passed a familiar place on the shore. He turned sideways and lifted his hand in greeting, leaning forward and waving quite vigorously into the distance. Suddenly he remembered where he was and returned to the commentary.

"This really used to be mining territory. Coal mining originally," he intoned. "All those houses were built by the mine owners for their families or superintendents. Now, well, I guess most of 'em are holiday homes. Worth a fortune, upwards of a million dollars each."

The voice had a soft American twang, still discernible after Bill's more than eight years in New South Wales.

He turned the boat round Coal Point, with Rathmines to his right, and as he did he looked to the starboard side and once again waved vigorously to a distant shore building. Slowly the water taxi moved along the lake coastline. The varied, abundant mass of tall trees rose in huge banks behind the houses and retirement homes, their branches reaching over the homes for the cooler waters of the lake—those absurdly near the top of the hills crowded one on top of the other seeking their place. Where there were no homes, those same trees themselves ventured right down to the water's edge.

The boat moved on. Above it, the vivid sun blazed from a virgin sky, and mobs of bright flowers burgeoned because of it in a riot of yellows and reds and, in particular, an intense, almost touchable, turquoise.

Bill never got used to the daily beauty. In particular, he still got a big kick from the early morning sunrises over the lake, and from the reflecting shadows of dusk below stripes of yellow dying sun and darkening blue skies.

He loved the look of the lake, and of the wildlife living in and from it. Every day he revelled in the visit of the mother duck leading her brood of four identical babies out of the water and to his back porch for a feed of bread, then on across a lawn to the stiltraised house next door under which they had been born.

Bill smiled fondly as he recalled the anxiety clearly discernible on the mother duck's face as she led three of the babies in search of the missing fourth one day. She had squawked frantically until she found him at the water's edge, sheltering under a bush. If he'd been a God-fearing man he'd have called it a miracle.

But Bill was not God-fearing. His life had been fun, but there had been moments that put him off that idea, and not even the beauty of the lake could alter his views.

He was a fairly tall man, and in some ways could be called good looking. He had a shock of pure white hair above grey eyebrows which bushed over pale blue eyes, and he wore tattered shorts and a T-shirt with "Lake Macquarie Water Taxi" above a logo on his right chest. There was an ornate watch with a fading silver strap on his left wrist, and an almost matching feminine-looking bracelet on the right.

Bill had been born in America some fifty-five years ago on the borders of Massachusetts and New York State, and he had worked the boats for the last eighteen of them. But before that, he had left high school early and learnt to fly with the US Air Force before taking a civilian job as a crop sprayer in the deep south.

His partner back then had been an Irishman called Eamonn who had lost his left arm in an air battle in World War Two, and they shared an old rotary-engined Spearman biplane.

"Eamonn could do everything with just that one right arm," Bill always told people, "But he always said that in crop spraying, if the power cables didn't get you the chemicals would."

Eamonn, though, had been shot dead by an irate husband in a bar one night.

After the funeral, Bill left the south and returned to New York for a couple of years, and it was there that he met, wooed and won his wife Sarah. She was an Australian, but at the time in no hurry to go home. Instead, after they had married the two of them had spent all their joint savings to move to the Caribbean.

Bill had started off there working as a crewman on a huge launch used for corporate entertaining of executives, with hostesses who looked good in swimsuits but didn't know one end of a share price from another. Slowly but surely he raised the money to buy his own small boat.

For a few years he had worked all hours ferrying people or cargo round the islands, then suddenly work boomed and Bill took on more boats and staff and turned his business into a highly successful operation.

Then just over eight years ago, with their two sons in their very late teens, Sarah had got homesick and Bill just upped sticks and moved her to Toronto on Lake Macquarie. They bought a boat and Sarah acted as his crew for three years, but now Bill worked alone on the lake every day, taking faceless and often mindless passengers on trips to places he loved every time he saw their natural beauty fighting against mankind's attempts to change them.

Today was like most other days. A group of passengers looking at, but not really seeing, the beauty of it all. Bill tilted his head to one side. *Their problem*, he thought.

By now, the taxi was almost level with Rathmines, and Bill turned the wheel to steer to port and across the water towards Swansea. Soon after, he turned it slowly again to ease the boat to the north, gliding smoothly over the water.

"They say there's an eagle's eyrie over there, on North Point." He nodded towards a clump of trees on a small island on his left and smiled again. "There are not too many of them around here. Hope they let him survive."

As he steered along the lake's edge, two herons, a pair of pelicans, some ibis and a sole black swan dotted the water a little way into the shore. A skein of geese flew overhead, and Bill could hear the "gissa-chip, gissa-chip" caw of ducks from the lake shore. Fish of all kinds frequently poked their noses up out of the water to feed on the myriad insects above them.

As the boat chugged forward, edging past Marks Point, Bill once again paused in his commentary on the flawless scenery to wave towards the shore.

A trimaran appeared and crossed in front of them, fairly close, and a throttled-back motorboat passed a few hundred metres away to the starboard.

"Too many boats," said Bill. "Lucky none of those Pacific liners can get through. We're quite safe." He waved heartily yet again towards a lone house on the north shore of Marks Point, steering with one hand to show how safe it was.

His mind was still virtually in neutral as he throttled back, with the tall masts of the Squadron sixteen-footers anchored in the Belmont Yacht Club coming into view. Bill picked his way between them, telling his passengers about the Squadron races. He had been a racer himself in the Caribbean, and he respected the crews of the tall boats and spoke of them with pride.

As he neared the yacht club quayside he cut the engine and, in accordance with the regulations, coasted in without a hint of wash. A pair of pert, blue-black starlings flew in as a welcoming committee, landing one on each of the fore rails at the bow. They quickly realised there was no food to be had, so after a bare moment they flew off again one at a time, returning to settle on the bow once more as Bill tied up and helped the passengers up the two steps of the ladder and onto the wooden slats of the quay.

"I'll see you back here when… oh, say two hours," he said.

A time was fixed, and Bill cast off again and took the two starlings with him as he left his passengers and eased his way alone back into the lake.

The five passengers made their way to the Belmont Sailing Club's outdoor cafe and sat ordering beers and a shandy.

"Were you the party Bill brought over?" asked the waitress when she brought the drinks. She was a middle-aged woman with a lined, care-worn face that made her look far older than she really was, and she was simply being chatty. But as she put the drinks on the plastic table the five nodded without looking up at her, studying the food menu instead.

When the waitress came back, they ordered—again without looking at her—and when she went back inside the cafe they gossiped about the taxi ride. "Smooth, peaceful" was the general opinion. Nothing about the scenery.

Eventually their seafood platter arrived, a huge two-deck contraption holding a mass of lobster, Belmont bugs, oysters, calamari and fried fish. Piles of fruit—melons, mango and strawberries—were mixed in with them.

As the waitress carefully put the food on the table, one of the five asked her about Bill. "Who is it he waves at as he goes round?" asked one.

The waitress wiped her hands down the front of her apron. "Well, Bill's wife died of a virus three years back. You probably noticed he still wears her bracelet," she told them. "He's been working the boat on his own ever since her death. He can't bear to go home to America. They both loved the beauty of the lake and everything around it so much."

She paused for a moment.

"But it's a lonely job on that boat, day in and day out. I think you'll find he waves to the Widow Johnson just outside Toronto, with the Widow Bremner at Rathmines and the Widow Marsh at Marks Point. He calls on them in turn every lunchtime he's working. A man has his needs, you know."

The five passengers fell silent.

"Oh yeah," added the waitress, "He comes here sometimes too. Ever since my husband died last year."

HOORAY FOR HOLLYWOOD

*T*he streets of Hollywood aren't really paved with gold. In fact, thought MaryAnn Brotherton, *they are really made of darned hard stone—hard on the feet and wearing to the nerves.*

But MaryAnn was there, with her memory recalling the songs and sayings and scenes of the literally hundreds of cinema films she had grown up with. There was *42nd Street*, and *On Golden Pond*, Lauren Bacall's sexily husky "You know how to whistle don't you" to a lisping, smoking, enigmatic Humphrey Bogart, her husband in real life as well.

Now MaryAnn really was there, in Hollywood, on the streets where Hepburn, Bergman, Bette Davis and Ginger, Spencer Tracey, Astaire, Niven and Errol Flynn had lived and worked.

She was in the land of Chaplin, Laurel, Hardy, Harpo and his manic brother Groucho. A world created by Hitchcock, Capra, Billy Wilder, and a whole myriad of other giants who had made real life on a screen for a world of drab nothing. She was there, out of the darkness of the cinema and into the sunlit world of Hollywood.

MaryAnn was on holiday with her parents. She was just seventeen, light-coloured hair a touch away from being film-star blonde, and with a face and figure that film publicists always used to call pert and pretty.

All her life she had lived in the Hollywood dream. Her parents, Bill and Martha, had fallen in love in the cinema long before she was born, had snatched their first kisses in the back row alongside Rita Hayworth and Cary Grant, and had got conventionally engaged while waiting for the bus home after seeing a re-release of the cascading waterfall of scantily clad girls in Busby Berkeley's *Footlight Parade*.

MaryAnn could not escape the silver screen world they had created and lived in. Nor did she want to. Cinema was, for her, a release from the traumas first of all of school, then blossoming adolescence and now into her teens. It was a world where, like her parents, she could flee the nastiness that faced her, and where she could relax in the knowledge that the good guy in the white hat would win, and that fairness was all.

And now, the three of them were there in the middle of it all. In Hollywood and walking down Sunset Boulevard itself. It was a triple dream come true.

Sure, the streets were not paved with gold. And the footprinted paving stones outside what was traditionally Grauman's Chinese Theatre (it's now Mann's) were disappointing. Even Betty Grable's leg print in the stone was just a print of a leg.

But this was Hollywood. And the so well-known gaudy reds and whites of the ugly Chinese theatre was the place where many of the pre-war grand premieres had been held—all crowds and cheers, stars and flashguns and glitter and glamour.

The Brothertons had seen the grave of Rudolph Valentino, still adorned with flowers on the anniversary of his death despite the long decades—although not, these days, still laid by the mysterious lady in black as yesteryear—and had visited the Hollywood Roosevelt Hotel where Michelle Pfeiffer had performed so exotically in *The Fabulous Baker Boys*.

They had gazed in awe at the fifty-foot-high Hollywood sign up in the hills above the town, put up in 1923 as a sales gimmick to sell houses in the area, and had strolled down Gower Street and La Brea Avenue to see the thousands of bronze stars set in the pavement to mark many of those other somewhat lesser stars who had glittered on their screen. They had wandered along Hollywood Boulevard totally absorbed, all three, in their own magic of the movies. They even thought in cinematic cliches as they walked, holding hands like silver screen college boys and girls.

They had seen the town's old cinemas—movie houses as they used to be—the Palace and the Orpheum. And they had seen where Cecil B DeMille had shot Tinseltown's very first movie, although admittedly now not on its original site at Vine.

Best of all they had seen the studios, and the sites of many of those now long since themselves faded out in a not-too-happy ending. Universal, founded by legendary Carl Laemmle, 20th Century Fox, Metro-Goldwyn-Mayer.

Yes, they had "done" Hollywood. Well almost, because the final treat was to be an actual tour inside a studio.

They had decided to forgo Universal, with its tourist-based tram tour of a 415-acre backlot showing off such modern delights as the *Jaws* monster, its *Jurassic Park* ride, the exterior of Norman Bates' *Psycho* abode, and the mock-realty of its *Earthquake* experience.

Instead, they chose the smaller Warner Brothers studios. Where Cagney himself had been "on top of the world, Ma". And so it was that the day after her somewhat disappointing look at the Chinese theatre's diminutive hand-and-foot-printed tiles, MaryAnn found herself in a long white cab being driven out to Burbank.

The driver, fat, relaxed and black, his peaked cap tipped to the back of his head, was chatting. "Yup, got me a script all ready to go," he answered Bill's sardonic question. "Thought Julia Roberts would be perfect for the lead but haven't asked her yet."

Eventually, he dropped the family off at the studio gate. They entered and were ushered into a waiting room with about six other excited fans, and were soon on their way round.

The sound stages loomed tall, not like factory blocks surprisingly—although they were, and are, just a series of fantasy factories—but somehow with a magic that silently whispered, "If you only knew what was inside."

They dropped in to make up, hairdressing, costumes, electrical and props. And finally they were taken onto Sound Stage 2. A small film was being shot, a TV commercial or some such, but with all the paraphernalia of a real film.

It all looked a tremendous muddle, and as the guide stayed silent Bill tried to explain to Martha and MaryAnn what was happening. He had read the books.

He explained about lighting, camera positions and angles, the sound booms. He told them how films are pieced together, with all the seemingly unconnected pieces filmed haphazardly then cut and slotted into the shape the director had in mind.

A voice called out. "Silence on set, we're going for a take," it said.

A bell rang, the overhead lights went out, and huge floods and dinkies and pups powered on to dazzle the set: a kitchen scene.

"Bring on the cattle," chuckled the assistant in imitation of Hollywood's great Alfred Hitchcock.

An indiscriminate actor and actress walked forward.

"Places please," said the humorous aide. "Roll'em."

The director leant forward, frowning in anticipation as the cameraman screamed, "Speed."

"Action!"

The actor took a step forward. "Where the hell are the… aah, heck. Where the hell are the… the onions…?"

"Cu-ut. Re-take."

After five attempts, he managed the line and the scene was over. MaryAnn and her parents, along with the other visitors, were ushered away from the set. The tour was over, and it was back to the hotel.

They were due to leave town at midday the next day, but that night they went to a small French bistro they had found for a farewell meal to discuss the thrills they had seen during their time in the town.

And it was there that the magic that normally lies dormant in Hollywood leapt up like those fanciful film scripts in so many people's imaginations.

They had just finished their main course when a stranger stopped by their table.

"Hi there, you visitors to town?" he asked. It was oh-so-obvious, but they told him they were.

"Well my name's Lance, and I represent the Hudson Brothers. Big producers, you know. This isn't a con, it's real, but I have been watching you." He indicated MaryAnn. "And I think you have a certain something. Perhaps you'd like to give the studio a call in the morning. It could be something you'd be interested in."

He produced a card from an inside pocket with a flourish and was gone. The Brothertons laughed and chatted about it as their desserts arrived and they waded in.

Over coffee the next morning, Bill produced the card from his own jacket pocket. "Why don't we just give 'em a ring? Might be a giggle, and it could give us something to do on our last morning in Hollywood," he said, feeling as he did so like so many of the producers he had seen in all those show-bizzy magical films.

MaryAnn and Martha didn't want to know at first, but he quickly persuaded them, and as it turned out within an hour a car had called to pick them up and they were at the Hudsons' studio block and in what was the largest room any of them had ever seen.

It was the office of studio boss Myron Schwartz, one of the legendary backroom nobodies that make Hollywood the money machine it had become.

Myron himself was of indiscriminate height, bulky yet lean-looking, tanned yet with an indoor pallor. His hair—was it receding or full?—was off his face, which itself was bulbous. He had fat lips, thick bushy eyebrows, and a nose that seemed to be slightly off-centre. In his hand was an unlit cigar, even though it was just half past ten in the morning.

He used the cigar to indicate that the Brothertons should sit and they did so, Bill lounging back easily but Martha and MaryAnn tilted forward on the edges of their plush armchairs.

"Hadda message from Lance—one o' the best," said Myron, his voice deep with a tinge of Brooklyn behind the mock refinement expected of a studio head. "See what he means. You, kid, well, ya look good. English kinda. It's fashionable. Ever thought of being in the movies?"

MaryAnn nodded, hardly comprehending what was being said.

"I'd like you to take a test. A screen test," went on Myron. "Gotta part in a movie. A big role. Starring. Needs a new face. And well, it looks just you."

By now Bill, especially, was taking notice. This had only happened in Hollywood films and his dreams, and now here it was in real life. "I think MaryAnn would love that," he said.

Martha gave a quick sidelong glance towards her daughter but didn't add anything.

"Have to change your name if you get the part," grinned Myron, his face lighting up automatically as it did in his several rather secretive big business producer meetings with starlets in hotel rooms. "Somethin' like… aaaah, Laverne Savage maybe."

MaryAnn gulped again. It was something that she knew would not only please her parents but was something she had secretly dreamt of throughout the years. She nodded agreement.

"But we're going home in an hour," was all she could say.

Myron smiled. "Don'chew worry your pretty head about that," he said. Then turning to Bill he started to make arrangements for the family to move into the Hollywood Roosevelt. At the studio's expense, of course.

The next few days were, to put it mildly, hectic. The Brothertons were driven to the studio daily, and while MaryAnn was touted round make up, lighting and the other departments for a variety of tests, Bill and Martha mingled with directors, producers, gofers and occasionally Myron himself.

On the day of the test they watched proudly as MaryAnn acted out a scene with a handsome, unknown studio "star". Make up girls touched things to her face, lighting men took metered readings close to her nose, assistants hurried to fill her every whim.

The director was caring and careful, and expressed his delight at her novice work. He ended up filming her full face and taking shots of her in profile and from any other angle he could think of.

The next morning, Myron joined them all in the viewing room to see the results. All agreed they were excellent, and even

MaryAnn liked what she saw. She tried to resist as she began to harbour small thoughts of filmic fame and fortune.

The next week flew by in a whirl of talks, with promises, counter-promises and bids that were mind boggling for the pretty, young teenage girl. And finally it was agreed. She would sign a contract to act as the female lead in Myron Schwartz's new epic *Mistress of the World* as soon as newspaper photographers and film reporters were able to visit the studio the next morning.

That night Bill and Martha celebrated, but MaryAnn—her mind in a whirl of confusion—stayed in her hotel room with the TV on but not seeing a thing as she thought of premieres and leading men and fame. She was about to become a film star.

The next day they were all together as the studio car took them back to Hudson Brothers' studios. MaryAnn was still in something of a daze, albeit in rather more control of herself by now, while Bill laughed and cracked jokes and Martha was a little silent.

They arrived at the studio early and wandered into the canteen for a last-minute drink, although MaryAnn decided to stick to a small orange juice while her parents drank two cups of coffee each.

There were, perhaps, just ten minutes before the time of the press call when they heard the talk from the next table. Another near-blonde with a pert and pretty figure and face was talking to a nondescript man that those in the know knew as a curmudgeonly agent.

"It can't be true. Myron just wouldn't cast anyone called Belinda de Lainchbury as the star of *Mistress of the World*. And surely he certainly wouldn't sign up anyone with a name like that in the key role then get her to change it to Laverne Savage," said the blonde. She laughed out loud, a strange donkey bray of a laugh.

Bill, Martha and MaryAnn listened intently, startled to say the least. They quickly paid up and went looking for Myron Schwarz.

His secretary would not let them into his office, but she did confirm that the film role that MaryAnn had tested for had been given to someone else. Laverne Savage, she insisted despite the protests.

So it was true, MaryAnn was out. She faced the fact with stunned horror, her new-found dreams in tatters and her immediate world fallen about her. With her parents just as horrified, MaryAnn slowly drooped her way out of the office, away from the studio and back to the Hollywood Roosevelt, only to discover that their room there had been cancelled and their suitcases already in the lobby.

They left the building, and while Martha tended the cases on the pavement Bill tried to get a taxi without the help of the street porter. The young girl wandered away alone.

The streets of Hollywood aren't really paved with gold, thought MaryAnn. *In fact, they're really made of darned hard stone—hard on the feet and wearing on the nerves...*

THE SERGEANT MAJOR'S BUCKET

The sergeant major's tea was always brewed in a bucket. Not any old bucket, but a large, brutally polished, gleaming brass bucket that seemed to weigh a ton and held a gallon of fluid.

It was my job to look after that tea bucket. To shine and nurture it. To keep it in metaled splendour and burnished glory. I could, I suppose, have written articles headed "I Was the Sergeant Major's Teaboy", but I was far too proud of the job for that and jealously guarded the bucket from any would-be usurper of my position of privilege.

To most people, the sergeant major was a bully; a hard hearted, brutal, fanatical soldier whose only instincts were for the military way, and whose only feelings were echoed in the shouts, screams and bangs of the parade ground. But to me, that brass-bound tea bucket linked us in a tight bond of unspoken friendship.

It was only right, I felt, when the sergeant major still entrusted me with the task of transporting his bucket when we were posted overseas and made our excitable, heroic way across the Channel from Dover to Calais, and then in convoy to the front line and the trenches.

Even when the snows fell in that winter of 1915, I kept the sergeant major's tea bucket shining. I stuck to a strict routine of cleaning and brewing, and the tea continued to be a source of pride to me, the sergeant major, and (I must add) even to the company commander himself.

For some reason, that winter Captain Throstleton took a great pride in the activities of all the men under his command, and the shining brass tea bucket, with its beauty and strength from lower rim to the tip of its arching handles, held pride of place in his rounds of inspection.

Once, Captain Throstleton even attended a brewing of the tea, a strange and rather mystical process that was guaranteed to give the tea a colouring and consistency far removed from the general dark, evil mess that was the usual in our front line trenches. He watched, fascinated I felt, as I collected the water in a selection of clean and borrowed dixie cans, and set them to boil over the large black stove that sizzled and flared in our dugout company office. He took careful note as I measured out the tea, taking it from a large sack in experienced handfuls and tipping it into the lovely, gleaming brass bucket.

Captain Throstleton muttered some appreciation as I poured the water, the boiling steaming water, over the tea, and added another fistful of sugar. He growled throatily with anticipation as I carefully, and somewhat artistically I liked to think, topped up the bucket with a large tin of sickly sweet condensed milk to give the sergeant major's tea a fine tawny colouring and a syrupy nature that was the pride of the company.

It was a moment of lasting pride to receive the accolade of satisfaction from the company commander of that winter, but it was like a song from heaven to hear my sergeant major smacking his lips as he twice daily drank the tea.

All through that winter and well into the spring that followed, nothing was allowed to interfere with the ceremony of the sergeant major's tea. The bucket and I carried on in a routine of brew and polish, polish and brew.

When the sun came over the slits that were the trenches and over the ravaged wastes of the so-called No Man's Land in the summer of 1916, I moved my tea bucket and my stove and my dixies of water out into the open, allowing the cleansing smell of the polish and the heart-warming aroma of the brewing tea to drift upwards and across and over the noses of the men who shared the trenches with the sergeant major and me.

It was manna from heaven, and—unfortunately—a signal to the enemy, for he, too, saw the glinting sun on the polished metal and began a cluster of firing that peppered our positions and made everyone duck their heads for safety.

When the firing stopped (a bird began singing instantly, I remember) I looked up. Four men lay dead, and the company commander who had joined us the winter before was injured and dying. He was groaning, and obviously beyond all hope.

By his side, in front of me, was the sergeant major, a glazed expression on his face and a blank look in his eyes. I looked at him closely without speaking for well over a minute, and he didn't move a muscle.

"You 'right, S'arnt Major?" I eventually asked, but still he didn't move.

I thought he had been hit by a stray bullet and went forward to him. He still remained motionless, but as I reached out to feel his heart or his pulse I saw a small tear building up, to fall slowly from his eye in an uncontrolled trickle down his chin.

I looked at the sergeant major and wondered. Then, slowly and with a feeling of dread building up inside my mind, I followed the direction of his glance. I turned my head slowly, and beyond the dead bodies and the injured, there it was. The bucket. Our beautiful, lovely, marvellous, gorgeous bucket.

It wasn't a very big bullet hole, but it was near the base and the tea had just flowed out of it and into the caked mud floor of the trench.

And the war was never the same from that day onwards.

JOURNEY INTO SPACE

The decipod landing gear of the spacecraft eased slowly from their in-flight recesses as the crew strapped themselves into their spacious inter-galactic seats.

Retro-rockets fired, and the craft sank slowly to the surface of the planet so far removed from their own. Touch down. A sudden silence.

"We're here. Now we rest before the team goes down to explore. Send the message back to base," said the craft's skipper, seemingly calm but with a raging excitement in his heart and brain.

The message was sent, crackling out its digital message over the billions of miles of nothing between whole galaxies of planets and stars. When it was done, a light flashed and the operator called the skipper. An incoming message from the craft's sister ship.

"Turn it on to cabin speakers," instructed the captain.

The message told him and his crew that their twin spacecraft had also landed on this strange planet—a mere five thousand miles away from them along its surface.

The captain replied, repeating his message to the base back home and telling his cospacemen that he and his crew were going to rest before beginning the next exploratory phase of the revolutionary trip. The other craft replied that it would do the same.

The next morning the two captains spoke to each other again at length before despatching their three-man search teams from the spacecraft to the surface of this strange and eerielooking lump of matter hurtling through galactic space.

Many hours later, the six explorers returned to their individual craft and reported back. "No initial sign of life," was their agreed joint view sent back to the space base at home.

Exploration continued for another six days. The captain of the leading first ship was daily told of high, lonely peaks; snow-covered ranges that looked as if they had risen from the ground and then been crushed inwards by giant hands. Huge ruts and cavities ran through them, and only a few—a very few—rivers ventured to wind in between. They were ghostly, alone and totally barren.

The further ship gave only reports of sandy tracts, desolate wastes as far as the eye could see. No water, a lot of heat and an unpleasant deadly feel over its serried layers.

After one more night's rest, the twin sky craft fired up their rockets and took to the heavens once more in their restless search for life in space.

Back home in their base several eons later, a bored clerk extended the three long, spiny fingers of his hand, pushing them out from their usual retracted place in the centre of his chest to scratch the tight skin on top of his huge cranium, resting abreast puny shoulders. He yawned, then pointed to the screen before him—as the words formed in his mind, they printed out on the screen to complete the log.

"No life on planet Earth," his finger and mind wrote on the screen.

Completed explorations by the space travellers, in what millennia later became known as the mountains of Afghanistan and in the Great Sandy Desert of Australia, had proved that to him and his leaders.

ONE NIGHT STAND

Quarter to eleven. And the dimly lit drinking club The Candlelight Lounge was very busy, but by no means overcrowded. Many of the drinkers were regulars—The Lounge had been trendy and chic for about three months and had already built up a steady stream of over-rich clients.

The club was a long oblong, with a well-lit bar triangularly set in one corner at the far end to the entrance glittering with mock silver and cunningly hidden facia lights, while the rest the club was fairly dim and painted a relaxing pale mauve, with tasteful full-length photos of dressed up celebrities scattered on the walls.

There were seats available at some of the tables and on the leather benches in the alcoves that lined two of the walls, deliberately lower lit than the main room giving the impression of greater solitude and secrecy. There was a constant movement of people moving to the bar to buy new drinks.

Dean Forbes sat on a comfortable high stool at the bar casually taking in the scene. He was one of the daily regulars.

Max the barman stood in his narrow space behind the counter close to him, using a silver jigger to measure quantities from four coloured bottles into an engraved shaker then waving it with a planned characteristic way, twisting it in a semi-circular roll as he pumped it up and down and backwards and forwards.

"Not much in today," Dean told him without turning his head.

"Never is on a Wednesday."

"Why Wednesday?" Dean turned his head to look at Max without moving his body.

"Perhaps they wash their hair," said the barman. He continued shaking as he reached behind him for a slim, elegant highly polished star-engraved martini glass. He nodded to a table on the far left of the room.

Dean turned to look.

"She looks quite tasty," muttered Max.

Dean saw the girl he meant. "A regular?"

"A tourist," said the barman.

Dan studied the girl, and continued staring as she looked up and caught his eye. They judged each other's looks and both liked what they saw. Dean made a hand signal asking if she would like a drink, and the girl nodded.

"What's she drinking?" he asked Max, still looking at the girl.

"This is for her."

"What is it?

"Don't ask, it's lethal," joked Max.

"Put it on my tab," said Dean.

"OK, Deano. It's expensive."

"When did you hear me complaining? Put it on my tab and I'll take it across to her."

Max shook the cocktail a little longer before pouring it into the chilled glass with a flourish from quite a height. He pushed it across the counter to Dean, who slowly stood, picked up the drink and walked across the room to the girl.

"I think this is for you," he told her.

"Oh, thanks. How much is—"

"On the house."

"But…"

"Don't ask. It's on the house."

"Well, thanks."

Dean sat down, uninvited, but with his eyes fixed on the girl. She was a light blonde, a real blonde, and she had a very attractive face—firm jaw, high cheekbones, blue eyes and eyebrows just a little darker than her hair. He noted that she had a minimum of make up to enhance her looks—a veneer of lipstick, a vague shadow of black around the eyes. Her skin looked smooth.

"I'm Deano," he told her, noticing her yellow blouse under a smart, vogue-ish, not-too-expensive copy of a haute couture blue trouser suit covering what he judged to be a modest but well-shaped figure. He was impressed.

"I'm Sooz… Susan," she replied.

In turn she was quietly, unobtrusively, studying Dean—a rather rugged face with a square-ish jaw, dark brown (almost black) hair, auburn eyes, smiling lips. He had a short fashionable stubble, and he wore a suit with a matching tie that was loosely lowered below a full tied height.

There was a beat, then Dean smiled and raised his glass—two-thirds full of an exotic sounding Italian lager. "Here's to new friends."

They both sipped their drink, and when they had done Dean put his glass down,

"I suppose the standard question at times like this is… do you come here often?" His grin widened at the supposed cliche.

"No, this is the first time. I'd planned to meet a girl friend after work, but she let me down. I thought I'd come in anyway to see what the place was like."

"So tell me about yourself."

"Not a lot to tell really," said Sooz demurely. "I'm twenty-three and seem to spend most of my time working…"

"Yeah, tough," said Dean, wiping his upper lip with his right thumb. "What do you do?"

"So, I'm the head of a small department organising events in the leisure industry. How about you?"

"Oh, me? A sous chef in quite a posh restaurant. I'm planning to open my own place soon. Any day now."

They both knew the other was lying, but it didn't matter, and for a few moments there was silence.

"Is it hot in here?" Sooz took off the jacket of her suit and hung it over the back of her seat, then undid the top button of her blouse.

Dean pretended he did not notice but suddenly, unusually, he was tongue tied and did not know what to say.

Eventually he asked, "What sort of events do you get involved with... organising?"

Sooz bushed slightly. "Well... er... I don't really organise anything. I'm just the PA to the senior organiser of events at a group of pubs."

Deano laughed. "Yeah, well, I guess I'd better admit it. I'm not really a sous chef. I'm the third chef in a pizza joint. Not really posh."

They both laughed; the original lies made no difference and they both relaxed.

From then on they got on well, talking about nothing really but commenting on the bar they were in and the other customers.

"They must be quite rich," said Sooz, picking up a drinks menu and glancing at it with little interest.

"That's why I only come here once a week," grinned Deano. "Got to try and keep up."

As he spoke, Sooz casually undid another two buttons of her blouse, apparently without thinking. Dean noticed, but didn't say anything.

They chatted aimlessly, and as they did so the bar gradually emptied, and soon there were only three other people sitting there apart from them.

"Looks like they'll soon be throwing us out," said Dean.

Sooz looked round. "Looks like it," she sighed.

"To mine?" he asked and Sooz nodded agreement.

As she stood to put her jacket back on Dean went back to the bar and settled his tab with Max. When he got back to the table he saw that the girl was at least two inches shorter than he was despite the four-inch high heels of her dark blue court shoes.

It was raining when they left The Candlelight Lounge, a heavy downpour, as if standing in a large shower bath.

"The car's on a metre a little way down," said Dean as they exited the front door, pausing under a triangular-shaped coloured linen arch. "Wait here in the dry. I'll go get it and reverse back to you."

"No, it's a one-way street. It'll be difficult. I'll come, you lead."

They ran down the road past five parked cars until they came to a small blue second-hand Ford Fiesta which Dean unlocked using his remote key as he ran. He saw Sooz into the passenger seat before he ran round to the other side and got in behind the wheel.

"I'm soaked," said Sooz as he closed his door. "I'll be glad to get this wet gear off when we get there."

Deano wasn't quite sure how to take that.

It only took about ten minutes to drive to Dean's flat, and by the time they had got there and parked, the rain had stopped—although there were several drops hovering in the air.

Once inside Dean gave Soos a towel to dry her hair before going to organise some music as "background noise". As she rubbed the towel over her hair she looked around.

The flat was on the second floor of a dingy block of flats in a rather well-worn district, and had two main rooms and through an open door she could also see a kitchen—all looking surprisingly neat and tidy for a bachelor home.

She looked round the room. There was an inviting settee, an armchair, two small coffee tables and a half empty bookcase. On the far corner from the settee there was a single book sitting on its glass top, and, still rubbing her hair she went for a closer look. *Nudes.* She opened it and saw tasteful but rather explicit photos of women. She smiled and closed the book.

By the time Deano came back Sooz was sitting on the settee, her legs curled up beside her and the damp towel draped over the arm furthest away from her. Soft music was playing through unseen loudspeakers in three corners of the room—lively dance type sounds—and Dean bent forward to set two half-full glasses on the table in front of her. He pushed one of them across to Sooz.

"Only wine I'm afraid. Red," he said as he sat down beside her, on her right.

"That's fine." She took a sip. "Nice."

They sipped the wine. "So tell me more about yourself," said Deano eventually.

Sooz wriggled herself into a more comfortable position, accidentally moving her body slightly closer to Dean, and thought. "Well," she replied eventually in their new-found honesty, "I was born in London, but my parents moved to America when I was four. My dad was some kind of computer expert and thought there was more opportunity in San Jose, but he was made redundant after a year and we had to move.

"I actually grew up in the poor downtown part of East Bay, on the wrong side of the Guadalupe River. It was a poor Mexican area and times were tough. It killed Dad and when he died Mum brought me back to England and as I grew up I trained as a beautician. I worked hard, and gradually drifted into the leisure industry—and became very good on the organisation side. Soon after that I moved to my present job working for the senior events organiser at a chain of pubs."

Dean heard her out, then heaved himself up from the settee. "Your glass is empty," he told her. "Back in a moment."

He went to the other room, and the music changed to soft romantic, gentle orchestrals. He returned with a bottle in his hand, almost full apart from the two small measures of their first two drinks. He poured more wine into both glasses, and Sooz picked hers up as he finished.

"What about you?" she asked. "Your story?"

"It's not very exciting," Deano replied. "Not like you. I had a boring time at school, and when I first went out to work I served chips in a burger joint. But, oh I don't know, it didn't pay much and I wasn't satisfied, so I felt I'd like to learn how to actually cook the burgers and earn more. I left, got myself a job in a small Italian restaurant and started to learn.

"I found I liked cooking all the food, not just burgers, and… well, now I'm the third chef in a small pizza restaurant. Hoping to learn more and possibly open my own restaurant some time."

His voice had a slight lilt to it—almost Irish, but not quite. Sooz couldn't figure it out, but it was soft and pleasant.

They drank more wine and chatted quietly.

"You've got so much room here. You need a lodger," said Sooz. Her tone was friendly.

"Enough room to dance?" replied Dean. Questioning.

They danced to the background music that was still playing—a smooch.

"I need to lie down after all that exercise. The drink…" laughed Sooz. Suggestive.

"Well, why don't you? I've got silk sheets." Amorous.

"I've never slept on silk sheets." Coquettish.

"Well, it look like it's raining again. You can stay the night if you want." Pleading.

As they talked Dean made sure both glasses were topped up with the rather smooth and comforting liquid and reached across unobtrusively to stroke her neck gently behind her right ear. Sooz snuggled closer.

They kissed, and when they broke apart Dean handed the girl her glass and they both finished the wine. The abandoned bottle stood guarding the empty glasses on the coffee table as they stood and, with arms around each other, drifted into the bedroom with the romantic music still playing on a loop.

They slowly undressed, keeping their eyes on each and dropping their clothes on the floor. As he saw Sooz in her brief underwear Dean took a deep breath, appreciative, and when they were fully naked Dean moved close to Sooz. She pushed a lock of blonde hair from her eyes.

"Do you do this kind of thing often?" she asked, her voice barely above a whisper.

"No. Do you?"

"Of course not."

They both lied—him perhaps a little more than her.

They got into the bed, a low narrow double bed with storage space underneath a sprung mattress. Dean pulled a quilted blue duvet over them, but Sooz immediately threw it off.

She faced him, her arms round his neck and they kissed.

Then they made love, slowly but with passion. Dean didn't even think about precautions—he wasn't bothered—but Sooz was on the pill in any case.

When it was over Sooz pulled the duvet over them again, and sometime later after a rather sleepy cuddle they fell asleep with their arms round each other.

There must have been a noise outside because both woke up suddenly with the half light of the illuminated alarm clock on Dean's bedside table loudly clicking away the minutes and showing at 3:14.

"What was that?" asked Sooz sleepily, but Dean didn't answer, reaching across instead to hold her again and kiss her bare shoulder.

They made love again, sleepily but still with passion, then both fell back to sleep. The clock ticked on.

Sooz woke up the next morning in a strange bed puzzled for a brief moment before she remembered. She smiled. The smell of cooking was in the air, so she got out of bed and, still nude, walked to where she could hear sounds of activity. In the kitchen she found Deano making breakfast: sausages, fried eggs and baked beans.

He turned from the stove and saw her. He walked across and touched her shoulder, gave her a kiss and a brief cuddle. "Got to… er… turn the eggs," he said. He had been going to say the sausages, but thought that might be too suggestive. "Don't want to overcook them."

Sooz sat at the kitchen table, and after a few minutes Dean brought a silvered toast rack with four slices of toast lined up in it, then went back to the stove to bring the food across. A huge plateful for each of them.

Sooz only had half a slice of the toast, dunking it in her breakfast cup of tea—she normally had coffee to give herself a morning lift—and they sat quietly eating like a long married couple.

When he had wolfed down his own food, Deano pulled her plate across and ate that as well as his own. "Got to keep my strength up," he grinned as he wiped the back of his hand across a greasy mouth.

They finished their teas, and when they had both finished Sooz stood up unselfconscious of her nakedness and went back to the bedroom, leaving Deano to clear up in the kitchen. She found her clothes neatly folded on a chair, then went to the bathroom and had a quick shower. When she got back to the bedroom Dean was there, now naked himself.

She started to dress while he looked on, eyes fixed on her body, but once she had put on her undergarments he lost interest and began to dress himself again.

Neither spoke as they put their clothes on—Sooz the same outfit she had worn the previous day, Dean in the same suit but with a clean shirt and different tie, again loosely knotted below the open top button—but when they had both completed the process she turned to him.

"I've got to get to work," she said in a rather flat voice. "Where are we? Is there a tube station near here?"

"Don't be daft," replied Dean rather brusquely. "I'll drive you. Where do you work?"

She told him.

"Oh, that's in the complete opposite way to where I've got to be. I'll take you to the station."

Sooz nodded.

"Whenever you're ready," added Dean.

Sooz looked round to check she hadn't left anything, then led the way to the door. Dean gave her a lift to the station, and once there, before she opened the car door, she leant across and gave him a light peck. Their lips barely touched.

"See you around," she said as she got out of the car.

"Yeah, in The Lounge," he replied as she shut the door, then before she had even crossed the pavement to the station entrance, he put the car into gear and drove off.

They never did meet again, and a year later she got married to a man she met in the same bar and gave up work. Dean stayed on as a third chef in the same pizza restaurant.

REMEMBRANCE SUNDAY

The eleventh hour of the eleventh day of the eleventh month. It was a time for memories. Nauseous but nostalgic memories of bloody war, death and carnage the like of which no man should ever have to know or remember.

But this was Remembrance Sunday many years on. And the old man was on parade once more just as he once paraded as a young man hearing the bugle call to arms to fight for his king and country.

It was a cold, raw day despite the pale November sunshine. Heavy overcoats hung with medals of bygone campaigns, and the heroes of yesteryear tried not to shiver as they had when they went into battle.

The old man remembered his first call to action. It was just a year into the war, and it had been a similar sort of day: chill and frosty. And he recalled clearly in his mind the sergeant's order to fix bayonets and move forward.

He could not forget the fear in his heart then. The thought had gone through his mind as he moved forward behind the cold steel blade that he could be killed at any second. It was a sombre thought.

Then he looked to the left. Ben and Charlie. To his right were Don, Fred, Harry and Billy. They looked resolute, but he knew that under it all they felt the same as him. Then one or other glanced at him, and they smiled at each other. The advance moved slowly on.

That was just the first of the fights. They had charged with bayonets, advanced cautiously through town streets, fired from trenches. No battle was any easier than the first.

But always there were the seven of them together.

In the evenings, when the calm of war overtook the exhausted young men of both sides, they had squatted together in trenches cut into the cold, icy ground as they brewed tea, had eaten cold meals from their billy cans, lain awake in damp bedsheets that had to be rolled and carried on their backs when they next went into action.

Always together. Him and his mates. Them and him. Him and them. They began to feel invincible.

Then it happened.

They were going across a field with the village about three hundred yards ahead when suddenly the artillery shells came flying in. As they screamed overhead the soldiers automatically ducked their heads as they would against rainfall, but this was far more deadly. Then they heard rifles firing, and one of them shouted that if you could hear the shot the bullet was past you. It was a reassuring thought, and they all smiled grimly.

The shells and the guns continued, and over to their right a huge gap appeared in C Company, but the old man hoped that his mates would be all right.

There were still more shells, more gunfire. Then they were on the fringes of the village, and the enemy was there in front of them. Face to face.

As the old man prepared to march off past the Cenotaph, he remembered.

A machine gun opened fire from behind a clump of rubble on the right, and he recalled seeing Billy thrust his bayonet forward; heard the surprised gasp of the stabbed enemy. Fred and Ben were shouting and shooting; Don rushed ahead of them towards the still-firing machine gun, and he remembered standing to shout a warning before he followed, screaming out loud as he charged. The old man watched as Don got to the enemy gun and it went silent after some screams. He won the Military Medal for that.

Soon there was no more fighting. The battle was won.

The marching started, and the old man stepped forward with the thousands of others: men, women, some children, proud widows. Uniforms of every kind and colour. Poppies red in the pale November sunshine. They were all there to pay their respects to the dead of the battles; their no-longer friends.

Marching past the Cenotaph on Remembrance Sunday the old man remembered. He was twenty again, alongside his mates going into war. But where were Don and Billy? Charlie, are you there? Fred, Harry, Ben?

He pulled back his shoulders once more and marched erect. *Where are you now?* he asked inside his mind.

Later, as his eyes swivelled to the right, to the saluting dais far over, he could still not pick out Don, Charlie and the rest. *Where have you all gone?* his brain asked inside. Then he snapped his eyes back to the front.

The old man felt suddenly alone. They had always been together, from the moment they joined the army; now they were, for some reason, apart. He looked round, and in an instant he saw them—ahead of him, perhaps six or seven rows and on the other side of the marching column.

They were all there together now; bowed, wrinkled and ancient. Don, Billy, Fred, Charlie, Harry, Ben. He wanted to call to them, but he couldn't shout their names; the occasion was wrong. He wanted to be with them again; they all looked dim, remote, so far away, and he wanted to reassure them that everything was still all right, that they were still as one.

He brought his already stiffened shoulders back even firmer, stood ever more erect and proud, and the parade moved slowly forward, all the old men rolling with a curious side to side sway to the beat, beat, beat of the big drum. Thousands of them. They were old and battered and frail on the outside, but as the martial songs played all of them became nineteen, or twenty or twenty-one inside.

They proudly marched, rows of medals clanking in rhythm to the bands. The old man drew his own shoulders back still stiffer yet again, and he swung his arms vigorously alongside the rest. He could see the others: Don, Billy, Charlie, Fred, Harry and Ben. They looked beaten like some of the others, and he knew the battles they had fought had worn them, torn them inside. As he marched proud, the old man recalled the chatter between them all those years ago; the fears as they waited to go into action. He remembered one of them asking him what he wanted from life.

"To be able to march past the Cenotaph on Remembrance Sunday," was the reply, but the old man could not remember who had asked it.

In his mind the old man was still a young man. As he marched, his eyes on the others, his friends, his battle mates, ahead of him, he reached down to feel the ache where he had been shot in the machine gun raid. It was a small, clean wound at the front, but he knew the bullet had shattered as it passed through him and the hole where it had left him diagonally opposite at his back was jagged and wide.

Then he knew. He was dead; shot when he stood to shout a warning to Don in the attack on the machine gun. He was the only one of the friends killed in the attack on the eleventh hour of that eleventh day of the eleventh month.

PRESS CALL

The cameras clicked, photographers jostling for position to get yet another of the same shot of the secretary of state. Reporters looked bored but kept a wary eye on each other least one got something exclusive that they couldn't report to their own office.

And in the middle of it all, Josie Moore stood shy and just a little bit afraid.

It was her first major press conference since becoming an inexperienced and rather naive reporter on a small local paper just two months before. So far, she had managed a few small stories, interviews with local house mums whose child had won a school prize or something.

Now she was here. In London. With the secretary of state, her local member of parliament, about to make a major pronouncement on an important issue of the day. Something that concerned increased international trade for her hometown, more jobs and prosperity, something that, if it went wrong, could even bring down the government of the day.

Josie was abashed.

All around her the big-name reporters of the national daily papers, the profound pontificators of television, and the brilliantly expert analysts of the weekly magazines were waiting to ask intelligent questions of import. And she could think of nothing that she could even dare ask the secretary about such an important subject.

He came into those popping flash bulbs, tall, elegant, smooth and full of importance. He smiled urbanely at everyone as assistants eased a way through the press mob for him, now and then inclining his head graciously at one or two of the more influential journos he knew. All of them, bar Josie, were shouting something vital.

Eventually the aides managed to quell the riotous mob and had them seated in long rows of hard-backed seats. The secretary, himself, was in a rather plush easy chair on a slightly raised dais, while his smart-suited but harassed press officer was standing in front of a lectern smiling inanely.

The secretary was formally introduced; he made his prepared statement. This was a great triumph for British business. The technology was here, the sales skills were here. He had personally seen to it—driven through the deal almost single handed against opposition. Blah blah.

He waited unabashed for the inevitable questions with a smile fixed on his face but with a blank behind his eyes. The reporters began to ask their hard-bitten questions, singly at first then in a growing torrent. What did this mean? What was the effect going to be? Josie scribbled everything down as fast as she could, hardly understanding any of it; barely even the questions let alone the answers. But she was trying hard to keep up with the big boys and girls.

Then suddenly the press officer stood again. "The secretary of state has to go. A cabinet meeting I believe it is, isn't it, Mr Secretary?" he announced.

The secretary of state nodded importantly. He muttered something to the press officer that no one else could hear.

"He'll take just one last question from each of you," said the officer. He pointed to one end of the rows of chairs. "You first."

The famous reporters and eminent men and women of words began their intricate probing. Josie listened, a growing dread building up in her when she realised it would all too soon be her turn to speak out loud and ask the secretary of state something with everyone else listening. She gulped, her mind in a turmoil.

Slowly the questioning moved round the room.

"How much will it cost?"

"Is it necessary?"

"What will the effects be on the world markets?"

"How will the man in the street cope with the regulations?"

The grilling went by with answers that did not answer; the secretary of state was far too wily a politician for that.

Then it was Josie's turn. She gulped. Took a deep breath. Blushed.

"Is it true that you are sleeping with the main contractor's wife?" she asked wide eyed.

GRAVE 136X

Guiseppi "The Gimp" Gorgonzo had no sense of remorse or pity when he put out a contract on Stoolpigeon Stu, a gangland informer who had perpetrated the worst, most dastardly, crime he could have committed: telling the gangland leader's deadliest enemy, Wideboy Wilson, about a job he was planning.

Stu—his real name was Stuart, but no one in gangland could possibly have lived with a moniker like that—could probably have got away with telling the police, but grassing The Gimp up to Wideboy was a sin of the most serious gravity, tantamount to depravity in Guiseppi's book.

Guiseppi The Gimp could not abide anyone who would not play by the rules. Although he was one of the city's most ruthless villains, there were ways to do things, and crossing the line, breaking the rules, his rules, did not feature high on his list of things that could be crossed.

Guiseppi had made his name in the murky world in which he operated when he had one day personally tied some then-big-time rival up with garden wire around his ankles and wrists, then given him five or six little taps around the skull with a baseball bat to dissuade his heavies from putting the boot in as he tried to take over some previously undisputed territory. The fact that it broke said head was an extra little bonus in the business of persuasion.

It was quite a feat considering the opponent was six-foot-three tall and built like the proverbial outhouse, and Guiseppi a not so grand five-foot-three in his stockinged feet and with a limp he'd got when a gangland ruck went wrong while he was just a kid of maybe twelve or thirteen.

It was the limp that gave Guiseppi his nickname. A gimp, of course, was the Americanised moniker given in those bad, bad days to anyone who was lame, and the young Guiseppi had always retained a personal preference of giving a likewise handle to anyone he worked with.

Right now, The Gimp was in the middle of a power struggle with Wideboy Wilson, who was surely the fattest man you'd ever seen, as to who ran the town.

He had tried playing it fair by calling in some long overdue debts from his friendly local policemen, but that hadn't worked because Wideboy simply came up with even bigger brown envelopes packed with cash. He'd tried winning over Wideboy's own men with subtle threats of mayhem, menace and mauling, but that had not worked either—they just laughed at a gimp.

So, as any reasonably minded person would have agreed, a contract was the only real solution.

To carry out the assassination, Guiseppi called in Laramie Lefty and Guns Levine, two men with a growing reputation for efficiently performing such deeds with great success.

Lefty, you should know, won his nickname of honour when he had his right hand chopped off in the famous gangland battle of Cicero in '92 or '93, since when he had only found it difficult when he had to hold a gun or knife while smoking to try to look menacing. Guns Levine was the simple follow-my-leader killer who loved to play with his toys, and even had a cigarette lighter specially made up in the shape of a Luger pistol—a top of the range model, of course.

Well, they were given the briefing and went to work with an almost indecent haste.

They spent just a morning plotting Stoolpigeon Stu's movements, then went along to the local cemetery to see where they could lose the body after the deed was done.

It showed a certain amount of professionalism, and it not only gave them an instant hiding place but saved them a lot of hard work when they saw that Grave 136X had already been dug up in preparation for a regular burial.

That night they went round to Stoolpigeon's house, knocked on the door, and shot him dead on the doorstep. Then they rammed the body upright on the back seat of the car they had stolen especially for the purpose—just in case they were stopped, they could tell the police he was asleep or drunk—and drove as casual as you like to the graveyard.

It was easy to pick the lock of the gates, and after Guns had dug down almost six more feet, Lefty took less than no time at all to commit Stoolpigeon's earthly remains to Grave 136X. Then, after Guns had replaced the extra earth he had removed, the two men returned to their car.

After a couple of beers in a nearby pub, they borrowed someone else's motor to cover their tracks and went back to Guiseppi's house to report that their job had been completed.

It wasn't that simple. The Gimp, who was as loyal as could be to his full-time staff, was not so trusting when it came to casual employees, even those with the reputation of Lefty and Guns. He demanded some sort of proof that the job had been done.

"Why don' you bring me da body?" he demanded. "I ain't gonna pay ya until I see da body."

Neither Lefty nor Guns thought that argument would win him round—the fact that he had five more of his dedicated henchmen behind him helped them make up their minds—so they left with a promise to do just as Guiseppi demanded.

They went for a couple more beers, then the two killers sat in yet another borrowed motor with a takeaway curry as they discussed their return to the burial ground to dig up Stoolpigeon Stu's body again. Before long, the food and the beers took their toll, and both fell asleep.

By the time they woke, dawn was breaking. Their return to the graveyard had to be carried out with care, and when they arrived it was just in time to see the guests arriving for the first funeral of the day.

Lefty and Guns respectfully took their hats off and bowed their heads as the hearse drove by, followed by a small armada of mourners' cars each with darkened windows.

"I get very emotional at funerals," said Guns as, to their horror, they watched the funeral party stop near to their own destination, and a service of interment took place with the mourners standing close by Grave 136X.

The two assassins had to literally kill time as they waited to return to get Stoolpigeon Stu's final remains to prove to their hard-hearted freelance employer that they had done the job he had requested.

They went for a drink, and time passed. Daylight was fast fading as they returned to the cemetery and climbed the six-foot wall surrounding it. By the time they were inside it was almost dark, and they both had weird, supernatural feelings as they wandered through the tombstones to find Grave 136X.

It was dark and eerie as night settled on the burial ground, and even though Lefty and Guns were hardened criminals they were scared, although neither would admit it to the other. As they walked cautiously through the rows of headstones they both had private thoughts of victims gone by, and the wind sighing through the trees had the sound of muted, heavenly, machine gun fire in their minds.

Soon they got to Grave 136X, to find that it had, indeed, been filled up when the last "real" funeral, the one they had watched, had taken place in it. There were a couple of spades left carelessly by the side of the grave, so both took off their jackets and began to dig.

The clay-based earth was dry and was hard to break up and they were both sweating profusely as they dug down, but they eventually paused to lift out the "new" corpse that had been placed there in its now-frozen all-embracing white shroud "parcel" six feet under the surface. They rested the rigid remains on one side and continued to burrow.

It was getting on for dawn by the time they had found the last mortal remains of Stoolpigeon Stu where they had interred them the previous day, buried further down in Grave 136X.

Lefty sat on the pile of earth they had removed, panting. It was hard work digging with just one hand. But with the sky beginning to light up with a new day, Guns managed to persuade him to begin work again. The two men started to fill in the grave once more, taking care halfway through the operation to replace the legitimate, but now frozen, body in its hallowed, allotted place.

"Hey, a stiff stiff," said Guns, reawakening all the old Hollywood slang terms he had picked up from The Gimp in an attempt to lighten the macabre moment.

The sun was high and the birds chirping overhead as they finished their gruesome task and with aching limbs carried Stoolpigeon Stu's body back to their car. They had no sooner dumped it in the boot and sat down to rest when Lefty found he had lost the earring given to him lovingly by San Fran Fran, his long-time regular girl of two months standing.

"Not only will she kill me if she finds out, it could be evidence," he told Guns as he insisted they had to go and find it.

The earring was nowhere to be found on the ground of the graveyard, and finally the pair had to return to Grave 136X to try to trace it. Once more they set to work digging up the official corpse, underneath which they found the missing piece of ear adornment.

After replacing the body again and finally filling up the now well-tilled grave once more, they returned to the car and went for breakfast. A full fry-up for Guns, who for some mystic reason could not face up to the mangled meat with tomato ketchup of the hamburger favoured by Lefty.

It was mid-morning by the time they returned to The Gimp's house to show him the dead body of the man who had so despicably betrayed him. And it was with a feeling of physical relief that they rang the doorbell and waited as footsteps slowly made their way to answer their call.

There was Goodtime Gloria Lorenzo, Guiseppi's ever-loving girl, her face looking old without make up, tear stains down her cheeks, and a happy glint in her eye as she had just been having words with Guiseppi's solicitor who had told her the extent of the fortune she had been left.

"Where's The Gimp?" asked Lefty.

"He's not here," replied Goodtime Gloria. "He's at the cemetery."

Lefty looked at Guns. Guns looked at Lefty. Both were puzzled.

"But we've just come from there," they said in unison.

"Yeah, I know. But Wideboy took out a hit on him," replied Goodtime Gloria, who did not know of the earlier contract her erstwhile boyfriend had made with the two gunmen in front of her.

"His mob shot him in the middle of the night a couple of nights ago. I was advised by his mouthpiece to plant him first thing yesterday so there was no body for the cops to investigate. You want t' pay your respects, you'll find him in Grave 136X."

THE STORYTELLER

The storyteller walked into the day nursing centre eager to get started.

The centre had been set up to give solace to the terminally ill, and he had been called in to help with some of those who attended irregularly. His job was to get them to write down or tell of their feelings, to communicate with the nurses and with each other. Not many cared.

This day in particular his heart sank when he saw there was just one patient in attendance.

The patient suffered some form of crippling illness that meant her body was bent and doubled up. Her arms were bent and virtually immovable across her frail chest, and her legs were curled up, one interlocked with the other in a small arc below her. She couldn't stand, move or, indeed, do anything for herself.

But despite her physical condition and the fact that she could only sometimes manage a groan of a word or two, her mind was still active and she despised the fact that she just couldn't get through to others or them to her.

Today she was all that the storyteller had.

"Hello," he smiled.

The patient grunted back her welcome.

"What can we talk about?"

There was a desperate look in the woman's eyes that showed him he had said the wrong thing. Talk was not an option.

The storyteller covered his mistake easily. He smiled again, a smooth professional smile. "Shall I tell you a story?" he asked.

The patient tried to answer, but in the end gave not so much a nod as a small dip of the head to agree.

The storyteller gave a small cough, his mind whirling into action as he tried to think of a subject. "Let me tell you of the prince and the pretty girl," he said.

"There was this handsome prince who lived with his parents, the king and queen, in their great palace," he began.

"It was a huge, stately old palace with high crenelated walls overlooking a square that was more often than not filled with adoring subjects eager for a glimpse of their top family. Although they loved the king and his consort without reservation, the local citizens, it must be admitted, always preferred seeing the prince when he either left the palace or returned to it after some mammoth regal occasion.

"The prince, you see, was... oh I don't know, about twenty-six and tall and handsome. One of the most good looking men you could ever hope to see—so handsome that it was almost to the point of being obscene.

"As well as being good looking, he was, too, smooth, polite and interesting. He was a man who loved living, even though his own life

was irrevocably locked into a never-ending round of state occasions and official functions.

"He took an interest in all his father's subjects, but his heart ached for just an occasional bit of what he thought was their real living. He dreamt constantly of having the same normal life as those subjects had: getting up and dressing himself in whatever clothes he wanted, going to work in a normal job, coming home by tube or bus, going to the pub. He yearned for normality in his goldfish bowl life.

"Well, on this day he was being driven out of the palace on his way to some opening or other when he spotted the girl. She was at the front of a crowd five-deep lining both sides of the road from the huge golden gates of the palace, and the prince spotted her at once because of her outstanding beauty.

"She was of medium height, and with fair hair that was pulled back in a low quiff over her smooth high forehead and fell at the sides in a glorious array around her perfectly shaped ears before turning in onto the nape of her neck. She had a delicate nose, and her mouth—smiling now as she spotted the prince—gave the impression that she laughed an awful lot. There was a look about her that she was serene in character, but was lively underneath it all and a lot of fun.

"The prince's car was soon past her and on its way, but for some reason the prince himself could not get the girl out of his memory. Her face stayed in his mind's eye throughout the day, and even while unveiling a plaque and making small talk with a group of self-opinionated local officials later on he could not help recalling her appearance at the palace gates.

"That evening, as his large official black car swept him back to the palace, she was there again, still smiling, still as beautifully memorable

as he remembered. The image stayed with him throughout that evening's state banquet, and was there when he was woken the next morning and given the list of functions he was to perform that day.

"To the prince's delight, the girl was outside the palace gates once more as he was rushed through later that morning. And throughout that second day, too, he could not rid himself of her image."

The storyteller paused to take a sip of water from a glass on the table. The patient was looking at him intently, and he could see in her eyes that she was starting to become interested in the story—that she wanted to know more.

"Shall I go on?" he asked with a slight smile.

The patient's eyes told him to, and her hand lifted painfully to hold his. The storyteller took it lightly and he continued.

"That evening the prince could not wait to finish his work. He broke off his engagements as soon as he could so he could get back to his palace early, and as he drove back he saw the girl was there again. This time he seemed to catch her eye as the car drove past, and he grinned and hoped the smile on her face was in direct return.

"Then as soon as the car pulled up, he dashed out and ran through the palace to a secret door he knew at the back and slipped through it quietly. Within minutes he had run breathlessly to the front of the vast building to join the crowd lingering in a square outside.

"It did not take him long to find the girl, and while he caught his breath he moved forward imperceptibly until he was standing right next to her. Then he was speaking to her, and although at first the girl did not know who he was it did not take her long to realise that this was the prince himself.

"The prince drew the girl away from the crowd slowly, and they walked softly side by side to the back of the palace talking together easily as they slipped in through the secret door. Then they were in the magnificent state rooms, and the girl's eyes opened wide with the unaccustomed splendour of it all.

"'Don't worry,' said the prince, completely at ease among the vivid reds and golds of the palace rooms. 'You are here as my guest… my friend. I want you to be my friend, you know. I think we can be.'

"The girl nodded, her eyes still unbelieving but with a look of adoration building at the back of them all the time."

The patient's hold on the storyteller's hand grew noticeably stronger as she gripped him apparently in anticipation of the romance. It soon began to unfold.

"That evening was the best in the prince's short life. He and the girl dined alone on the finest food the palace could provide, and they laughed a lot. They found out things about each other, secret things that crop up between two people, and they soon found they had a lot in common despite their different backgrounds. They talked and discovered each other well into the night.

"All too soon it was time for the girl to leave, although it was not quite the witching hour. The prince reluctantly walked her to the secret back door, and for a moment it seemed as if they would kiss.

"'Not tonight,' said the prince eventually as he looked into the girl's adoring eyes. 'Tomorrow. You will come back tomorrow, won't you?'

"The girl nodded, her inner feelings almost bursting as she realised what was starting to happen to her.

"'Until tomorrow then,' said the prince, then suddenly the girl was gone and he was alone in the huge, crowded palace.

"That night the prince was full of hope that she would return the next day. In his mind he felt that at last he had met someone who would give him the chance of the normality he craved in his life. He hoped that somehow she would be able to stay with him, and that maybe that would allow him to live his life among the trappings of pageantry in some way almost as normally as all those others in the kingdom who lived their ordinary lives day by day.

"The girl, too—at home with her parents—dreamt sweet dreams that were also full of hope."

The storyteller paused and licked his drying lips to refresh them. The patient's eyes were now closed, although her hand still gripped his tight.

"It shows," he said, "That no matter who you are you must always have hope. Hope is eternal."

The storyteller ended his tale and turned. Standing behind him was a nurse who had come in and heard the story he had been telling.

"I think she's fallen asleep," he told her.

The nurse stepped forward and looked. "No," she replied, "It's more than that."

She reached forward and gently eased the patient's hand from the storyteller's. "She's dead," said the nurse softly. "I think she heard what you said though. Look at the smile on her face. It's beautiful. I think you gave her a final moment of hope that helped her die with peace."

The storyteller stood slowly and turned to walk away. Hope? Everlasting hope? He had already forgotten the old lady and his professional mind was already on his next job later that day, hoping it would work out.

THE SHRINE

Everyone who visited the narrow terraced house at 23 Acacia Avenue was amazed at the way that Henry Ackroyd kept it as a shrine to his dead wife Mabel. The house was second from the left as you looked head-on to the block of five, and from the outside there was nothing to differentiate it from any of the others in the plain, mean street.

But inside it was different. There were photos of Mabel in every single room and every visitor (few though they may have been) marvelled at the emotional feelings that Henry called up as he tried to keep her memory alive.

Photos? There were pictures of every size: postcard, portrait, an enlarged head-and-shoulders two feet tall and eighteen inches wide above the fireplace in his main living room. They were glossy or matt. Some edged in white, and all in shiny frames—gold and silver and one in a plain white wood.

Everyone in the district knew about it, and all thought it rather touching that he kept the house as a temple to Mabel. It was, they said, a lovely way to keep her memory alive.

I had heard about the shrine house, of course, but when I first visited as part of a routine courtesy call from the local GP surgery, I was in awe at the scope of the photographs.

Henry had them on view in every available space in the house. In the living room, dining room, both bedrooms, kitchen, and even in the toilet at the top of the stairs. Henry had hung them so that they covered virtually every inch of the drab striped wallpaper, and on top of every space he could find, Tables, a sideboard, even a couple of chairs had Mabel's photographs sitting on them.

After many minutes having Mabel's face staring at me wherever I stood I felt I had to say something. "You must have loved her very much," I said as Henry sat unmoved in front of me.

He looked back at me, impassive, but didn't answer.

"I, er, I think it's wonderful you've kept her memory alive in this way," I then said, trying to fill the uncomfortable silence after my first comment. This time there was a reaction.

"Oh yes, it keeps her memory alive all right," he said. "I don't ever want to forget her."

He paused, obviously thinking of the woman he had once loved and whose memory he now cherished so much.

"She must have been a lovely woman," I started to say, but Henry exploded.

"Lovely? *Lovely*?" he shouted, his voice rising in anger, "She was a cow. A real bitch of a woman." He put his face in his hands and fought to control his emotions. "I hated her with every fibre of my body," he finally added.

The outburst confused me. "But if you hated her…" I gestured at the photographs still staring at us from the walls and furniture, "Why all this?"

Henry sat up and looked at me earnestly. "I hated her, but I want to remember her," he said, his voice now on an even keel. He paused, seeming to summon up some unwanted memory, then he explained.

"Mabel was the first worst woman you could imagine. She complained about everything, and no matter what I tried or said, she blamed me for every perceived ill. She was a dragon. She nagged me incessantly and she made my life a misery…"

"If she was that bad, why did you stay with her?" I asked.

Henry shook his head. "She had money in a savings bank—left to her by her parents. Thousands and thousands of pounds," he eventually told me. "She refused to spend any of that money and expected me to provide for everything she wanted—and she wanted the best. I had to pay for her every whim from my own poor salary.

"She had expensive tastes and I couldn't earn enough to satisfy her wants, so she nagged me even more. I thought of leaving her, but the thought of all that money got to me and I stayed. But it got so bad that at one time I even thought of killing her, but of course I didn't do that."

Henry licked his dry lips. "I'm afraid my greed finally got the better of me, and I devised a way of finally getting her to release the money so I could use it. Somehow I managed to get it into her mind that she should make a will, and once she had got the idea

I got her very drunk on the wine she loved and somehow put the idea into her mind that she should leave all the savings to me. After months of trying I got her to sit down and write the will."

He indicated the sideboard. "It's in the centre drawer—Mabel's will—leaving her fortune to me. To me. Payback."

I was puzzled. "But all these photos… the shrine?" I queried.

"Well," said Henry, "Mabel had the last word. She suddenly died of a stroke brought on by the drink—before she signed the will. It's a useless document, and the powers that be won't let me touch it. So yes, I want to remember her. To remind myself what a nasty bitch she was."

A COMMITTED COMMITTEE

They were small, all of them an exact three old-fashioned feet in height and with their heads large in proportion to their bodies, which were shrivelled and barely useful. A few wires could be seen coming from the lower neck region of some of the heads, disappearing into perfectly formed small holes in the diminutive right shoulders.

There was a group of eight of them, and all were somewhat grey in appearance and spoke in harsh, metallic, stuttering voices. When they laughed, it sounded something like "Aaark, aaark…"

This was the Reflection of Better Organisation for Tomorrow committee of the World Parliament, formed in equal numbers by representatives from the all-powerful United States of America, United States of Europe, United States of the Orient and the United States of Africa—all of whose words were absolute world law and could not be argued. The committee had been set up by the Presidential Computer Base and its ancillary web to find ways of improving life for the future as the world moved into the new millennium—the year 4000. Today was the first day of 4000, and R.O.B.O.T was holding its umpteenth meeting without yet having formed any clear-cut policy for improving the world's vast over-population.

They had, it's true, devised all manner of concepts over the past year. An Ovoid—a peculiar-shaped building to commemorate the anniversary of that out-dated notion of time—and a hover ride that would take citizens high into the sky into the still-cool atmosphere above planet Earth to peer at the stars rather than having to take a tiresome trip to one in a daily spacecraft.

But there was nothing definite as yet.

"Hey, I've got an idea," said one of the Europeans (from the country of Britain as it happens) suddenly. "Why don't we create… a human being?"

The others looked at him coldly, their single mid-forehead eyes jointly suspicious.

"What's a human? How would it work?" asked a younger American member.

"You know, like they used to have centuries ago, before global warming killed Earthland," enthused the English speaker.

"Remember the history books? Men and women. We could easily recreate their flesh, living tissues, to make one. Maybe even give it a brain so it could work without instruction. Needn't be much more than the size of a walnut and it would be able to give it all the instructions."

An African spoke with a slight hesitancy. "A walnut? Yes, I remember them. Saw one in the Year 3000 Museum once. Could pack a pile of nanometre chips into one that size."

The English committeeman seized the moment. "But that's the point. You wouldn't need any form of chip," he said.

"No chips...?"

"No, the human's brain would be made so it could do it all," said the USE's main representative.

"I'm sure we could develop one like that without too much trouble. And we could even give this human... wha'd'yercall'ems? Er, yeah, eyes. And something so it could pick up smells. And we could give it a hearing organ, and maybe even a voice box with a slit through which it could communicate."

And Oriental butted in. "But wouldn't that be a bit unnatural? You couldn't get a smooth communication like real speech," he intervened politely.

English was not to be put off, and he continued urbanely. "Yeah it would. And you could even use the speech slit to shove replenishments in to keep the mechanism going. And liquid to oil it. You know, like they used to all those centuries ago."

He sat back with a quiet whirr, smug at the thought that he had put forward the only real idea that the world group had been able to come up with in its three thousand years of hard talk.

The others on the committee looked at each other as his suggestion was absorbed.

"Aaark, aaark," said some.

"Grunt, grumble," added others.

But no one knew quite what to say until an American stepped in.

"Nah, a human being would never work," he summed it up.

And R.O.B.O.T got on with its serious millennium debate.

BEDTIME

Barb was lying in bed one night. Husband Horace was falling asleep next to her, but Barb was in a romantic mood and wanted to talk.

"You used to hold my hand when we were courting," she said wistfully.

Horace wearily reached across, held her hand for a second and tried to get back to sleep.

"Then you used to kiss me," she added a few moments later.

Mildly irritated, Horace reached across, gave her a peck on the cheekand settled down to sleep again.

Thirty seconds later Barb continued. "Then you used to bite my neck…"

Horace sighted, then he threw back the bed clothes angrily and got out of bed.

"Where are you going?" Barb asked.

"To get my teeth!"

THE VERDICT

Bugsy Malone was in trouble. Not for the first time, he had been arrested and now languished in the New York City jail.

But this time he was worried. The cops had slung a murder rap at him for the first time and Bugsy knew they could make it stick.

"But it wasn't really moider," he protested to friends who visited him. "It was a moicy killin' o' my ol' friend Luigi the Wop!"

Bugsy, however, pleaded his innocence in vain. He was arraigned before a grand jury, and now awaited his trial uneasily.

He needn't have worried. While he wasted away in remand jail, his boys were working on his freedom. And their main method was to see a small, pale-faced gentleman called Alfie... juryman number five at Bugsy's forthcoming trial.

"Ya godda work for Bugsy," one mobster told Alfie.

"Ya godda get him free," echoed a second.

But Alfie wasn't interested.

"He's innocent," insisted the first mobster.

"We'll fill ya whole fam'ly full o' lead and dump 'em in the Hudson River wid da fishes if ya don't help," pleaded the second.

Alfie listened.

The mobsters outlined their plan. Alfie was to stick out for a verdict of accidental shooting when the jury retired, no matter what. There had to be a unanimous vote for murder, they told Alfie, so if he did what they said, all would be well.

Money changed hands, and Alfie was left alone at last—conscience stricken and feeling slightly worried.

The opening day of the trial came, and Bugsy was brought into a tense and excited courtroom. Attorneys on both sides argued their cases back and forth, and Judge Henry Machin nodded frequently in an effort to stay awake.

Then at long last, the jury retired.

For four days and three nights the courtroom was a hive of expectancy, until on the final day the twelve good men and true returned to give their verdict, with Alfie looking just a little bit shaken.

"Accidental shooting," said the foreman, his voice sounding tired.

"Eighteen months," snapped Judge Machin, dreaming of his evening meal.

The trial was over, and Bugsy's boys were jubilant.

"He'll be out o' dere in no time," they told Alfie in the corridor outside the courtroom. "But what took ya so long?"

Alfie shrugged. "I did exactly what you said and stuck out for accidental shooting," he replied. "I won 'em all round OK too. Ya know, if I hadn't, they'd have hung an acquittal on him!"

IVO'S STORY

The throbbing grunt of the engine echoed from the black mountains rising from the sea as Ivo steered his way back to the village. Another day over. The tourists moved and returned backwards and forwards across the bay, clicking their cameras and "oohing" and "aahing" at the sheer beauty of the rugged Dalmatian coastline.

Ivo had seen it a hundred thousand times in his life as a ferryman, of course, but it was only at times like this in the cooling sun of the evening, after the day's work was done, that he really appreciated it. The mountains on the left, with their rolling, boulder ridges, the cypress and pine trees at their feet falling clean into the dropped rocks of the beach.

He could picture the village of Cavtat, where he worked, around the headland. A row of lights would now be glinting on the enclosed waters of the bay through the bushy palm trees, and the parked boats would dance on the water giving it a lazy end-of-day feeling.

At the other end of the village, the square-shaped church towers would be pointing up to the heavens, and behind it the close-packed traditionally tiled houses would seem to be huddling together and to Mother Earth as if to keep warm in the cooling night air. Not that it was cold, but once the blazing sun had dipped over the mountains a certain keen chill seemed to touch the flesh.

It would be romantic for the visitors, but to Ivo—who had never had room for romance—there was just a vague and not-understood stirring that something good was reflected by all the beauty.

Not that he was going to go round to the main village at this time of night. He was on his way home to a house way back in the foothills. He would drop anchor and tie the prow of his boat in the old harbour around the other side of the promontory of St. Roko on which the village stood. The prettiness there was not quite as keen, but it was still a lovely sight as the smooth waters lapped in between the two strips of land taking the boat into the harbour.

There, with the evening bus waiting its catch of tourists to go round the bay to the restaurants there, the others would also be ending their work and slipping into the mood of the evening. It would be a good time of day.

He had seen it so many times before. Had come into land there for many years since growing up so many years ago, even then with his thoughts of boats. A hundred thousand times, he wondered. More like a million as he had toured day after day for nearly sixty years.

In his nostrils was the distant smell of hibiscus, and the smoky reminder that evening meals were being cooked in all the hotels and pensions along the way. The sea rolled and occasionally thudded against the solid wood hull of his boat as he thought of his own meal. Warm minced beef cooked on a smoke fire in the Serbo-Croatian style, and later a beer or two and a chaser in the village, in the bar where the harbour people drank and discouraged strangers who spoke in foreign tongues.

It was in the bar at about half past nine that Ivo, his own tongue loosened by a glass of the burning slivovitz (it always tasted better after the first), began telling his stories.

He told, in particular, his tale of the pale-skinned girl on the ride home from Dubrovnik, and how she had teased and flirted with him and given him a kiss. Full on the lips, he insisted.

It was a story he often told his fellow boatmen, and he fantasised it in such a way that it could almost be true, but to the others, it was just another story to make them laugh.

Ivo was the village "ancient", the man to make all men laugh. A storyteller to thrive on free drinks and to take the mind of his fellows off the hard work of the day. Every village in the area had one, and tonight Ivo was in good form. His ebony-brown face creased in smile as he described the supposed events of the day.

"Ha, ha, ho, ho," roared the men of the sea as they sipped their drinks and encouraged him to more.

Ivo let the raw alcohol of the plum brandy burn in his throat as he embroidered the oft-told tale.

Soon they all went home and slept the sleep of the weary. It was a long day in the season, and they all (including Ivo) slept sound until the first screech of the wheeling gulls and the darting swifts calling for their own small bit of space woke them the next morning.

Ivo dressed in his corduroy slacks and tartan shirt and sipped a heavy black coffee to rid his mouth of the night before. He was out early to take the first tourists across the bay, and they dutifully looked and loved as Ivo sat impassive, a hand-rolled cigarette as usual between his lips as he steered between the small village harbours.

Cavtat to Plat to Mlini to Cavtat. On to Dubrovnik, and then across to Lokrum. Then back and back and round and out again. All the while, the thick wooden tiller in his left hand tugged against the strength of the sea as the boat carved a swathe through it. A good strong boat and a good strong sailor.

The beauty of the coast left him unmoved and unfeeling. Tonight, on his way home, he would savour its goodness, its sweet smells, and its oneness in his mind.

Only Ivo did not think like that; he was an unemotional man.

But it was when he was on his way home that it happened. He was throbbing along slowly across the bay in the cool of evening when a huge splash and a scream just around the headland jerked his thoughts away from the mountains and the sea and the tall trees reaching to the tilting sun. Ivo pulled on the ragged string that controlled the throttle, and the boat's motor roared and splashed the screw through the water. The boat bounced on the waves as it skidded round the promontory of rocks.

Ivo saw the girl immediately. She was splashing round in the green water, her hair bobbing on the waves and her mouth a wide slit in a bronzed face as she yelled—her voice wafting away beneath the lap of the waves and the insistent roar of the boat's engine.

Ivo was conscious that a huge seagull rode the waves just to her left, and that an insect, too far from land and destined for death, buzzed just above the water.

"I'm coming," he called, not caring that she probably could neither hear nor understand. "Hold fast, I'll soon be there."

It took him little more than a minute to close on the drowning girl, and as he yanked up the throttle string to close down the engine he was already reaching with his other hand for the silver-tipped hook he kept "just in case". He reached across, missed the girl the first time, but caught her the next.

Soon he had her on board, and as she swayed to keep her balance in the bobbing hull she suddenly began to shiver. Violently and uncontrollably.

Ivo reached out to help her stop. "It's all right, little one," he said, and tried to grin.

The girl did not understand, but she realised he was trying to help. She kept on shivering.

"I'm sorry," she said in not-understood English as Ivo offered a huge, crumpled handkerchief so she could dry herself. "I slipped. Don't ask me how. I was trying to get round the rocks and I missed my footing. The waves carried me out." The shivering eased a bit.

"It's all right now," said Ivo.

The young girl and the old man understood the look in each other's eyes and there was no need for more words.

The seagull took off from the waves as if the sideshow was over. The insect had long since disappeared, and there was no sound except for the soft "plip-plop" of the sea against the side of the boat. The girl used the handkerchief on her face, but water still dripped from her white dress and Ivo, noticing that it clung, pretended that it didn't show through and nodded reassurance again.

"You're the ferryman," said the girl. "You took me across the bay to Cavtat yesterday. Yes, I'm sure it was you."

Ivo found an oily rag and offered it as an extra towel. Then he laughed. "You can't use that," he said.

The girl gave him a smile. She understood.

Ivo put the rag down again and took off his shirt and offered that instead. "Here. Dry yourself," he said in speedy Yugoslav.

The girl shook her head, but when he offered it again, pushing it fractionally towards her twice, she took it and used it sparingly. The fright had gone from her now.

As she rubbed her lithe young body, Ivo started the engine again. His own ageing frame was bronzed like his face and arms, and the girl noted that, although his ribs showed through, he had muscles at the shoulders from his days running the boat through the sea.

"Where?" he asked, and the girl somehow understood.

"Srebreno," she told him.

Ivo slipped the engine into gear and tugged at the throttle. The boat eased forward again, and he pushed the tiller away to sweep it to the right in a long arc. The prow bobbed on a wave, then straightened as he aimed it for the harbour ahead. The girl put his shirt down at his side and looked back at the rocks she had been climbing.

"It was the most amazing thing, as if I was being pulled down by a magnet," she said out loud.

Ivo nodded. "Yes," he answered, because he did not understand what she said but felt he should reply.

Soon the boat had pulled into Srebreno, and Ivo throttled back. As the boat bumped the harbour wall, he jumped ashore and held it steady with a rope. He beckoned the girl out, helping her clamber onto the harbour wall.

"Go now. Dry yourself properly," he told her.

The girl smiled, but hesitated. A gust of wind caught her still-wet skirt, and she shivered again momentarily.

"Go," said Ivo, his hands waving her away but a smile on his lips and in his eyes.

He prepared to jump back into the boat, but the girl put her hand on his arm.

"Thank you," she said simply. "Thank you very much."

On an instinct she leant forward and kissed his lips lightly. Then she hurried away.

Ivo watched for a minute, then he slipped back into the boat and was well out into the bay again before he put on his dampened shirt.

That evening he was again in the bar, and the drinks flowed free. Ivo was in the middle of a crowd, and as the glasses emptied fast he told the tale. The girl, she kissed him, he said. On the lips.

"Yesterday she had fair skin, but today she was tanned," taunted another boatman who had never loved the sunset. "Ivo, you are a hoot."

He drank his drink and told the others about the "ancient", about the old boatman who always had a tale to tell.

"Ho, ho, ha, ha," they roared.

Eventually Ivo went out of the bar and sat in his boat. It was dark now, but knowledge told him of the black mountains that still reared high above the trees and the sea above him. He could smell the hibiscus and the honeysuckle. The lights from the bar danced on the water.

"It happened," he said to himself. "It did. This time it really did."

He took a deep breath, and held it while he listened to the water splashing against the sides of the boat.

A burst of laughter came from the bar.

"Yes," he said. "This time it really happened. To me."

PICTURES OF LOVE

They were young, good looking and very much in love. Tony and Annabell.

The trouble was that Annabell's father thought they were too young, and he would not even allow them to meet. He insisted that Annabell was worthy of a far better future with someone richer and with more prospects than young Tony.

Annabell's father, Alexander James Cunningham, a key figure in a city insurance bank, could not stop the young couple meeting though. They did so whenever and wherever they could, holding hands in cinema back rows, cuddling in shop doorways, or kissing hidden in the trees at the entrance to the long driveway to her house.

It was, though, a romance that seemed doomed to die.

At least, that's the way it looked to the romantic young pair whenever they held their illicit assignations. They saw themselves as a kind of modern Romeo and Juliet, and when they were together in the cinemas or the doorways or on cold dark evenings in the trees by the driveway to her house, Annabell and Tony would talk tragically of themselves as modern star-crossed lovers.

Things had been going on like that for some months when Annabell's father discovered what had been happening literally under his nose. He came home late one evening and saw the two of them embracing as he swept his large company car through the tall iron gates and up the drive towards his mansion.

When Annabell eventually came indoors, he confronted her immediately. "I told you not to see that boy," he raged.

Annabell looked at him defiantly while her mother wondered whether or not she should intervene.

"I will not have my word disobeyed," went on the irascible Alexander James Cunningham. "I said you must not see him, and I meant it. You will do as you are told, and from now on you are forbidden to see him ever again."

Annabell tried to argue, but he would brook none of it and eventually she gave up and went to bed, holding her tears back until she was safely locked in her own room where not even her mother could go to console her.

The next day she rang Tony and told him what had happened, and they agreed to meet that afternoon to talk things over.

The meeting was arranged in a supermarket just outside the village where they lived, and they fixed up to meet by a photo booth outside its main door. It was a place they had used before, because they could hide together behind the curtain of the booth without fear of discovery.

The morning went slowly until the appointed time for the meeting, but then they were together slipping into the booth to hold hands and wonder what they could do.

"He can't do that," said Tony with the innocence of youth when Annabell told him of her father's insistence that they never meet each other again. "Doesn't he realise we're in love? He can't just stop us even seeing each other ever again."

Annabell nodded her agreement. "He says we mustn't ever meet again, and I don't think I could bear that," she told her youthful paramour. "I think I'd kill myself if I could never see you, hold you, again."

Tony smiled; a thin, wan smile. "If you're going to do that, I'd better have a picture to remember you by," he said facetiously, putting coins into the slot in front of them.

"You mustn't even joke about something like that," said Annabell seriously. "We're going to be together always."

"Yes," agreed Tony. "Always."

The camera flashed and caught them as a couple, then they took turns to lean to one side so there could also be individual single photos taken by the machine.

As it whirred and they waited for the prints to drop out, Tony took Annabell's hands again. They kissed lightly.

The three pictures dropped, and Annabell took her hands away and picked them out of the pocket. She put the photographs in her pocket and Tony put his arms around her shoulders and held her tight. He wondered what he could suggest.

"I know, we'll elope," he finally said.

The idea appealed to Annabell, and they instantly set about making their plans.

When they left the booth, both were in a much happier mood and it had been agreed that they would meet again at ten o'clock the next morning. Tony would hire a car, and they would run off somewhere to be romantically married—possibly by the sea or in the hills to the north. They left each other and went to their homes.

The next morning, Annabell was awake early, scarcely able to hide her excitement but scared that she would show her feelings to her father. As he went off to his office and her mother prepared for some outing with her friends, Annabell slipped to her bedroom and packed her clothes, making sure to include the pretty party frock that she had worn the first day she had met Tony, her dance dresses, and another bit of evening frippery she felt would be appropriate for her romantic elopement wedding ceremony.

Soon she slipped out of the house to make her way to the village where she had arranged to meet Tony for the start of their idyllic flight at the entrance to the supermarket.

She was singing aloud as she skipped happily down the drive of her home, and did not see her father's car approaching along the road leading up to it. Mr Cunningham had forgotten some papers, and had irritably turned from the traffic jam leading to his office to return home to get them. When he saw Annabell carrying a suitcase and heading for the village he had a suspicion and decided to follow her to find out if he was right. If it was as he thought, he felt, it would be time to confront the boy and finish things between him and his daughter once and for all.

Annabell did not realise she was being followed, and when she got to the tryst Tony was waiting for her. She got into the car beside him, kissed him full on the lips, and they drove off.

Annabell's father was too far behind to stop them leaving, but he immediately gave chase. It was a few miles down the road before Tony realised they were being followed.

"Your father... he's chasing us," her told Annabell.

She turned in her seat to look over her shoulder, and her eyes widened. "He mustn't catch us," she almost whispered.

Tony put his foot down hard on the accelerator, and the car jumped forward. His speed built up, but Annabell's father's car was more powerful and easily kept up. Tony pressed down even harder on the pedal, and as the car swerved round a bend he lost control and the car bounced against a hawthorn bush at the side of the road, rolled over, and ended up upside down skewed across the road.

Annabell's father watched the crash with horror. He slammed on his brakes, but by the time he got to the overturned hired car it was too late. The young lovers were, indeed, star-crossed lovers and both were dead.

Cunningham was inconsolable. It went through his mind that his daughter's happiness was all he should have cared about, that her apparent feelings for the young Tony were just a passing fancy and he should have left her to grow out of them in the fullness of time.

His wife was equally shocked, and neither knew what to say to each other. Theirs was a sad, lonely house that night.

The sun still rose the next morning though, and it was shining high in the sky when a lone policeman cycled up the now lonely drive with Annabell's suitcase, along with a plastic bag containing her few other personal possessions hanging from his handlebars.

"We felt you should have these," he told the grieving parents as he handed the case and the bag across.

Later that day, Alexander Cunningham took the bag to Annabell's room to look at its contents out of sight of his anguished wife's eyes. He knew that she blamed him for their daughter's death, and he did not want to hurt her even more.

As he spilt the contents of the bag onto his daughter's bed, the photographs taken in the supermarket booth fell on top. Cunningham picked them up and looked at them. He threw the picture of Tony back onto the bed along with that of the two young lovers together. But the single likeness of Annabell stayed in his hand as he looked round and saw an old frame on his daughter's bedside table, with a school photograph of Tony locked into it. He took the picture of the boy out and threw it on top of the other two photographs on the bed before carefully putting his daughter's photo in its place and taking it downstairs to show his wife.

"This is probably the last picture she ever had taken," he told her quietly, handing over the framed reminder.

Mrs Cunningham took it, tears in her eyes, kissed it once, then hooked it carefully in replacement of a watercolour hanging in a prominent lone position on the central wall above the centre of the mantlepiece.

The tortured Alexander James Cunningham looked at the lone photograph continually that evening until he miserably followed his wife to an early bed.

Neither slept well that night. It seemed to Alexander that he could hear whispering noises from the garden outside, and a couple of times he even got out of the warm bed to stand, shivering, looking out of the bedroom window down the long drive to the road. His wife knew what he was doing, but kept her eyes tight shut although protective unconsciousness would not come to her either.

Sleep did come eventually, but it was with still weary eyes that they both got out of bed, put on dressing gowns, and went down the stairs of their cold, empty house. Neither felt like breakfast, and Alexander went to sit in an armchair instead.

Suddenly he heard his wife gasp. "There," she said, and he looked up to see her pointing at the mantelshelf. "The picture..."

Alexander followed the direction of her finger. And there, in the centre of the mantelpiece, was the picture of their Annabell. Only this time she was not on her own—the supermarket snap was now the one of her and Tony together.

A GIRL LIKE SUE

She was not so old, just thirty-five or thirty-six maybe. But she had an aged body that was now fairly useless. It hurt, and these days it did not do as Sue Wakeling asked. Not that she asked it to do much. Her body was diseased, riddled with multiple sclerosis.

Sue lay in her hospital bed and tried to sleep, but sleep would not come. Her mind was filled with ragged thoughts of days gone by, but she could not concentrate completely because of the hurt her body gave her.

A sharp pain in her shoulder made her try to move to a more comfortable position, but she could not. Her head ached just above the receding hair line, and she could feel an itch on the right side of her nose. She tried to lift her dead left hand to it, but it fell back. When the irritation continued, she tried again and managed to get her right hand up to it, very slowly and with great difficulty, but she could not extend the fingers and had to rub at the sensitive spot with the gnarled, curled knuckles of an old lady's hand without feeling.

Sue still did not realise exactly why her body was like that. When she had first been struck down, the doctors had tried to explain things in the way that doctors do. They had tried to simplify details so that she could understand, but there was no way even then that her mind could wrap itself around the complicated medical jargon they inevitably used.

What she did know then, and only very occasionally now, was that the continual pain was there day and night. It kept her awake when she wanted to sleep, and sometimes the sheer agony forced her mind to switch itself to unconsciousness when she wanted to stay awake to see the sunshine through the hospital window and convince herself that she was still alive. That did not happen very often.

Sometimes she recalled and understood. Parkinson's disease. Somewhere in the deeper recesses of her memory she recalled the doctors telling her that it was a chronic, progressive disease of the nervous system that gradually destroyed the protective shields around the nerves in the brain or the spinal cord. Its effects, they had told her rather clinically, would slowly spread from those vanished sheaths to disable all her body.

As the debilitating illness had inevitably done as they had predicted, Sue slowly became a kind of living, soulless automaton. She drooped to a zombie-like state in which her mind came and went as her physical body sank into uselessness.

Most times now, she could not remember anything from her past; even events from just a few moments before became historical. Mentally, she drifted along the sea of life like a leaf floating on the waves and waiting only to sink to the depths.

Sue had been a vivid, animated girl when she was younger. She had a natural energy that literally exploded every time she moved; she walked with a rippling energy she could barely suppress, and when she ran she erupted into violent animation. She was lively, vigorous and vivacious in her every action, laughing at every facet of life.

As a youngster, her sheer love of life and her bounding energy had marked her out from a very early age as an athlete, and she had taken to sport with a zest that matched her enthusiasm.

She easily accepted the fact that she was different from the other children in her school. She revelled in that difference, giggling as she pointed out that not only was she "a star" but that she was a leftie—the only left-handed girl in the class.

Before she was twelve, Sue had won events against girls half as old again as herself, and it all seemed so easy that she quickly turned from the explosive sprint races to long-distance runs. Even they were not enough, and as she got even stronger in her body she began to add field events such as putting the shot and throwing a javelin.

Eventually, when she reached her mid-teens, Sue had become one of the most accomplished young heptathletes in the world. She performed the seven events of the competition with careless ease, and finally she was picked to represent her country in international competition.

No one was surprised when Sue won in those cosmopolitan arenas, and the knowledgeable experts marked her down as a good bet to take a gold medal at the Olympic Games, and then to become a world champion.

In the build-up to those top challenges, Sue took part in as many events as she could, both at home and around the world. She travelled with all expenses paid to compete in the most exclusive parts of the globe. She saw America, Africa, Australia. She visited scenic pleasures such as Victoria Falls, the Great Barrier Reef and the Grand Canyon. Her every whim seemed to have some acolyte dancing to her wishes. She lived what seemed the very good life, but she was worth it because of her happy nature, sunny personality and sheer, raw, precocious talent.

Between the sightseeing tours and everyday fun times, she had to train and perform on the athletic stage, but that was something she found easy. She loved the two-day heptathlon competitions; four events on the first day and three more the next. She organised her training methodically, loving the practice as she ran two-hundred- and eight-hundred-metre races on the flat, hurdled her way along a brisk one hundred metres, jumped both high and long, and continued to putt the shot and throw the javelin with a left arm that was as strong as most men of her age.

Sue was on top of the world, loving every split moment of her dynamic, industrious life of movement and pleasure and often laughing out loud at the thought of all that was right with her world. To a young girl who, although moving rapidly to the top of her chosen career, was still only just beginning a life, there seemed no end to the gratification of existence.

Her sports life was ordered and orderly. She knew the next Olympics, when she would be just nineteen, would probably come too soon for her to compete with a chance. So she set her sights on the following games, when she would be twenty-three and in her prime.

Then suddenly, right out of nowhere when she was just two years short of that, Sue started to fall ill. As a young adult it came hard to her, but as the sudden severe blurring of vision during one competition turned to weakness in both her legs and in her throwing left arm during many others, she got her first feelings of mortality.

At first, she began to wonder simply whether they were symptoms of an over-worked body; warning signs that she had run and thrown and jumped and leapt too much and too often. But as the early signs cleared, she rid her mind of those distressing, anxious feelings and continued to train and compete, carrying on with her daily round of travelling and, after those earlier worries, enjoying life once more.

Then the illness began to creep back, and soon Sue could not take part in her sport. She saw doctors who were solemn, doctors who were optimistic, doctors who feared the worst. As her travelling and competing began to slow down and disappear, she sought more medical advice that was at first still diametrically and contentiously opposed.

But as her body slowly began to lose its youthful energy, Sue knew she was seriously ill and eventually MS was diagnosed. She was treated, but all the treatment did was to slow down the wearing out process that was slowly but surely strangling her body.

By the time she should have been competing in the Olympic Games, Sue was permanently confined to her house. She could barely walk, let alone run or jump, and she needed a stick to get from one room to the other.

It was not long before the insidious disease caused her to move her bed to a downstairs room, and it was from an armchair there that she watched the following Olympics. Then the illness seemed to rush ahead so that she became bed-ridden completely. By the time she moved into her thirties and had seen another Olympics come and go, the illness had such a hold that Sue was moved to a medical centre near her home, and as the years moved slowly and inexorably on and the need for more bed space became more pressing in the hospital, she was shuffled from one sanitorium to the next. Her condition deteriorated, and both she and the physicians knew she would never get better. She had rare moments of clarity, but in the main her brain was warped into a blank nothing. She did not know, or even care, where she was; her past was a blank like her future.

Now, as she was lay in her hospital bed with her body useless and her mind all but failed, she had a sudden brief flash of comprehension as she realised her nose was running. Once again she could not raise either hand to wipe it, but a moment of sudden lucidity reminded her of… of what? Of running. Running noses now. Running, running, then. She tried again to lift her left hand to her nose, and in that same fractional moment recalled that she had been left-handed all that time back. She threw the javelin and putt the shot left-handed. It was a brief second of time, and Sue quickly lapsed once more into a comatose state—that near permanent state of her brain within a body that was just alive but did not work.

Soon after, a nurse came into her room. She looked down carefully at Sue, lying there still and helpless and with her eyes flickering slightly and, without giving more than a passing professional thought, walked across the room to switch on the television set in the far corner. The Olympics had been showing, and she had been watching the end of one session as she relaxed in the staff room with a coffee minutes before returning to duty. The nurse wanted to see the ending of the heptathlon but had been hustled out of the coffee room by a rightly enthusiastic new sister. She did not know that the now just thirty-five-year-old Sue had once been a champion in the event; the subject had never arisen. Sue was, after all, a patient, a helpless patient who needed constant attention and could never have been a vital, well-trained, fully fit athletic girl.

The nurse glanced back at Sue, whose head was now pressed back into the pillow with her eyes shut. Then she turned her attention to the television picture. To her disappointment, sports coverage had ended and the early evening news headlines were now being given. She listened to the headlines, then went back to Sue's bed and tidied the blankets, plumping up the pillow and tucking in the sheet all round.

The volume of the TV set was switched right down, so she barely heard the news reader announce coverage of the big

Olympic surprise. She went back to the set and turned the sound up a fraction, and as the pictures switched to recorded tapes of the events she had been watching earlier she heard a commentator say that the last competitor was preparing for her last throw in the javelin, the last event in the heptathlon. A young teenage girl who had been a rank outsider in her first games, he said in hushed, reverential tones, had done so well over two days that now just one good throw would give her the gold medal.

The nurse watched as the girl ran up, javelin poised in her left hand and back over her shoulder. She threw, the spear soared away, and the camera followed it to Earth. The commentator was screaming, although the nurse could barely hear him, that it was a world record.

"Sue's won the gold," he shouted as the cameras panned back quickly to show the girl leaping with unconcealed youthful enthusiasm and joy. "The youngest ever, and the first left-hander ever, to take the top medal in the event."

The nurse watched for a few moments more, then when the pictures returned to the news reader she switched the set off and turned to go. As she did so she glanced once more at the patient in the bed.

Sue's head had lolled over to one side as she died while the javelin flew.

THE CHRISTMAS PARTY

The flares soared high into the dark near-dawn sky over No Man's Land, and the British Tommies lurking in their trenches thought that although they were not quite Christmas tree lights they would do.

It was Christmas Day, and the war was just five months old. After breakfast, the usual gruel-tasting muck with a watery tea whose only good point was that it was hot, the soldiers turned their minds torpidly to the daily routine.

Then suddenly, as if in a kind of dream, they heard the sound of carols. Christmas carols.

"Stille nacht, heilige nacht…"

The sounds were coming from the German trenches, facing them and just about a hundred and fifty yards across the wasteland.

Some of the Tommies started to sing a hesitant reply… but it only took a moment or two before a red-faced major appeared from his dugout to quieten them. Still the singing continued from the other side, the rather muted snapping of rifle fire, the retort of an occasional machine gun, and the screech of shells overhead providing a mystical, rather bizarre, accompaniment.

By mid-morning, the carols had stopped. The Germans had carried on with them for about two to maybe two and a half hours before they started to stutter and fade away. But the memory of them lingered, and the feeling of Christmas remained in the air.

It was about eleven o'clock now, and suddenly an observer on the eastern flank saw a white handkerchief fluttering up over the German lines. A voice called out. *"Kameraden. Freunde. Nicht schiessen."* Comrades, friends, don't fire.

As the lookout shouted, more heads nudged hesitantly over the sills of the British trenches, and the Tommies watched as a handwritten sign was held up over the German dugout: "Hapy Chrismas." It was misspelt, but the message was there.

A couple of British soldiers quickly scrawled the same words and held their placard up, then a voice called out over the cold mud between the two sets of troops.

"Why don't we all stop shooting and come out to collect our dead and wounded?" called a British lieutenant in good German, and a few moments later the reply was received agreeing that it would be a good idea.

Soldiers scrambled over both trench rims to go out to collect between fifty and sixty bodies, mainly dead, to take them back to their own side either for a decent burial or in the cases of the few still half alive to send on to a field hospital somewhere behind the lines. Then it was back to the trenches and the confrontational face-to-face war.

An hour or so went by, and then, almost in awe, the British sentries watched as a few Germans rose into No Man's Land and took a few, just a few, tentative steps forward.

"*Nicht schiessen.*" The words sounded loud in a sudden silence.

Like the British, the Germans all looked very young. One or two held their hands forward and slightly raised to show they were unarmed, and a couple held cigars forward as if as presents. Some of the British, startled by the sight, began to raise their rifles, but a sergeant quickly called out in an authoritative voice.

"Stop, you can't shoot unarmed men," he said.

The rifles lowered.

"*Frohe Weihnachten,*" one of the Germans called.

"Happy Christmas," replied one of the British, and suddenly soldiers from both sides of the battle-scarred divide began to clamber above the ridges of their trenches to join together in No Man's Land.

There was still the bark of gunfire away to the right, far to the right, but suddenly the two opposing armies were together in the mud-spattered chaos and confusion of the shell holes, shaking hands and wishing each other a happy Noel.

There was laughter, and the Germans offered more cigars and a few bottles of beer. The British had only a few mouldy apples and some oranges to give as presents in return, but all were given and accepted in the spirit of the day. Christmas Day.

Very quickly the gunfire to the right stopped, and soon the noises of battle were replaced by different sounds from the left. There was jolly singing, the words mainly in French, and almost as if by some magical intervention one of the British soldiers produced a mouth organ and began to play a recognisable harmony. The soldiers from both sides joined in, singing the well-known words in their own tongues.

They had been together for over half an hour before the red-faced major appeared. "Stop this. Stop it immediately," he screeched, his face apoplectic and his whole being showing anger. "You mustn't mix with the enemy. We are at war… You must kill the Hun."

As he screamed, an adolescent-looking German officer stepped forward from the opposite side of the desolate land between the trenches. "Please, it is Christmas," he said. "You will join us for a drink to the Boy Jesus?"

The major stamped rapidly back to the safety of his own dugout. The men of both sides cheered.

Soon there were more than two hundred soldiers from both sides, standing together, laughing and sipping at the strong German ale that was produced, then all stood together and someone said a prayer for Christmas Day.

As it ended, the men began exchanging souvenirs—of British bully beef, German sausages, buttons, cap badges, and that funny spiked German military helmet, the *Pickelhaube*—and then a ball appeared. A leather football that quickly led to the men splitting into two teams of maybe fifty in each. Steel helmets were dropped as goalposts, and the game began. When it had reached five goals each, the German officer who had produced the beer called for a stop.

"It is, maybe, time for us to end… all level," he said with a huge grin spread across his face.

By then it was getting on for half past three, and the sky was quickly darkening, with just a thin strip of light low on the horizon outlining the stark skeletal remnants of the dead trees.

Slowly, reluctantly, the two opposing forces retreated to their own lines and the stinking reality of the trenches.

The day was drawing to a close, but through the evening just a few lone voices could still be heard drifting above No Man's Land. *Stille nacht, heilige nacht*, silent night, holy night…

Midnight came, and Christmas Day was over. The next day, more than one hundred men on each side died from the sporadic gunfire between the two trenches.

* * *

This story is a fiction based on eye-witness accounts of life in the trenches around Ypres in Belgium during the "Great War to End All Wars". It has been officially accepted and is stored in the official Ypres (Belgium) WW1 Museum in its "Christmas Truce" section.

THE ARTIST

Way up high in the Montmartre area near the Sacré Coeur church, a street artist worked his patch in the hot, bright sunshine of mid-summer, half-heartedly and often carelessly sketching the faces of the many tourists who thronged those narrow crammed-in streets looking for an unusual souvenir to take back home.

He was in his usual spot in rue Norvins, just off the crowded Place du Tertre (he chose the spot on the corner of rue Poulbot as the Place was always too crowded and too full of fellow street painters), and as always had spent his day painting faces of mainly youngsters (particularly young girls). He regarded it as "merely schoolroom copying", because deep inside Maurice Montelban yearned to be a "real artist"! He had, literally, dreams of making great paintings, and often went to museums to look over the works of the great artists from the past and thought of himself becoming one of them, although coming up to his thirtieth birthday he frequently wondered if that would ever happen.

After a slow morning, his third or fourth "client" came along, an extremely pretty teenage girl with her boyfriend asking him to draw her portrait—a pencil drawing as it was cheaper than a full painted watercolour. Maurice nodded agreement, and the girl sat daintily and rather self-consciously on the folding stool before him as the boy went off for a beer in a cafe on the corner to wait for her. Hundreds, seemingly thousands, of tourists poured past, most ignoring the sitting but a few glancing at it mindlessly before wandering off to buy a souvenir to take to a friend or relative back home.

She really was a beautiful teenager, and as Maurice started sketching the facial image as usual, in his mind he was planning out a real and potentially great painting. As his fingers automatically drew the outline of the girl's face, then started to fill in the shading to make it look like something it could never be, his imagination took over, and a great work was envisaged.

Maurice finished the portrait, and the boyfriend returned. The boy was annoyed—the beer had been warm and tourists had continually tripped over his feet and his table—and as he looked at the drawing of the girl he disliked it on principle and refused to pay, saying the result was rubbish.

Maurice was too hot and bored to argue, so he simply sighed and prepared the pencil and paper for his next client: a small girl of seven in a yellow cotton dress and with freckles. His mind was blank.

When he had finished work for the afternoon, Maurice packed his easel, pencils, paints, pieces of paper and unsold drawings into a case and went to the same cafe the boyfriend had used, ordering a Pernod and adding water to it from the small jug the waiter had left to transform the greenish drink to a milky colour. As the sun started to sink below the ancient buildings of the quarter he thought back on the day's unsatisfactory work, then recalled the beauteous, captivating teenager from the morning.

His mind worked on a "proper" portrait of her. As he sat reminiscing, and sighing frequently, a piece of paper slipped edgewise from his case. He bent to tuck it in, but it snagged and he had to pull it out completely. It was the drawing of the girl. A sign? He looked at it, then gulped down the rest of his liquorice-tasting drink and hurried back to his single third-floor room nearby in the rue du Mont-Cenis.

He sat at his permanent easel there for just a moment, then mixed colours and started painting. He worked non-stop through the night, ignoring food and sleep as he recalled a glint in the girl's eye, and as if it were somehow transmitted to his hand, managed to get it accurately on the canvas. She had an enigmatic Mona Lisa-style smile that he captured, and the overall look on her enchanting face was recreated.

As he painted, he conjured up an image of the smoothness of the girl's forehead, the high cheekbones, the touch of shade below them. He mentally pictured her vivid blue eyes, the curve of her eyebrows, the faint, but permanent, upward curl of her mouth showing her humour. He brought to mind how a small lock of her auburn hair continually slipped in front of her right eye making her blow upwards from the side of her mouth to clear it—and somehow he managed to convey that in his work as well.

As the portrait progressed, he added a touch here, a daub there, a bright flash sideways or downwards. All the time the girl's face and personality grew on the canvas, an exquisitely unerring and friendly, happy picture of a young girl in the full bloom of her youth.

He finished as the sun came up and looked at the painting with satisfaction. At last, a work he could be proud of. A "real" painting worthy of his talent.

The next day the girl came back on her own to the corner of rue Poulbot, and asked Maurice if she could possibly have the previous day's sketch, offering to pay for it herself and apologising for her boyfriend's rudeness. Maurice shyly showed her the new portrait and asked her to sit for a few moments so he could finish it off. She did so willingly, and for the next half hour or so they sat together working on the final touches of the painting. A huge crowd gathered to watch, all of them admiring out loud the magnificence of the work. It was a great portrait, and at last Maurice was happy.

It would be nice to say that the curator of one of the great art museums happened to pass and see the work, offering an honoured place in his gallery alongside the older and more famous works. But the truth is, a curator did go past, barely glancing at the painting and making rude comments about "draughtmen".

TE-CHE-HEE-LA

t was the best place for swinging and that transatlantic jitterbugging.

The Roxy dance hall in London. In the West End. Everyone was there it seemed, and it was jumping. The band loud and blaring, trumpets and trombones vying with each other to strut their stuff, the guys and gals swinging each other round and round and about and sometimes over their shoulders.

Young factory girls took time away from making the ammunition for their men in the front line to go there and take a bit of a rest—and to meet the gum-chewing GIs who really knew how to dance. Young guys with slicked-back hair and quiffs, who talked like those film stars up there on the big screens, had lots of money to spend, and were able to give them rarities like nylon stockings, make up and other luxuries like that.

Ah yes, the Roxy.

It was there one Friday night that Diana Morrison from a bleak terraced street in south London met Private (First Class) Danny Donovan from Lawrence County, South Dakota. And they fell in love.

Danny was one of the American soldiers in England with his infantry unit, and while waiting to go into battle was simply intent on having a good time. London in the early 1940s had survived the Blitz and seemed a good place to do that.

He had gone to the Roxy with a load of his pals, and he was the last of them to pick up a girl. But unlike them, instead of just grabbing the first girl he could he had waited until he had seen someone he really liked the look of.

Diana filled the bill as soon as he noticed her. She was just a little shorter than him, with her deep brown bobbed hair showing just a hint of red under the flashing lights of the dance hall. Her eyes were also brown, and she did not seem to wear quite as much lipstick as the other girls. She was, he reckoned, about nineteen or twenty, and there was an air of innocence about her that was so different to the other London girls he and his friends had picked up since their arrival in the town a couple of weeks before.

Once he had spotted her, Danny was quick to go up to Diana to ask her to dance. She took an instant liking to the smooth-faced uniformed American soldier, taking in his slicked-back black hair and green eyes in an instant, and she readily agreed. Within moments they were together on the floor dancing to the twelve-piece band, with its five trumpets blaring, two trombones blasting, two saxophones wailing and a wannabe Artie Shaw clarinettist tootling away as a demented drummer matched a chubby bass player firing off riff after pulsating riff.

A multi-faceted glass glitterball hanging from the roof was lit by two spotlights that sent shards of reflection down onto the tangled mass of swinging dancers below, the only light in the near stygian gloom of the dance hall that was only slightly better than the darkness of the blackout that still hung over London after the years of daily Blitz and bombing. Soon they were laughing out loud as Danny took Diana through some of the most intricate jive moments she had ever seen.

As all the other young girls used to the drab days of war, Diana found it colourful and exciting. Like the others, she was dressed in all her finery for the dance, all of them in cheap knee-length, brightly coloured cotton dresses that whirled as they gyrated with the young men of battle, the American "doughboys" all wearing bright badges on their khaki uniforms. Danny and his pals all had the big red flash on their arms as they were attached to the 1st Infantry Division. It seemed to add to the intensity of a scene slightly dulled down by the drab light blue uniforms of the few British airmen, the darker blue of the Royal Navy, and the drab, heavier khaki of the home soldiers on leave.

Mostly though, it was all exciting and glamorous for the girls after nearly four years of war.

For Diana, dancing with her newly met Danny it was love at first sight. As she cavorted the new American jive dance with him she knew he was the one for her, and even when the music stopped she let him carry on whirling her round, although he slowed down when the lone clarinettist, accompanied by a pianist who had joined the band, heralded the next number: a slow, smoochy blues that meant they held each other close.

Danny's arm was held firmly around Diana's waist, and she held a hand loosely to the back of his neck.

It was an enchanting first meeting, and when the band took a rest they sat in a corner with glasses of lemonade, he smoking a strong American cigarette while they chatted about themselves.

Danny was unlike any of the other boys that Diana had ever met. He was not like most of the "grunts" who went to the Roxy; he was quiet, modest, almost shy. At one time, while they were talking he sneezed, and blushed—actually blushed—when he found he did not have a handkerchief on him. Diana noticed but did not make a fuss, simply reaching in her bag and brought out a small white handkerchief with a sewn flower embossed in one corner to give to him. He blew his nose and put the hankie in his pocket.

At the end of the evening, Diana went home with the friends with whom she had arrived while Danny returned to his camp with his pals. But it was the first of their many meetings in the couple of weeks that followed. Danny met Diana every single day, and although at first they mainly continued to go to the Roxy with all his companions, their dates gradually drifted further away from them and her girlfriends.

They far preferred to be alone together, either going to the cinema—the movies as Danny called them—or going to a special cafe where they would listen to the wireless, the radio, and he would give her jars of American instant coffee—"java"—butter and sugar to supplement her wartime British rations.

Sometimes they would just walk and talk about things, arms around each other's waists, and Danny would call Diana his "little English fairy".

During their times together, Danny would excite Diana by telling her of his home and early life in America, in a small Midwest township called Spearfish.

"It's a great place," he'd tell her. "The Queen City—with three big peaks like the jewels of a crown above her."

Spearfish, said Danny, was on the edge of the Black Hills of South Dakota, virtually at the heart of America. "Well, it's just a couple of miles from Belle Fourche." He pronounced it "Bell Foosh". "And that's the actual centre of the USA. The town leaders are tryin' to make sure it gets an official marker to that effect when the war's over," he said.

Diana was thrilled by his stories of Middle American life. As a Londoner it sounded somehow romantic to hear of a small township of just some two and a half thousand people.

"Although it's got a new university that's growing real fast," said Danny.

He would tell stories that the young girl could easily imagine, weaving pictures of the ponderosas' vast expanse of buttes and spires that stretched as far as the eye could see, and of the pine-covered mountains that were so deep green they looked black from a distance.

"The Black Hills, the Lakota Sioux call them Paha Sapa, the Holy Mountains," he told her.

Diana was enthralled by Danny's stories of the places around his homestead.

"You'd love t'see the Great Plains with the mountains and the Bridal Veil Falls," he would say. "It's nice and warm at this time of the year too. Not too hot, and I guess it's not too cold either." He pronounced that "eether".

Danny used his imagination to tell Diana stories of The Badlands, of the way he had discovered them as a youngster when he went hiking and camping to places like the caverns and tunnels at the Wind Cave National Park. He spoke of the crystals growing underground at the Jewel Cave—he called it the "Jool" Cave—and of the gigantic faces of four great American presidents still being carved out of the solid granite mountains at Mount Rushmore after decades of effort.

Diana was fascinated by his stories of the herds of elk and wild horses that still roamed the plains, and of the rare creatures like the black-footed ferrets or black-tailed prairie dogs. "There's a whole host of wildlife," he enthused, sometimes bursting into song, "Oh, give me a home where the buffalo roam…"

Danny explained one night that Spearfish had developed around a creek where Lakota Sioux ("the Soo") used to catch fish with their spears, and said the town itself had developed after the Indians had routed a small group of gold prospectors.

He made his hometown sound like a boy's adventure tale, with stories of cowboys and what he called "Injins", of frontiersmen like Wild Bill Hickock, Custer, and of the pioneers' Gold Rush.

"Nowadays it's a quiet town though," he'd tell the wide-eyed girl.

Most of all, the stories were about the American Indians who had obviously caught his imagination as a young lad, a fascination that was still with him and led him to talk about virtually everything to do with them.

Many of his tales were of giants like Crazy Horse, Sitting Bull and the great Native Indian nation of the area—the Sioux, the "nadouessioux" or little snakes, split into seven mighty tribes—and of their unique pow-wows and the kaleidoscope of singing and dancing that went with them.

"When I was just a bitty bit of a boy, I went camping in the Devil's Tower. That's an old volcano crater that rises almost a thousand feet up, just south of Rapid City," he told Diana. "It's awesome there, and full of Indian legends… the fights, the raids. It set my mind on fire. I could see it all, and it was right there round my own home."

Danny told stories about the ancient Sioux ghost dances, about the battles at Wounded Knee, and about the petrified forest of Lemmon, and the more he told them, the more his own imagination caught fire with them.

The stories were so vivid that Diana could picture it all equally in her own mind, and she felt she knew the place, the towns, the reservations, the teepees and the prairie, although how much of that was down to her many trips to "the pictures" and their scenes with John Wayne and other film cowboys defending their small homesteads from Indian raids rather than Danny's stories, not even she could tell. Sometimes, most times, not even Danny could tell where the truth ended and those same films began.

Despite the fantasies, or perhaps because of them, Diana found Danny to be an attentive lover. She was intoxicated and mentally seduced by his romantic side too, especially when he gave her flowers for the first time in her life. They were simple Michaelmas daisies with an unusual blue shade that tended towards purple, and he told her they reminded him of the purple coneflowers of the South Dakota mesa. Those native American flowers he told her were to be her "special gentian love flowers".

From his point of view, Danny had also fallen head over heels in love with the pretty young girl, and he bought the unusual daisies one day after they had seen them on a market stall and she said she liked them. It was just one of the many little touches in his romancing of the starry-minded young girl that made her fall in love with him.

One night, after he had been telling her more stories about the Sioux, he kissed her, and as they broke away from each other he looked at her intently, still holding her face in his cupped hands.

"*Techihila*," he said. The word sounded like "Te-che-hee-la" with the accent on the third part, and somehow Diana did not need to be told what the Sioux word meant. Danny didn't really need to explain that it was, indeed, the nearest the Lakota Indians came to saying "I love you".

"They don't have words for that," he said softly, "But it's what a fighting brave would say to his woman when he left her to go into battle."

Later, when she got home late to find her sister Margaret still awake in the bedroom they shared, Diana told her about it. "We'd been dancing at the Roxy all evening, and the whole place was jiving," she said in the build-up. "Then suddenly everyone seemed to pull to the sides and one couple were in the middle," said Diana full of wide-eyed, girlish enthusiasm.

"They jitterbugged while everyone shouted them on. I told Danny I could never do that, I'd be too shy, and guess what? He just pulled me into the middle of that circle and we danced. He threw me up in the air and over his shoulders, all round. It was great. Everyone clapped and shouted, then suddenly they were all round us dancing away as well. The way I felt wasn't like anything I've ever known before. It was just… well, just the best."

She paused for breath. "He said he loved me… in Sioux. And I know I've fallen in love with him," she added loosely with a sideways look at her sister.

"But he's a Yank, how could you?" asked Margaret coldly.

"He's so different. He's not brash like the other GIs, and he doesn't even chew gum like most of them. He's a real gentleman," replied Diana almost breathlessly. "And when we're out, he treats me just like a lady, not a factory girl. He's real swell."

Margaret noted the American phrase but didn't say anything. Soon after, they went to bed agreeing to differ, and Diana lay there wide awake for seemingly hours, the word *"techihila"* going round and round in her mind.

Two days later when her mother mentioned that Margaret had told her about the boy and said she didn't like the idea of her daughter going out with "a Yankee", Diana rebuked her sister for telling tales and she was never as friendly towards Margaret or their mother again.

Danny and Diana were together for about two months before he got the call to action. He told her about it as they returned from a night at the cinema during which they had seen a romantic musical film, *Meet Me in St. Louis*, and as they strolled down the street to her house they were both singing the film's hit *Trolley Song*—he imitating Tom Drake's shy personality and she trying to match Judy Garland's alluring, smiling voice.

They turned into her road, and almost to her front door before Danny stopped and turned to face Diana. "Honey, it ain't goin' to be for long, but I am goin' to have to go far away," he told her.

Diana stopped singing and looked stunned. "What do you mean? Going away…" she asked him.

"Well, I can't say too much, but there's this big operation comin' up and my lot will be right at the heart of it," he said. He kissed her. "But don't worry. I'll be back," he vowed.

Diana did not know what to say. "When?" was the only question that came to her mind. She knew that this kind of thing happened in a war, but for some reason she had put all thoughts of it happening to her and Danny back into the darker recesses of her mind. "When?"

Danny held her tight. "This darned war can't go on forever," he said softly, once more sounding like the Hollywood stars they both adored. "But I'll be back, no matter when." He smiled, a tender smile. "I guess it won't be too long, but let's give me, Ike and the boys a bit of room to manoeuvre. Let's say it'll be within, what, five years? It won't take that long, but as I say, I will be back. No matter when. I promise."

They kissed again, and Danny noticed the blackout curtains of Diana's front downstairs window fluttering slightly, a vague light coming through them as though from some other room at the back shining through an open door. "I really have to go," he said. "You'd better go in now." He kissed the silent girl again and turned away.

"*Techihila,*" he said, so softly she thought she might have imagined it.

Diana wanted to cry, to hold him and stop him leaving, but she simply stood on the same spot without moving, not even blinking as she watched him walk down the street and round the corner.

Her mind was a bit of a blank as he disappeared, and she had a strong, illusory but tangible feeling that she would never see him again. She did not move for perhaps five minutes after Danny had disappeared from view, then she turned and went into her house and straight to bed, lying awake with her mind a blank until she finally fell asleep at around four in the morning.

It was two weeks before Diana heard about the D-Day landings on the radio, and she immediately realised that was where Danny had been sent when he was taken from her. The next day a letter from him fell on the door mat. She picked it up when she went downstairs in the morning, and recognising his handwriting, put it in the pocket of her flimsy dressing gown to read later. When she went to work, she waited for her midmorning break before going to the lavatory and reading it in the silence of the cubicle.

The letter was long and chatty, but not really informative about where Danny was when it was written. It was dated the day after the D-Day landings, and as she sat all alone, Diana read with horror how the American GIs from Danny's division had sailed in to the beach in choppy seas that made many of them seasick, and under heavy enemy attack had leapt from their landing craft facing a two- or three-hundred-yard dash across the open crescent-shaped beach with enemy machine gun fire raking across their advance.

"We Yanks drew the short end of the straw," he wrote. "Where we landed was overlooked by a high cliff where the Germans were waiting, and they had their guns well positioned to catch us so they just poured machine gun fire down on top of us as we dashed across the beach.

"There were thick belts of barbed wire in our way to slow us down, and the trouble was that we'd bombed the place days before, then shelled it before we went into land. We had to dodge round our own craters. We took heavy casualties, more than three thousand I heard."

Danny said that once they'd reached the bottom of the cliff, he and his buddies had tried to use grappling hooks to fix ropes they could climb up, but the Germans had simply thrown hand grenades down on top of them.

"It was real scary. Anyone who says he wasn't frightened is a liar," he wrote.

Later, Danny's letter told how he had been heartened by the sight of a padre, Father Joe Lacey, who'd landed with them. "The boys had called him a small, old, fat Irishman on the way over, and they said he'd never be able to keep up with us," he wrote, "But Father Joe was right there, kneeling down under fire to help the wounded and pull the dead bodies out of the water to make room for the next wave to come in.

"He'd told us to get on with the fighting and leave the praying to him, but I guess most of us still said a prayer or two as we tried to get ashore. He was an inspiration."

Diana read it all with an overwhelming and growing fear. She just could not imagine Danny, her Danny, being in danger like that, and even as she read she knew that although he had survived the initial landings he was still in tremendous danger. She became increasingly worried, really worried, for him.

She was close to tears, her mind in a tumult of confusion, as she finished reading the account of the terrible battle to gain a foothold on enemy-held territory.

But then, on the sixth page of the handwritten letter it all changed and a half smile formed on her lips as she read that Danny had wanted to propose to her on that final evening but had been too scared.

"I couldn't raise my nerve to ask you when I left, in case you said no," he wrote. "I was not brave enough then. I guess I was saving my courage for this battle because I knew I was on the big one although I couldn't tell you about it for obvious reasons. It was hell, and I still can't say where I am now, though I still need all the guts I can get. But now I feel I can ask you: will you marry me when I get back?"

Diana read that line three times with moist eyes, happy that Danny said he hoped she would accept the letter as his formal proposal.

"Like most of us here I'm scared," he told her, "But I hope you'll say you will marry me when it's all over and that will give me the courage to get through it. Believe me, if you will, I'll be back, I promise you that. I will be back."

Under his name at the bottom of the letter, Danny had put in a row of twelve Xs and below them he wrote, *"Techihila."*

She read the letter twice, then still sitting on the closed toilet seat, she shouted, out loud, "Yes, Danny, I'll marry you. I will."

The days that followed saw Diana in a paradise of happiness. She knew what she felt, and constant re-reading of the letter told her that Danny felt the same.

It was only when, a week after getting the letter, that she went to the cinema with a friend and in the newsreel between the two features saw the first pictures of the invasion landings. While they obviously concentrated on the British Army efforts, there was enough footage there to show Diana how horrifying it must have been for her Danny landing on what the news reader called "Bloody Omaha" beach.

As she watched the film, she gingerly opened her handbag in the dark and put her hand inside it to hold Danny's well-worn and well-read letter. She thought how he had been too scared to propose to her, but had shown courage in the face of that terrible battle.

As the newsreel ended, Diana was appalled with what she had seen and could not help thinking about him even when the main feature began. The old feeling of the inevitable permanent loss of Danny returned.

A couple of years later the war ended, and although she waited for some time—counting the five years Danny had promised—Diana heard no more from her young American sweetheart. Danny became a part of her past, a memory she told herself was part of her growing up period, although she always remembered him with a sorrowing love, even when she got married and had a daughter and eventually three grandchildren.

It was a good life, although her husband and both parents died within a year of each other, and Diana moved back into her old family home with its memories and, for a while, its sorrows.

Life continued, until one day fifty-five years later—a whole lifetime—there was a knock at her front door one sunny June morning. Outside was a man of around fiftyish, slightly portly, hair receding, but with a vaguely familiar look to his smiling face.

"Hi there. I hope you're Diana Morrison," he said in a strong Midwestern American accent.

"Diana Backley. I was married."

"Sorry. My name's Denny Donovan, Danny Donovan's son. I've seen your name in some of the papers Dad left behind, and your name was always Morrison." The man had been holding his hand behind his back, but then brought it round and offered Diana a small posy of Michaelmas daisies. "He said you always liked these." He smiled.

Diana took the flowers, automatically smelling their poignant aroma before suddenly remembering her manners. "I'm sorry. Forgive me. Please come in."

The man smiled again and nodded, and Diana stood aside to let him through the door.

She led the way into her living room, offering tea or coffee. "No thanks, I never did get to like British tea, and I'm afraid I find your coffee none too strong either."

Diana thought it was the kind of thing that Danny would have said and he pronounced the word "eether" just like his father had.

The stranger told Diana his name was really Dennis, and that he was Danny's only son. "No one ever calls me Dennis though. Guess it's because I'm supposed to be like Dad and it's the nearest they can get to him."

He studied Diana's face for a moment. Then he pursed his lips and carried on. "He told me about you when I was young, but I've never had the chance to come over here to meet you before. But this year I got the chance, so I decided to take it and try to track you down," he said.

"Your name was on a note they found in Dad's pocket when he died, and I discovered an address in a pile of old papers I found when we moved house a couple of years back. They were letters and things that Dad had written but never posted, and he'd left them in an old case tucked away in the loft after he passed away. Dad always wrote about you with some affection."

Diana did not know what to think. Her mind was going over and over trying to sort itself out, and the only image it could latch onto was that of herself watching Danny walk down the street and round the corner when he went off to war. She felt once more the same illusory feeling that she'd had then that she would never see him again.

"Danny's dead?" she asked.

"Yeah, I'm afraid so. He went just a year ago; strangely it was on the anniversary of the invasion of Europe during the war. The doctors reckoned that the wounds he got then were so bad that he never really got over the effects."

Diana had a hollow feeling inside, but she managed to maintain a presence of calm. "I never knew he'd been wounded," she said, almost as though to herself.

"Oh yeah, he was quite badly smashed up a couple of months after the invasion, in a huge battle at some French place called St. Lo." He pronounced it "Saint Lo" as Danny would have done. "He was hit three times in the chest and arms; they flew him back to the States where he was kept in a military hospital for more than eleven months until he was able to go home."

Denny paused and looked at Diana carefully before going on. "Guess he was one of the lucky ones, 'cause he was only injured. More than eight thousand GIs were killed in that fight," he said eventually.

"Grandma Donovan always told me though, that he was never the same, that he appeared somehow detached when he got back to Spearfish. She said he seemed to almost become like a Lakota Injin—his mind was filled with stories of them. Whatever it was though, she said he always looked to have something going on his brain that no one else could understand."

Diana stood up. "I must get myself a cup of tea," she said, hoping the break would give her time to collect herself properly. "If you'd like a coffee, well, I've got some American instant if you like. I got to like it during the war, and there's a shop near here that sells it."

"Well, perhaps I could go for a cup of coffee then, if you're sure it's not too much trouble," replied Denny, standing as Diana left the room.

While she was in the kitchen, he looked around him at the pictures and artefacts that littered the homely room. Then when Diana returned with the drinks and a plate of biscuits, they sat again and talked for a long time about Danny and his life after the war.

Denny said his father had virtually been forced by his own and his mother's families to marry. "It seems it was the way things were just after the war. All the vets had childhood sweethearts, and I guess they were all expected to carry on as if the war hadn't happened," he said.

Denny told Diana he had been born a year after the wedding, but his mother had been knocked down and killed by a hit and run driver when he was just three months old. Danny had raised him with help from his own parents, and for the first years of his life they had lived in a happy small town family atmosphere with his grandparents.

He said that he had always automatically assumed from the way those grandparents spoke that his father had loved his mother "in a way".

But, he said, he vaguely remembered that one birthday his father had said something he hadn't understood, saying that he had only really loved "the English fairy" he had left behind.

"I never really knew what he meant, I was just too young," said Denny, "But thinking back on it, I guess he was just depressed when his old wounds were aching and for some reason was trying to tell me something I'd know when I grew up. About you. Maybe that was what was on his mind." Denny looked at Diana again cautiously. "I guess he never told Mom," he added. "She never knew, but I did."

The summer sun was starting to sink behind the trees in the street outside the suburban house as Denny went on to tell Diana that his father had died of a heart attack bought on by his overall bad health. "He got through the landing on Omaha, but he never knew how badly he was hurt in that battle soon after," added Denny. "And he had the heart attack while he was in the agency booking a ticket for a trip he was planning, to come back to Europe and England. Most of us thought it was to look at the beaches again.

"Later on, well, as I said I found a whole pile of papers. Among them there was this old travel itinerary he'd planned for a trip back to London soon after the war. I thought it must be some kinda reunion he was planning, but there was a note he'd written with it that had your name on it. I guess I read it all with a bit of a lump in my throat, because suddenly it all seemed to add up. The English fairy an' all."

Denny smiled at Diana. "Just one thing about it though. Those papers had all the details of where you lived, but that note had a strange thing in it. Dad had just scribbled something in pencil by the side, something about being in London four years and ten months after returning home. What does that mean?"

Diana's eyes were moist as she explained. "When he went away, he told me he'd be back. But because he didn't know how long the war would last, he just said it would be within five years," she said.

Denny involuntarily reached out and put his hand on her arm. "He never quite made it then," he told her tenderly. "He was married and I'd come along, but it seems Dad thought you were meant to be together as he promised. But I guess fate took a hold."

Diana blinked away the growing tears and got control of herself. "I'd say you were right. It was just never meant to be," she said softly.

The two of them chatted for a while, the younger man and the older former girlfriend of his father, and soon it grew dark. Denny stood to leave and they agreed to meet again, and as she opened the front door of the house to let him out he remembered something.

Reaching into the back pocket of his trousers he pulled out a battered, crumpled envelope. He handed it to Diana, and she looked down to see it was addressed to her in Danny's writing.

"I found this too," said Denny. "It's addressed to you, reckon he'd have wanted you to see what was in it."

He stepped outside the door as Diana looked down at the envelope.

"Among the other bits I found was something about the Roxy dance hall," said Denny, on the doorstep. "I was going to go to see it, but I found it's closed down now. That's a pity."

She watched him walk down the garden path, and it occurred to her that was the way she had last seen his father too.

When Denny was gone, Diana closed the door and went back indoors and sat in an armchair. She studied the wrinkled envelope he'd given her for a few moments, then opened it and pulled out the letter. It was from Danny, his handwriting that of a young man obviously under stress, and Diana instinctively observed that although the envelope was badly creased and had that air of antiquity that old reports usually have, the letter itself seemed fresh and newly written.

She guessed it had been written some time during the invasion battles, and she began to read those long ago words that told her simply how Danny felt about her. Diana read the letter, not really knowing how she felt about it.

As she read, she felt something else inside the envelope. It was the small white handkerchief with a sewn flower embossed in one corner that she had lent Danny when he sneezed on their first date.

She sat there looking at it silently for several minutes before putting it on her lap and turning back to the letter. It finished with a simple sentence.

"I love you, and remember, lover, no matter were I go in this darned war, I'll be back," it said. *"Techihila."* She noted that he had misspelt "where".

Diana sighed, and idly looked at the envelope again. She realised there was still something else inside it, and put two fingers in to see what it was. She pulled out two purple-coloured leaves from an artificial flower decoration. A gentian love flower.

Her face was still, but her eyes were moist as she sat quite still thinking about Danny and his son, who had just left her. She recalled what the boy had told her: Danny had died trying to get back to her within the five years in which he had promised to return.

Then she smiled softly to herself and remembered the other thing Denny had told her as he left: "The Roxy is closed down now," he'd said.

"Yes," she said out loud, "It shut down five years to the day after Danny left to go to war."

THE END

And that's it! I hope you've enjoyed meeting some of my friends. I know they will join me in wishing you all: happy story-reading.